Published by Long Midnight Publishing, 2019

copyright © 2019 Douglas Lindsay

ISBN: 978-1702013819

www.douglaslindsay.com

SEE THAT MY GRAVE IS KEPT CLEAN

DOUGLAS LINDSAY

LMP

Prologue

So here I am, a gun in my hand, one bullet, and Michael fucking Clayton standing right in front of me.

Michael Clayton, for his part, seems unconcerned. He's smiling, the smile in his eyes more than on the lips. He genuinely believes I'm going to use the bullet on myself rather than him. That was why he gave me the gun in the first place.

The weird fucking thing is, he's right.

1

'Got something that'll be right up your street,' says Ramsay.

Walking into the station. Nine-thirty-four. Late. Again.

Woke up at half-two, could feel one of those fucking birds pecking at my brain. Right inside. Like it was there. Lay there for I don't know how long, finally got up, made a cup of tea and turned on the TV. Not much on at four in the morning. Watched half an hour of the Cubs at the Nationals. Tied game, into overtime, bottom of the fifteenth. The *fifteenth*. Jesus. Even that didn't put me back to sleep.

Went back to bed, lay there like a lemon as the day got light, finally got back to sleep at seven, or something, just when I should have been getting up. And now I'm late and will have to deal with Taylor's eyebrow, or however it is he's going to express his disapproval.

Stop to talk to Ramsay on the front desk.

'Why do I think I'm going to be offended?' I say.

Ramsay laughs.

'You look like shit, by the way,' he says.

'I know. Give me the thing.'

'There's a guy in Room 3 wants to complain about the people who live across the street.'

I lean on the counter, settling in for the duration of the story.

'Those kind are certainly my favourites,' I say. 'Mowing his front lawn too early on a Sunday?'

'Shagging his wife up against the window of their bedroom,' says Ramsay.

I take a moment to process that one. Not just the fact someone somewhere is shagging his wife up against a window, or that someone who's watched it wants to complain rather than get the popcorn in, but the fact he's been saving it for me.

'Are you making that up?'

'Takes all sorts,' he says.

'And you think it's a job for a detective sergeant?'

A defensive look crosses his face. I don't think I've ever, in all my career, played either the detective or the rank card. Don't know where that came from. Obviously not in the mood for exhibitionist sex acts.

'Taylor said you weren't busy and you could handle it.'

'Did he?'

And just like that I've ruined it for him.

'Whatever, Sergeant,' he says, 'if you're going to be a dick about it. I'll give it to Anderson.'

He sits down, back in front of the computer.

'Sorry, Stuart, you're right. It's up my street. Bad night.'

Tap my head, as though he's supposed to know what that means. As though I've been telling people about the fucking birds which, of course, I haven't. Why would I tell anyone about the birds?

'Room 3,' I add. 'I'm going, I'm going. Straight there.'

Walk away, waving off any objections he might have, but I don't think there were going to be any anyway. He was going to have a laugh, I ruined it, and now we're moving on. We're all grown ups here.

* * *

The crows are back. I don't know why.

I mean, in my head. They're still outside, of course, all over. More and more of them every year. But those crows never went away. The crows in my head though, those fuckers had gone.

After all the shit a year and a half ago, my head was

3

full of them. This cacophony of noise. Crows, with their jibber-jabber. In my dreams at night, in my waking nightmares in the day.

I'd go and sit in the park at the top of the town, just to get some air, listen to the wind in the trees, and there would always be the ugly sound of the crows. Everywhere.

But it didn't last. Not the ones in my head. A couple of months maybe, and then they flew off somewhere. I don't know where they went. Just disappeared. The fucking plague. Had it one day, gone the next.

The real crows, the ones in the park, sitting on the roofs, waiting for spilled kebabs after closing time on a Friday night, they were still there, but they didn't bother me anymore.

I could look at a crow and think, yeah whatever, your uncle nearly had the chance to eat my brain, but it didn't happen, and so we've all moved on. Fuck you, you shiny, jet black asshole.

But now, the last couple of weeks, they're back. Back in my head. Back in my dreams. Talking to me. I think they're talking to me, but I can never remember what they say. And those crows out there, the ones on the telephone poles and sitting on walls. They're looking at me again. I can feel them. Piece of shit, carrion scum bastards.

So, why are they back?

Jesus, how the fuck do I know? But there's something. There's one possibility. One thing standing out and crying, *me, me, look at me, this is why!*

It's got to be that bastard, Clayton. Michael Clayton. He's out there somewhere. Never went away. That's what the crows are telling me.

Could we have snared the fucker if we'd gone for him after the absurd Plague of Crows crap?

We got the killer, and the suits upstairs were happy to assume it was a one-woman job. She was a serial killer. Serial killers don't usually have evil masterminds behind them. We'd done what was needed, we'd caught her, and killed her, red-handed. The killing stopped. They weren't about to go back out to the public and say, you know that case we cracked, you know how we said you could stop living in fear, you know how we were all self-satisfyingly licking our own balls – even though cracking the case was actually nothing to do with us suits in the first place – well we've only told you half the story. There was someone else involved and they're still out there, so if you thought you were safe walking home from work tonight, think again. You're all going to die.

They were never going to say it, and sure enough, they didn't. With Clayton having established his credentials as a walking law suit, and the main piece of evidence against him being the time he pitched up at the hospital and more or less confessed to me, the suits chose to leave him alone. Perhaps they would've been more credulous of my story if I hadn't been so doped up on morphine at the time of the confession. Ultimately, I'm not sure I believe it myself. Can I even be certain he was in the hospital room at all?

Nevertheless, he's back now. At least, that's what I'm assuming, but I don't think anyone higher up the food chain, starting with DCI Taylor, will take my word for it based on conversations with crows in the middle of the night. I need more.

I'm not going looking for it, though. If the crows are speaking the truth, and he is back, then the asshole will know where to find me.

Maybe the morning I wake up remembering what the crows have said to me in the night, will be the morning I die.

That would be a relief.

* * *

The complainant is sitting across the desk from me, holding an iPad. An older version. One of the ones weighing eight or nine kilos. So far, he's yet to show me anything.

I'm dying for a coffee, but since I made such an ill-gracious hash of receiving the assignment from Ramsay, I kind of rushed in here, not stopping on the way.

I have my notepad. Haven't written anything yet.

'What makes you think it's aimed specifically at you?' I ask.

'Because no one else, no other house I mean, looks directly on to their front window. I know what they're doing. They wait until there's no one about on the street, and you know what it's like up there. Those streets can be very quiet, particularly these days when parents don't let their children outside without a bodyguard.'

He's in his early sixties, small round glasses resting on the end of a large nose, mostly bald but with longish grey hair at the sides and back. Needs a cut, I'd say. I think he's trying to cultivate some sort of professorial look, but I've already learned he's in insurance. I elected not to go any further.

'Big houses up there,' I say. 'What do they do?'

He snorts.

'I doubt *she's* ever done *anything*. *He* was at RBS. They made him redundant, and he walked away with one point three million.' He articulates the figure like he might be getting lip read, enhanced mouth movement/lower volume combination. This guy really is a twat. Still, here now. All in.

'Show me the photograph,' I say.

'There's more than one.'

'Excellent.'

He turns on the tablet, tips it up so I can't see him type in the pass code – which is fair enough, because obviously being a police officer I'm this close from reaching over there, grabbing the thing the fuck off him and never giving it back – has to concentrate while he works out how to retrieve a photograph, and then turns the tablet round, making sure to hold on to the device.

'See?' he says.

There, right enough, is a picture of a woman, her breasts squashed against the window. Her face is squashed too, although the look of pleasure is still apparent. The man behind is not in shot, but for a single hand holding her stomach. A large lady in her fifties, a mass of curly hair, dyed auburn.

I study it, noting the high quality of the double glazing – if these were 1930s windows, that woman would be going for a Burton, shards of shattered glass embedded in those large, compressed boobs – before looking up at him.

'That's some pretty graphic evidence,' I say. 'When was it taken?'

'Oh, that was the third time.'

'The third?'

'These people aren't messing around, Sergeant.'

'And do you have photos from the first two?'

Pursed lips.

'The first time, well to be honest, I was shocked. And I wouldn't have dreamt of taking a picture. I thought they must just have got carried away. But then, sure enough, a few days later, they did it again. Right there, up at the window opposite where I sit and do my jigsaw puzzles.'

He does jigsaw puzzles. Oh well, they can be fun. Or something. Meditative. That's the word. Not fun. Maybe it would help me if I did jigsaw puzzles.

'What kid of jigsaw puzzles do you do?'

'What?'

'Do you do those, you know, five thousand piece things, or…'

'Oh, usually fifteen hundred. Anything else is too… Wait. What does that have to do with it? Are you mocking me?'

'Not at all, Mr Gregson. Sorry, so you took the picture the third time?'

He looks suspicious, and then says, 'Yes.'

'And this was in the last couple of days?'

'Oh no.'

'No?'

'No, this was three weeks ago.' His eyes have widened. 'The other pictures, they're from other times. I have a lot of pictures.'

'How many times have they had sex in the window, Mr Gregson?'

The lips tighten a little again, the way one's sphincter does any time a doctor mentions the word *suppository*.

'Ten.'

'And why has it taken you so long to come to speak to us?'

He leans forward on the desk.

'I didn't know what to do. Mr Hartwell and I, you know, we're on the Bowling Club committee together. We all know each other. I've eaten Mrs Hartwell's cake.'

Keep a straight face now, Sergeant, none of your sniggering. This isn't a *Carry On* movie.

'Have you seen them socially since the window sex began?' I ask.

'Of course.'

'And...?'

'Nothing was said,' he says primly.

'So, why d'you think they're intentionally letting you watch them have sex?'

He looks back at the picture of the woman, and then turns the tablet back to me. He starts slowly dragging his finger across the screen, flicking from image to image. Mrs Hartwell pressed against the window. Mr Hartwell side on, his wife on her knees fellating him. Mrs Hartwell sitting on her husband's face. Mrs Hartwell, seemingly with her legs between her husband's armpits, her head resting on the ground, as he fucks her. There's the clincher. I don't get a really good look at it, but it's the kind of position you only do for show. Can't possibly be comfortable for either of them.

There are a lot of pictures. He keeps going, flicking through. It's probably up to me to stop him.

'Wow, you got an ejaculation shot. Nice timing.'

He presses the off button, and brings the tablet fully back under his control, looking uncomfortable.

'You want me to go and speak to them?' I ask.

—
8

'Yes!'

'OK, I can do that. Don't you think… they must have seen you taking the photographs, though, right, especially if you were taking it on that thing? It's hardly discreet.'

'Yes, of course they saw. They clearly loved it. Look at the pair of them. They're like rabbits.'

'Perhaps they were thinking you were enjoying it. You took all…'

'Good God!'

'Have you asked them to stop? Have you, for example, drawn a curtain so you can't see them?'

'It's summer. I don't draw the curtains until after ten.'

'All right… Why do you think they're doing it, then?'

'Clearly they want me to join in. But I'm not going to. They can't have me.'

Time for coffee. I push the chair back, stand up. Despite the fact the woman in the photograph is so unattractive she could have played one of the dwarf women you never actually get to see in *Lord Of The Rings*, there was a time when I would have been turned on looking at those pictures. Not any more. Well, not at the moment.

'Thanks for coming in, Mr Gregson. I'll go and see them and report back, and we'll see where it's going to go.'

He doesn't look convinced. Perhaps if I'd said I'd go round there with a SWAT team.

2

Clayton lies on the sofa, staring at the ceiling. The psychiatrist sits three yards away. She holds a notepad, and a small pencil, the kind golfers use to mark a scorecard. She seems uncomfortable, but Clayton is oblivious.

'You wanted to talk about school,' she says.

Clayton taps the ends of his fingers together.

'Yes,' he says. 'I did, didn't I? And you're absolutely right, because where else does it all start? One wastes so many years of one's life in those God-awful institutions. And they wonder why we're so messed up. Why we need help.'

'Most people don't need help when they leave school. Not psychiatric help, anyway.'

He snorts, closes his eyes.

'What was so different about you?'

He makes a theatrical hand gesture, tossing her words across the room.

'There's no point in doing this if you're not going to talk to me,' she says.

'Yes, yes, of course,' he says, his voice mellower than she'd been expecting.

She watches him, he does not look at her. His eyes are closed, she knows from experience with others that he is reliving a moment, finding the words, wondering whether or not to tell her the story. The less she says now, the more likely he'll eventually talk. She wouldn't be here, after all, if he wasn't going to.

'All right, all right, of course,' he says. 'Of course.'

He clasps his hands, his fingers rhythmic, constant small movements, and nods to himself again.

'There were three things. I was quiet, of course. Didn't have many friends. Wasn't bullied much, although I was soft. Too soft. But they didn't realise. I think... yes, I think they were scared of me. Because I was quiet, and I watched. One day in music the teacher asked who could play the piano.'

He seems embarrassed by the memory.

'There was silence for a while, and so I put my hand up. I don't know why I did that. I was fourteen. I played *Jesu*. Much too slowly, and several mistakes later, I retreated. And then, suddenly, Adam Pearson walks to the front of the class, looking shy. Shy. As if. Played the piano like, I don't know, some 1940s bluesman. Jesus. Looking back... he owned the room. Magnificent playing. Truly magnificent.'

'Surely it needn't have impacted on you,' she said. 'Your classmates must just have, I don't know, ignored you. And it soun...'

'They were laughing. Not out loud, but they were laughing.'

Fingers are tensing, getting annoyed. She knows the signs. Now he's started, he won't stop.

'So, then fucking Pearson, or someone, I don't know who, gets Gillian Thompson to come up and speak to me in the common room. Asked me what book I was reading, as though–'

'What book were you reading?'

'What?'

He turns and looks at her, his brow furrowed at the interruption.

'What book were you reading?'

'*The Shining*. What difference does it make?'

She shakes her head, indicates for him to go on.

'I barely spoke to her. Just showed her the book. She goes back to her friends and they start laughing. I mean, what was she doing, talking to me? Gillian Thompson?

Seriously? She was taking the piss.'

'Who was Gillian Thompson?'

'The class bike. She was pretty, mind. Pretty. No business talking to the likes of me.'

'And the third thing?' she asks.

Classic case, she thinks. Such trivial grievances. So often the way.

'I asked her out. I thought about it, I thought about why she came to speak to me, and I asked her out. She said no. And then Pearson, who I'd hardly, I don't know, hardly noticed before then, he laughs at me. He tells everyone. They're looking at me, this overweight, unattractive nerd, with his Stephen King novels, and buried in his algebra books. They were laughing at me. It was him. Pearson. I knew it was. It was like... when he played the piano in class, he wanted some dweeb to get up there first, somebody rubbish, so he would look even better against them. I mean, it wasn't like he needed it. He was good enough.'

He stares straight ahead. His eyes are looking at a picture on the wall in front of him. A pale wall, the picture a still life, fruit in a bowl, a brace of partridge on a kitchen table.

'Pity,' he says.

She waits for him to continue, but at the same time knows he's come to a natural break in the narrative.

'What is?'

'Sorry?'

'What's a pity?'

'That he died, of course,' says Clayton.

A beat.

'How did it happen?' she forces herself to ask.

Clayton smiles, waves one of his dismissive hands, catches her eye for the first time in a while, and then rests his head back on the settee.

'He lived up near the school, the house backed onto some old fields. The fields are a housing estate now, of course. There were trees on the other side of the field, a nice wood. I think it's still there. Had a lovely feel to it. A small stream. Probably full of used needles and condoms these days, but it was decent back then.

'I watched him for a while. Adam Pearson. I hid in the woods and watched him. It was the following school year, perfect time. Late September. The nights were getting shorter, but the leaves were hanging onto the trees, and there was plenty of cover in there. I could see his bedroom window. He would have the curtains open, the light on. Played guitar, did his homework, listened to music. So fucking normal.

'When he'd been in town, he'd often come home across the field at the back...'

He lets the words drift away. Taking himself back. She swallows. Strangely, despite everything, she hadn't actually seen this coming. What story had she thought he was going to tell from his childhood?

'I honestly... honestly didn't think I was ever going to kill him. That wasn't what this was about. I was going to break his fingers. That was all. Break his stupid, long, thin, fucking, piano-playing fingers.

'Came up behind him in the dark. Oh, I was nervous, nervous all right. Shitting myself. Had a brick in my hand. Shitting myself he was going to turn round, but it was raining and windy. The trees were moving. Perfect cover. In my dreams I'd imagined taking a movie moment. You know, pausing just behind him, saying, 'Adam?' and seeing the look on his poor, pathetic little face when he turned round, just before I fucked him over the forehead with the brick. But I admit it! I'm no film star! No hero! I chickened out, and hit him over the back of the head.

'He fell. I hit him again to be sure, and then dragged him by the legs into the woods. He'd had his hood up, and for a second I thought how wonderfully funny it would have been if it hadn't been Adam. If I had just skulled some poor innocent passer-by!'

He laughs, shaking his head in amusement, and then the laughter dies, and he stares melancholically back at the picture of the dead partridges.

'But no, it was Adam, poor Adam right enough. And so I did what I set out to do. I broke his fingers. I thought they would snap easily, you know, just bending them back.'

He turns and gives her a curious stare, not quite understanding. She swallows again. Feels the hair standing on her arms.

'I couldn't even do that. I was pathetic. Oh, I think I managed one little finger. Just one. So, I attacked them with the brick instead. And... well, that's all. That was how it happened. Maybe if I'd been able to break his fingers easily, I could have done it and left it there. But I got carried away. Started hitting his fingers with the brick, and then one time I missed his hand, it was up here, you know, his arm bent so it was up by his shoulder, and I hit his face, his stupid, pretty fucking face, and he flinched and I thought, shit, he's going to wake up. So I switched from his hands to his face and head.

'I don't mind admitting I was crying. Quite upset by the whole sad affair. Some would think it was me who should be pitied. And there I was. Couldn't stop. I kept hitting him in the head with the brick...'

His voice drifts off again, as if swallowed up in sorrowful remembrance. The tone, she thinks, would not have been unlike someone describing the last time they saw their father alive. A lament to a lost time.

'No,' he says, 'he never did wake up.'

With those words, the memory is snapped, he frees himself from it and says, 'Ha!'

Clasps his hands together again.

'There you are.'

'Didn't the police come to the school?'

'Of course!'

'Did they interview you?'

'They interviewed everyone. I was just another kid, just another quiet kid, who sat at the back of the class and didn't really have any friends, and didn't say much. No one noticed me.'

'You thought a minute ago everyone was laughing at you.'

His eyes rest on her, his face impassive. The look that goes right through her. The look that explains why he's sitting there, now, in front of her, and she's got a notebook in her hands. The look that chills her right down into the pit of her soul.

'I think we're done for the day,' he says.

3

Standing at the window in Taylor's room, waiting for him to get off the phone. He's speaking to Connor, who's spending the day through in Edinburgh discussing budget cuts. And when I say discussing, he'll be getting told the score. The title of the lecture by the Chief Constable of Police Scotland is "How Bad It Is, And By How Much Are You All Just About To Be Fucked". Or something. They'll be drawing lots to see who's out of a job by the time they get to the door of the lecture room.

Connor said before he left he'd been told his job is safe, so we don't even have that little piece of hope. All we can cling to is that someone was lying to him because he's a dick.

Taylor isn't saying much, so I've tuned out. Looking out at the day, a warm late morning in June. I can see two of our lot standing outside having a fag. There's a young couple across the road on the way to the pub. They are familiar to us, which is why I know they're on the way to the pub. As time goes by, we will play a bigger and bigger part in their lives. Not that it's usually detective work. There's never much detecting to do with the likes of them.

Taylor hangs up. I don't immediately turn round. There's an attractiveness about the day. The sort of day that makes you want to be up a mountain, or by a river. Or both. A packed lunch, a cool drink. Peanuts. Maybe a flask of tea for later.

'What's so interesting?'

I turn, dragged away from my passing daydream.

'What's the news?' I ask.

'They haven't really got started yet,' says Taylor.

'They've had the introductory speeches, then they had a break. The superintendent felt the need to check in during his spare twenty minutes, for which I'm grateful, because obviously we've all been running around like headless Muppets in his absence, waiting for some direction.'

'Perhaps he was doing it to demonstrate to all the other knobs how vital he is to the station.'

Taylor stares with some resignation at the floor.

'Probably bang on.'

He looks up. He's tired. Everybody's tired.

'You were late,' he says. 'Again.'

'Sorry,' I say.

'If it's alcohol–'

'Just not sleeping. Lying in bed, a total basketcase. This morning I turned my alarm off because I was wide awake, but made the rookie error of not getting out of bed when I did it.'

'At least you picked the morning the boss was in Edinburgh, but, you know–'

Hold my hand up.

'I'm on it. Two alarms tomorrow, one on the other side of the room.'

'Anyway, I want you to realise I gave you the guy with the photographs as punishment. And you're going to follow it to the death.'

Well, that serves me right.

'Have you been round to talk to the happy couple yet?'

'Just about to,' I say. 'My original plan was to come up here and try to get out of it, but I see now…'

He waves his hand to the door.

'Can I do some proper work when I get back?'

'If you can find some.'

I stop at the door.

'What d'you think about the cuts? They'll look for volunteers, or there'll be compulsory redundancies?'

Taylor holds my stare. Can tell right there he's been wondering about it himself.

'Don't know how it's going to go,' he says. 'But this

time, well, as they say in American movies, this shit is real. Maybe Connor will have something to tell us tomorrow.'

Small wave of the hand in acknowledgement, then turn and off out the door.

* * *

Sitting in the front room, looking out over Gunville Road, taking tea with Mr and Mrs Hartwell. Thought I might as well. It's lunchtime and I'm hungry, and they weren't offering food. Tea and biscuits will have to do.

'My wife is an attractive woman,' says Hartwell.

I nod in agreement, although really, what the actual fuck? The only way that sentence makes any rational sense is if the woman sitting on the sofa holding his hand isn't his wife.

'Yes,' I say, obviously hoping no one's recording the conversation, 'but you realise you can be charged for this. If Mr Gregson pursues his complaint, there's a fair amount of shit could come your way. You could be in a lot of—'

'Oh, Jesus, don't get us started,' she says.

Her hand parts from her husband's and she leans forward. The top she's wearing is low cut, and suddenly the great chasm between her breasts is presented for my analysis. I look up as quickly as possible. As if I don't have enough mental scarring.

'That man is an egregious little prick.'

Lovely.

'So, why—'

'We're not harassing him, Sergeant, he's harassing us!' explodes the bloke. 'He's been pestering Lucinda for years. Well, fuck him. Really, fuck him. If he wanted to see my wife's tits, I thought, well here you fucking go.'

It's hard to know where to start.

Lift the mug up to my face, and decide to hide behind it for a while.

* * *

Back at my desk, the case of *he said she said* to write up. Neighbourly disputes, even ones with added porn, are just a gigantic pain in the arse. Give me a straightforward, drunken chibbing any day.

Morrow's not as his desk. The place seems kind of quiet. We all know the axe is coming, and it's affected the building. It's like there's less work to do, the Crime Gods looking down and saying, *you can't complain about cuts, yous've got fuck all on.*

Taylor walks past, slows down.

'All well?'

I give him the look, but don't reply.

'Did they put on a show for you to demonstrate the simple naivety of their actions?'

'Where's Morrow?' I ask, by way of moving the conversation on.

'Down at the station,' he says. 'A woman flung herself in front of a train.'

Again? Crap. Feel the weight of such a depressing thought.

Our train station is one of those that makes a perfect suicide spot. The Glasgow to London trains fly through without stopping. Fuck knows what speed they're doing, but Jesus, there's something innately terrifying about them. So much power. Puts the shit up me, I have to say. I always stand well away, like I feel the force of it is going to suck me on to the track.

Other people seem to not give a shit.

Taylor stands for a second, as we both contemplate what was going through her head in the moments before she took the step, then he double taps the desk and walks on.

—

4

Having coffee across the road with Sgt Harrison. She's my new go-to guy for intimate conversation. My gay best friend. She's a bit messed up, and I'm a complete fuck up, so we kind of get along. And, of course, she's damned attractive, coupled with the fact I never even make the effort of trying to get her into bed, so it all works out.

Everyone at the station thinks I'm playing some sort of long game, believing I can wear her down, make the score, and then move on. And when I say everyone, I mean Taylor. I doubt anyone else cares. All those constables these days, they're all twenty years younger than Eileen and me.

When I think of the two of us sitting at a table, I see the attractive fortysomething lesbian and the office stud. The constables will see two old fuckers clinging on to each other like sad, middle-aged has-beens in a Woody Allen movie.

'So, this happened,' I begin, as we settle down across the table, a coffee and a muffin each. My turn to download, given that yesterday she owned the conversation with a fantastic tale of a couple of hours in bed with a nineteen year-old student who, when lying back naked at the end, smoking a joint, had told her it had been like having sex with her mum. Eileen hadn't hung around long enough to establish whether that was a simile arising from actual experience, but thinking back, she wouldn't have been surprised.

'Tell me you're having sex again,' she says. 'I can't be the only complete tart left at the station.'

It's been eight months. Haven't had sex since the night

I spent with Philo Stewart. It's not that, after her murder, I made some sort of vow of celibacy. Just haven't felt like it. Haven't gone looking for it, and it hasn't happened.

'I spend all my time with a lesbian,' I say, 'how is it I'm going to get laid?'

'I manage, despite spending time with you.'

'Well, yes, but people probably think we're both gay. Which works for you, because you are.'

'No one thinks you're gay.'

'Whatever. Can I tell you what happened, or do you not want to hear it because it's not got sex in it?'

She laughs, breaks off a piece of muffin. Recently had her teeth whitened. Nice job. Let's hope she doesn't get her face punched in by one of our clients. That's the kind of thing that happens, after all.

'Sure,' she says. 'But, you know, I thought when we started hanging out, I was at least in for some vicarious hetero-sex. I mean, I've given you a lot – a lot – of lesbian stories, so one of these days you're going to have to start pulling your weight.'

'OK, I'll have sex, just to keep you happy. But can I tell you the thing?'

'Tell me the thing.'

'Thank you. So, I was up at Philo's grave at the weekend. Sunday afternoon.'

She's nodding, knows I go up there. One day she might look concerned at me and tell me I have to get over it and move on, but not yet.

'And, her husband shows up.'

She lets out a low whistle.

'Uh-oh. First time that's happened?'

'Yep.'

'Did you see him coming?'

That, of course, cuts straight to it. If I'd seen him coming, there wouldn't have been half the trouble.

'You didn't see him coming, and you were talking to her. Out loud.'

'You're very perceptive,' I say. 'You should be a

detective.'

'So, how did it play out?'

'Well…'

Break off a piece of muffin, take another mouthful of coffee.

'What exactly were you saying?'

'Hmm… that's the thing. It was… I think… he implied what I was saying was worse, because it was just general chitchat. I mean, obviously it would have been bad if I'd been pouring my heart out about how much I missed her, and what a great life we could have had together. But I wasn't. Well, not at that particular moment. I was just having a chat.'

'And was she talking back?'

'In my head…'

'And were you leaving gaps for her to talk back?'

'Yep.'

'Hmm, not great. And what… were you standing over the grave, kneeling down beside it…?'

I laugh, but not in a butgusting, just heard Frankie Boyle use the word *cunt* sort of a way. Just laughing at myself, because I know how this all sounds.

'I was sitting on the grave, leaning back against the headstone.'

'Jesus, Hutton.'

'Drinking wine.'

She puts her hand to her face. There's something of the Emma Thompson concern about her when she does that – you know, Emma Thompson's concerned face, she uses it in every movie – and I get to see it rather often from Eileen.

'Not from the bottle?'

'Oh no, I had a glass. Two glasses.'

'You poured Philo a glass.'

'Yes.'

'Did you have a picnic?'

'Just a bag of crisps.'

'Classy.'

'Hey, they were Kettle Chips.'

'Ah, right. Quality. You weren't naked, were you?'

'If I had been, I think it would've been on the news.'

'OK, right, we've established the scene. What happened?'

'He was upset.'

'No kidding?'

'No idea how long he was standing there listening. I mean, cheeky bastard, it was none of his business. Then he storms up, kicks over the wine, stands over me calling me a fucking, cheating, marriage-breaking cunt. Those were his words.'

'Cheating, marriage-breaking cunt?'

'Yes. I mean, technically the guy who broke up his marriage was the bastard who killed his wife, not me.'

'Technically. What did you do?'

'I sat and let him rant for a while, then I thought we were getting to the stage where he was going to kick me in the face, so I got up.'

'What was he saying?'

'Oh, you know, the kind of things you'd expect. Who the fuck was I, how dare I…blah blah blah. Called me a cunt several times. I'd thought him a fairly mild-mannered chap, but seems I was wrong.'

'I think maybe he was provoked.'

'Mmm.' Take another bite of muffin. 'I didn't react to him, although I suppose that might've made it worse. He was looking for a fight, and he didn't get it. But it's a fair cop. It's just about the most intimate situation in which he's ever going to find us. It's the one-of-you-is-dead equivalent of being caught fucking on the kitchen table.'

'How'd it end?'

'Not so well. I apologised, which he didn't seem keen on hearing. I didn't apologise again. Didn't, in fact, really feel like doing it at all by the end, because I have to say he was pissing me off. I loved his wife, she loved me, and he was a pussy. That's just how it is, it's not officially my fault. Nevertheless, I have some sympathy for him under the circumstances. But the whining... Anyway, when I wasn't rising to the bait, he finally pushed me. He pushed me and took a step back at the same time. I haven't seen someone do that since primary school.'

'And you?'

'I successfully fought the basic urge to fuck him one in the face. Didn't say anything, turned and walked away. Was prepared to run because I know the shit would've hit the fan if I'd got into a fight. I don't mind leaving the police, as you know, but I'd rather do it with a redundancy payment, than out on my arse.'

'He didn't come after you?'

'I expect he thought about it, but no. Lets me get so far then shouts, 'You left your cheap bloody plonk, you bastard!''

She laughs again.

'And you know what? It was a Chablis! Fucking Chablis. Cheeky bastard. And he'd kicked the bottle over 'n' all, so there was hardly any left anyway.'

She's still laughing behind her coffee cup.

'Well, well done for walking away. You took the moral high ground. Apart from the fact you shagged his wife and drank wine on her grave.'

Nearly finished the muffin. As usual, at such times, one begins to accept it won't be long before one has to return to work.

'Your teeth look great, by the way,' I say.

'Thank you.'

'Makes you look younger.'

'Thanks. That's what I thought, until Saturday night.'

'Doesn't sound like she was looking at your teeth.'

'Hilarious.'

5

When I get back to the station Morrow still isn't as his desk, then I notice him in with Taylor. I'm about to sit down when I get the shout of 'Hoy!' from the office. Marginally better than being whistled at. Maybe. Take a second, salvaging some self-respect about being treated like a sheepdog by not immediately responding, lift a piece of paper, toss it back on the desk without looking at it, and then walk into the room.

Morrow nods at me, Taylor indicates his computer screen.

'We got this from the station's CCTV footage.'

'What are we talking about?'

'The suicide,' says Morrow.

'Right.'

'Which wasn't,' he adds.

The usual crappy grey film runs. There aren't many people on the platform. North side of the station, where the southbound trains stop. Or fly by, incredibly quickly, in the case of the London-bound Virgin trains. There are five people in all. One sitting in the shelter, looking at her phone. Another older guy reading a newspaper standing at the far end. There's a teenager holding a skateboard. I'm assuming he's a teenager, actually, because of the skateboard, but who knows? Then there's a woman standing more or less on the yellow line running a couple of feet from the edge of the platform, her phone in her hand. You can't really tell just from this footage, but we've all seen her. The totally absorbed woman. Headphones in, lost in her own world, music on, either texting or scrolling through Tumblr.

Fucking Internet.

Then there's a guy, walking towards her, just behind, about five yards away. Short coat, beanie, longish hair sticking out from beneath it. The coat and the beanie immediately make him stand out on a warm day like this.

When the film starts there's no sign of a train, even though you can see a hundred yards of track, but these fellows come quickly.

And then there it is, the Euston express, whizzing towards us. When it's fifty yards short of the station the guy in the beanie comes alongside the woman with the phone, pushes her in the back, and she's falling over the edge just as the train passes the station.

Perfect timing.

Hard to watch something like that and not wince. The first time you see it at any rate.

It only just happens in frame, so we don't really see the aftermath. Something flies in the air, and the front of the train and the body are gone, the carriages hurtling past. The guy in the beanie turns, looking after her, shouting. The other three passengers seem to wake up to what's happened. The beanie guy is pointing after the train, as though alerting people. The footage ends.

Taylor clicks it back to the start and we watch it again. The same thing plays over, not revealing anything new on the second viewing. It is definitely apparent what we're watching is no accident, no inadvertent stumble.

'Murder,' I say, mundanely.

'Aye,' says Taylor. He clicks the computer screen back to his wallpaper, a dramatic low moon over the Canadian Rockies scene. Very nice.

'What happened to the guy in the beanie?' I ask.

'Gone gone gone,' says Morrow. 'The other three were still there when we got there. They said he was screaming, like, *oh fuck, I tried to save her*. Said he was going mental. The station guy comes down, but there's not exactly pandemonium, because by the time the train's stopped it's halfway to England it's going so fast, and there are only the three people, and since they didn't see anything…'

'Why d'you think he made the fuss if no one saw anything anyway? He had nothing to cover up.'

'Not sure,' says Morrow.

'Maybe it was part of the plan,' says Taylor. 'He was always going to do it to cover himself, and didn't want to risk looking to see if anyone was watching him. All part of the same flowing movement as tossing her under the train.'

'The driver?'

'Still waiting to speak to him,' says Morrow. 'The rail people came in and whisked him off. Said their people had to speak to him first, which I didn't think was an issue. Didn't think he'd have anything to tell us. Then I saw this.'

'OK,' I say, 'we need to get on to him. Who's the victim?'

'Tandy Kramer,' says Morrow.

'Tandy Kramer?'

'Tandy Kramer.'

Whatever.

'Have we notify–'

'We're only just getting started.'

'Right, gentlemen,' says Taylor, 'time to get into this, all hands. Sergeant, speak to the driver, and don't take any of their shite. We need to him to talk. Constable, get back down there with a couple of guys, look at CCTV from other angles, speak to anyone you can find, wrap the joint up even more tightly than it is already. Before you go, get me her next of kin and I'll get round there. And I'll speak to Ramsay, see who else we can rope in. Get one of the rooms set up. Let's see if we can get this one someway towards a conclusion before Connor gets to hear about it and has us running in circles.'

Not entirely impossible. But then, let's take a walk down to the shops with realism here. We're looking for a guy wearing a beanie with a wig sticking out from beneath, who then vanished. There's a decent chance

Connor's going to be dead by the time we even know who we're looking for.

6

8:17 pm, murder inquiry in full swing. And by full swing, I mean the media has got hold of it.

They say it ain't murder until somebody's dead. It also ain't murder until there's a journalist asking you stupid questions.

Have taken a break with Taylor to come to look at Tandy Kramer's body. Sure enough, with a name like Tandy, she's American. Student, studying at Glasgow Uni. We still don't know what she was doing out our way. Parents back in California have been notified, the father is coming over to collect the body. We're not really going to need to argue any odds about hanging onto her for any length of time. Cause of death is unlikely to be in question, although of course our good friend Balingol, the most miserable fucker to ever slice into a stiff with a scalpel, has to help out the investigation by extracting everything he can from the cadaver.

And on this occasion, he comes up trumps, right from the off, and he has more to work with than could have been expected under the circumstances.

When Miss Kramer hit the train, she wasn't plastered over the front, like Wily Coyote attached to a bomb or anything. It smacked into her and tossed her aside like a dead badger. Her body landed entirely in one piece, in the trees, about seventy yards further down the station.

And now, lying there before us, covered bar the head, she looks like she could be sleeping. Apart from the complexion. Her complexion is terrible.

'So, as you can see,' says Balingol, about to give us a tour, 'remarkably the head is unscathed. The train caught her in the side of the abdomen. Naturally, though, when you get an unblemished face like this in such a case, there's an opposite effect elsewhere. Sometimes it might just be on the inside, and sometimes it's like this…'

He pulls the sheet away, revealing the crushing of her body. Always have to take a moment when looking at something like that. No blood, no breaking of the skin, just her entire body bruised up to the neck, the abdomen crushed and distorted. One of those injuries resulting in a person being so grotesque and misshapen, it looks like a movie special effect. Like you're staring at a prosthetic.

Taylor doesn't look for long, then indicates for him to pull the sheet back up, which he does, once again leaving the face uncovered. She can be a witness to the discussion.

'So, she was killed by the train,' says Balingol, getting the obvious out of the way first. 'There was nothing to indicate she might have had trouble stopping herself falling over. A little alcohol, some indication of marijuana use, but nothing today. Probably last night. What she had been doing today was having sex, and I'm going to say with an older man.'

I let out an involuntary groan, and the two of them look at me. I catch Taylor's eye, but don't say anything.

'Out with it,' he says.

'It's going to be one of those granddad porn rings again, isn't it? Does no one have sex with someone their own age anymore?'

Taylor, unexpectedly, doesn't rebuke me for the line, perhaps indicating he's thinking the same thing, and we look at Balingol for confirmation.

'You can relax,' he says. 'I'm thinking maybe forty, forty-five. Nothing too outlandish.'

Taylor looks back at me, questioning.

'Any thoughts?'

'Still haven't got anything on why she was in Cambuslang,' I say, answering the question prosaically, 'but I guess now we know.'

'Aye,' he says.

Heavy sigh, a somewhat deflated, helpless hand gesture.

'Anything else to report?' he asks.

'She was pregnant,' says Balingol, with the casual, throwaway tone he might have used to tell us her height.

'Better and better,' says Taylor. 'Would she have known?'

Balingol makes the universal gesture of ignorance, for all the world like he's an Italian New Yorker or something.

'I'd say four weeks. Borderline. Maybe she did, maybe...'

And he leaves the rest of the sentence unsaid.

* * *

Sitting in the pub with Taylor, after going back to the station and running through everything we know.

We haven't got very far, and certainly tomorrow morning we're going to be presenting Connor with an unsolved murder, heading as yet in no particular direction, with a list of people still to talk to, and wondering if it might have had something to do with the fact she was pregnant, when the people we've spoken to so far didn't think she was in a relationship.

Two middle-aged, tired police officers in the pub. Just like the old days. We don't do this so much anymore, but Taylor must have decided he needed to wind down. Asked Morrow if he wanted to join us, but he excused himself. It might just have been me, but I couldn't help thinking he had a look on his face to say, 'On you go, granddad, I'm hitting the cool bars.'

More likely, he's probably going home to study for his sergeant's exam, whilst eating salad.

'If it's voluntary, are you going to apply for it?' asks Taylor, breaking into a five-minute silence.

'Redundancy, you mean?'

'No,' he says, dryly, 'the free rectal exam that's going round.'

'Funny.'

Long sigh.

'I'll look at the terms,' I say, 'but you know, it probably doesn't matter. That would just be giving myself more time to make the decision.'

'What would you do if you left?'

Take another drink, listen to the great sound of the ice in the glass, although it does herald the need to go and get another one shortly. Taylor's nearly finished his pint, and I'm hoping he's not about to hit the road when he's done.

'Become a football manager,' I say.

He laughs.

'Nice. You're going for that, rather than rock god, gigolo or President of Space?'

'I'm going to use the redundancy cash to do the courses, work my way up.'

He looks curiously at me.

'You've given it some thought?'

'Yep.'

'That what you've been doing while you've not been sleeping with women?'

'One of the many things.'

'Well, at least you've got a plan,' he says. 'More than I can say. So what sort of manager are you going to be? Brian Clough or Ally McLeod?'

Drain the glass.

'I'm going to be a civilising influence on the world of football.'

He laughs.

'It's not like it doesn't need it,' he says. 'Go on.'

'The trouble with football is, it's full of fucktards. Diving and whining little bastards with their tattoos and their stupid fucking haircuts, moaning at the referee, mobbing the referee, faking this, cheating about the next thing. And then when they score, you can tell they've spent more time in training perfecting their fucking dumbass, thumb-sucking, baby-rocking celebration than they did controlling the ball or passing to one of their own fucking teammates. But why do they do all that shit?'

'Because they're wankers?'

'Because they're empowered by their managers. That's where it starts. I'm going to be different. Day One, I'm getting rid of everybody on the team. Everybody. I don't want anybody there who's not one of my people. Then I'm going to bring in my own people. Youngsters I can mould. I'll civilise them. Tell them there'll be none of that shit. Soon as I see any of them do it, they're off. They'll play with dignity. They'll be no drinking during the season. My team won't be about how they look, with the hair and the boots and the whatever, but how they play the game. We'll do the training in the morning, and then in the afternoon they'll do stuff like learn French, play chess and practice kung fu techniques. I mean, for the meditative, life balance aspects, rather than the kicking shit out of people. It's good for overall health and fitness.'

'Great plan. Who are you managing here? Real Madrid, or a team of ten year-olds at a boarding school, who are going to have no choice?'

'Thought I'd start with Cowdenbeath or Albion Rovers. I'm going to create a new breed of thinking, balanced footballer. They'll be like Jedis. They'll be able to feel where opponents are, they'll be able to seek out teammates with a long through ball without even looking up. But more than that, they're going to be decent, non-fuckwitted, sensible lads, playing a fair game. We'll be successful, our guys will go to other clubs, and this dogma of decency and fair play will spread. I'll be remembered as the man who civilised football, and society along with it.'

'Fine words for a fucked up, sex addicted, chain smoking alcoholic. I'm sure you'll inspire a generation.'

Take another drink, although it's already finished, so just get the dregs and the melted ice.

'I'm having another. D'you want one?'

'Why not? You can tell me your plan to rid the world of nuclear weapons, bring peace to the Middle East and stop people talking shite on the Internet.'

7

I'm lying in a forest. I don't want to be back in the forest. It hasn't been long enough. Eyes open, but I can't get up. Unable to lift my head, although I can't feel what it is that's holding me down.

I can feel the damp earth and leaves and twigs beneath me, the cold air on my chest and legs. Naked again.

Have a sudden fear I'm not in a mild-mannered forest in Scotland, but somewhere else. Somewhere warmer, somewhere more continental. Somewhere the spiders are large, where the bugs are insidious. Then at the same time I notice the leaves in the trees, I recognise the smell in the air, and I remember I always have this thought. I always worry I'm somewhere large spiders are going to be crawling over me, before realising I'm in central Scotland. The Trossachs.

I remember it's not the spiders I have to worry about, then I hear it. The same thought process every time, with the same result. As though I can't hear the crows until I've run through the progression in my head.

There they are, right on cue. The crows. And I can feel the tension on my skin, the cold sweat starting up straight away. And I can't turn, but I can hear the fluttering of the wings behind me, the ugly squawk getting closer. As usual, I worry about my head. Is my head all right? Has my scalp been removed?

But my head feels normal. There's no extra chill where my hair should be, because it's still there. The rest of my body feels odd, naked in a forest, but my head feels normal. Feels as it should.

And then the fluttering stops with the sound of a bird

landing in the leaves, a few feet behind me. I try to look round, but I can't move. I try. Want to turn. Can't do it. The footfalls of the bird get closer, and then they stop. Right there. Right by my head, just behind my right ear.

I look round as much as I can, and can just make out the wing. The black wing. The crow. I can't remember what's coming. I should know, I've been here so often. It taunts me, and although I can't see it, I can imagine its head tilted to the side in curiosity. Or in mocking laughter.

And then there's the pain of the sharp jab. Its beak, stabbed into my skull, just behind the ear. A short break, and then another one. Another. Fuck, that's sore. Same spot every time, just behind the ear. Is that a weak spot?

Why there? Why not some soft part of the body? If he wants into the brain, why not go through the eyes? Stupid crow.

Again, another three jabs in quick succession.

'Fuck off!'

I can speak! Ha! I can't move, but I can speak. I'd settle for the reverse.

'Fuck off!'

Do crows understand profanity? It's the tone, isn't it? Trying to scare him with noise. It's all I can do. Maybe if I roar.

I roar. Throaty, all the noise I can muster. It hurts, but it's loud, before tailing off into a high-pitched yowl.

Silence.

I can see the bird thinking about it, its head still to the side, staring at me. But he hasn't backed off. Maybe I'm going to need to scream ag–

'What was *that*?'

A strange voice. I don't know what the voice is. I understand the words, but the voice in itself is inexplicable. An alien sound.

'Was that a scream? Were you, I don't know, impersonating a lion? Jesus. I've got to tell you, pal, whatever it was, it failed.'

'I was trying to scare you.'

That's all I can think to say. Really? That's all I've got? And it hurts to talk. My throat hurts after the roar.

'Oh, yeah, because that worked. Listen kid, you just lie there. I'm going to do my thing, you're going to do your thing. Whatever it is. But enough with the roaring already, my ears hurt.'

'What is your thing?' I say. 'Pecking at my head isn't a thing.'

'Sure it is.'

'That's not even half a thing.'

'Buddy, accept it. It's a thing. A whole, goddam thing.'

'I want you to stop!'

'Well, go ahead then. I'm only here because of you, so don't try fucking with my shit.'

'What d'you mean? What d'you mean you're only here because of me?'

'You're the one with the fucked up head. You're the one who wants someone to drill inside it and remove everything. You're the one who wants to forget. So I'm here doing what I'm supposed to be doing, and you're roaring! Jesus! What kind of fucked up shit is that?'

'Yes, I want to forget, but not like this.'

'Hey, kid, forgetting don't come easy in life. You can't just forget shit. It takes effort. Bad things have to happen. You need to think about what it is you really want. I'm not here because I want to be. Jesus, there are worms and shit to eat, why would I spend my time tapping away at solid freakin' skull here? Any time you want me to leave, you know what to do.'

'What?'

'You know what to do, kid, so just do it.'

I wake up. Eyes wide open. Don't sit up in bed, just lie there, naked, staring at the ceiling. The covers have fallen off. Cold. The middle of the night, still dark. Sweating.

I cough. My throat's sore.

8

Wednesday morning. The usual crew together in the hastily assembled ops room. It's not quite all hands yet. Too early to know what we're dealing with. Could just have been a drunken lout, although no one's putting money on that.

It's not that anyone's saying, dear God, a drunken lout on a train platform at eleven o'clock in the morning? Never in all my life! It's the beanie, and the hair. Looks wrong, feels wrong.

Taylor is majoring on the beanie.

'Yep, there are guys wearing beanies all year round,' he's saying, 'regardless of the weather, but the intent here, coupled with the peculiarity, and of course, there's hair sticking out the bottom of the beanie because it's a feature, and a couple of the others on the platform remember him wearing glasses… it all says disguise.'

Six of us in the room in all. Taylor, Morrow and me, three constables. Cairns, Jones, and Ablett.

Constables come and go, don't they? It's like this production line of spotty youths and flat-chested girls.

I know, I know, the size of their chests has nothing to do with it.

'Which also means we can rule out a random act of badness, some kid just having a moment of madness and thinking, fuck it, this'll be funny. He, or she, went there with intent. So, was it with intent to kill Tandy Kramer specifically, or was he happy to just kill?'

He looks around the room, glances back at the white board which has everything we know so far – yep, not very much – then turns back.

'I think we ought to hope it was the former, because that way at least it ends here. And it hugely increases our chances of doing a quick job. If it was random...'

He lets the sentence go with a wave, glances at the clock then looks at me.

'I need to be in with Connor. Can you start divvying up, Sergeant? We've got to pin down who got her pregnant, so we need to speak to men in their forties with whom she had even the slightest contact. We should look at the CCTV footage from later on. We won't be looking for the beanie, but it's possible the killer returned. It's going to be tough recognising him, but have somebody take a look anyway. And broaden the scope of her fellow students you speak to.'

Another glance at the clock.

'I'll go and meet the girl's father off the plane,' he continues, 'but that's not for another few hours. Right...'

He gives me the *get on with it* nod, and then leaves. I stand up and turn to address the crowd of four. This is where, if we were in a sitcom, they'd all start talking to each other and completely ignore me. No sitcom this. Just seems like it, ninety-eight per cent of the time.

* * *

Knock and enter. Taylor back at his desk, typing quickly. Eyes on the screen. I don't think I've ever seen him do that before.

'Are you touch typing?'

He turns. Looks more tired than he did thirty minutes ago. In no mood for the usual light-hearted frivolity I try to bring to any murder investigation.

He doesn't say anything, just answers the question with something of an impatient eyebrow.

'How'd it go with Connor?' I ask.

'They're not cutting staff,' he says.

The look of disgruntlement stays on his face.

'What d'you mean?'

'Just like it sounds.'

'But...'

'What?'

'I just thought... Everyone's been talking about it. Just presumed there were going to be cuts.'

'There *are* going to be cuts. But not staff cuts, just budgetary cuts. They don't want to lose any more police officers. Not yet.'

'Politics?'

'Damned politics. Absolutely. That's what it's all about. The government have passed down the instruction. There's less money, but they don't want any headlines about cuts in frontline policing. They don't want... fuck, whatever, you get the picture. There will be no cushy redundancy payments.'

'So how do they make the cuts without cutting staff?'

'They cut everything else. They close buildings, they put eight people in an office designed for two. They stop overtime payments...'

'That'll be a bastard.'

'Yes, it will. We exist on overtime. There are occasions when we absolutely need it. They won't stop it altogether, but it's to be cut by eighty per cent.'

'Fuck off.'

'No, fuck on,' he says, even though that's not an actual phrase. 'And so on and so on. There'll be a pay freeze, and an actual pay cut is not out of the question. Allowances are gone, any other kind of monies paid out, forget it. That kind of thing. But no staff cuts, so the fucking government can stand up there and say they're saving fucking money on the police, but front line services, all the bobbies-on-the-fucking-beat crap, hasn't been affected. Which of course, it fucking will be.'

'Jesus...'

'Yes. Jesus. No doubt they're just saving their damn money so they can flush it down the fucking NHS toilet. The minute they start charging people for fuck-witted stupidity, then they'll be able to balance their fucking budget a lot better. So, madam, you went hillwalking in a fucking blizzard, with visibility less than two feet, and you broke your leg? That'll be fifteen fucking grand for the hospital. You're seventeen and you drank two bottles of vodka a day for a year? You can pay for your fucking liver treatment, and if you can't and you die, then that, my dumbass friend, is natural selection at work. Congratulations, you're a living fucking anthropological project.'

Hmm, the boss doesn't usually swear.

He shakes his head, stops himself before he launches into another example of entitled Britain, absolving itself of all its problems and passing them on to the government.

'Bollocks,' he mutters, and then waves away the conversation. 'You'll just have to find another way to finance your Jedi football coaching course. Where've you got to?'

'Just off into the university with Morrow. He's going to speak to some more of her classmates, and apparently there are a couple of older fellows amongst them. I'm speaking to her lecturers and tutors. She had three different men for maths, and a couple of statistics people, one man.'

'Fine,' he says, then he glances at the door by way of saying it's where he wants me to go, turns back to the computer and starts typing.

'That's not your resignation letter?' I say, as I'm leaving.

He doesn't answer.

9

Used to have this lecturer at Glasgow. Maths. While back now, wonder if he's still here. He'd walk into the lecture hall. Wouldn't look at the class, wouldn't say anything to the class. He'd turn his back and start to write the lecture on the board. All he said was what he wrote on the board. No elaboration. He would stand for an hour, writing equations and shit, and then the hour would be up, he'd put his bag or whatever under his arm, and then he'd turn and walk out. No questions, no 'you should do this or the next thing for next week'. Nothing.

At the time, I don't know, I was nineteen or so I guess, I just thought, well that's weird. Looking back, it seems pretty sad. The guy must have been extremely screwed up. Or else, just in completely the wrong job. Perhaps he was one of those maths geniuses you hear about, you know, the type who are usually Asian and can get their BSc by the time they're six. Maybe he was one of those. I mean, what kind of job do you get when you're a maths genius? Most of them probably end up as lecturers, but they're geniuses, they don't want to talk to people. They want to sit in a room with shit scribbled all over blackboards, occasionally looking up from a book to ignore some gorgeous woman who wants to sleep with them because they're a genius.

Had to bring sex into it.

The first guy I speak to, Dr Dalzeil, reminds me of my maths genius of a lecturer, who may not, of course, have been a genius at all. Maybe, in fact, he was the cleaner and he was faking it. Maybe he knew fuck all about maths, and that was why he never took questions. He just stood up there, copying someone else's notes onto a board.

'Was she in my class?'

That's how Dalzeil responds to my initial question. But the way he says it, it's not evasive, it's not smug, it's not dismissive. It's confused. The tone says, what, those people who sit there have names?

'Yes, she was in your class. Had been all year. American,' I add.

'American?'

I have a photograph, which I hadn't thought I'd need, but I take it out my pocket and place it on the desk in front of him.

'I recognise her.'

'You've been teaching her for the last year.'

'We're not a school,' he says. 'I don't think... I don't think I'm expected to have any sort of relationship with the students.'

'Where do you live?'

'What?'

'Where do you live?'

'I have rooms. Near the bowling club. I mean, Burnbank. Burnbank Bowling Club. I can see the clubhouse.'

He has rooms. Do people have rooms anymore? Nevertheless, despite the fact that speaking to him is getting me absolutely nowhere, I do find him quite refreshing. And, as a bonus, I won't have to arrest him.

* * *

This guy's more like it. Has bit-of-a-cunt written all over him.

'Yes, terrible business,' he begins, as we ease ourselves into seats in his office. 'She was very good. Highest grade in the midterms, was fully expecting her to have the highest grade this month. I know what we think of Americans, but we do get some very able maths students coming over here.'

'Did she do any sort of extra, I don't know, did you

42

tutor her in some way, give her any extra help?'

'Never needed to. Most able student in her year. Very clever. Very clever indeed.'

'You never saw her out of university?'

'No, of course not.' He tosses one of those casual hands. 'Well, you know, perhaps out on Byres Road...'

This is him. I know it. It's no big deal, and from looking at the build of the guy, it's not him who pushed her in front of the train, but he was sleeping with her. I wonder how much to bother letting him wriggle around before getting the truth out the fucker.

'She was pregnant,' I say.

He holds my gaze. I can hear the swallow. Silence in the room, and then the sound of the gentle tapping of his fingers.

'Well, obviously that's not something I was aware of.'

'No?'

'Of course not. She was hardly... she was hardly likely to suddenly stand up and announce it in a lecture hall.'

'No, but she might have divulged the information over the kitchen table, or while lying in bed.'

The tension in the face drops. It doesn't relax, just repositions itself. Now we're getting to it, and he's not going to take that kind of shit from a police officer. We're about to get the lawyer spiel or the do-you-know-who-I-am spiel, or the I-have-friends-in-the-SNP spiel. Any one of those and he can fuck off.

'I don't know what you're implyi...'

'Where do you live?'

I could have found out this stuff before asking these guys, but didn't have the time, and it's easy enough to check if they're telling the truth. And anyway, there's nothing ultimately this guy can do about the gigantic piece of circumstantial evidence helping nail the fucker to the gatepost.

'Cambuslang,' he says. 'Top end of Wellshot.'

I stare across the desk at him. Hold it. Don't need to add anything.

'It means nothing,' he says.

That, my asshole friend, is bullshit, but there's still no need for me to speak. No way he has the balls to stare me out.

'She was one of my students, she died in Cambuslang, I live in Cambuslang. And on that basis, what? Is that enough for you to take me to court? Is that the sort of evidence the police choose to go on these days, because if it is…'

He looks off to the side, stares vacantly, then finally looks back at his silent interrogator.

'I'm not saying anything else,' he says. 'So, if you're just going to sit there like fucking Avercamp or something, then, I don't know, please feel free. I have a tutorial class to attend in fifteen minutes.'

Avercamp? I don't want to know.

'You'll need to cancel it or get someone else to do it,' I say.

'Why?'

'What were you doing yesterday morning?'

'What?'

Oh, he's looking very pissed off now. The cool, calm composure of an ice hockey player in the middle of a brawl. What a dick.

'Where were you yesterday morning? And remember, I can independently verify your schedule.'

'I was here.'

'In this office or at various places around the university?'

'In this office. I was working. I'm co-authoring a paper on the Birch and Swinnerton-Dyer conjecture. I don't suppose you even know what that is.'

Oh, fuck you, you pompous prick.

'What time did you get here?'

'I don't know.'

'It was yesterday. Think about it.'

He shrugs, continues the annoyed look of the unfairly hounded.

—

44

'What d'you want me to say?'

Give him another second. I've had enough. Fun over.

'Yesterday morning, not long before she was pushed in front of a train, Tandy Kramer had sex with a man in his forties. Given you're the right age, you knew Miss Kramer, and you live in the same town in which she very probably had sex, it's entirely reasonable for us to check the DNA of the sperm we found in her body against yours, which will tell us either way. So this it, maths guy. We're going down to the station. Right now. You and me. You can tell me whether you had sex with Miss Kramer, but remember, I'm going to have absolute proof of whether you're telling the truth. Now, get your coat.'

'I don't think you quite realise who I am.'

There is a pregnant pause.

Yes I do.

You're a dick.

10

'She was nineteen, there was nothing illegal. There's no university law expressly forbidding relationships with the students. Yes, it's frowned upon, but if you think I'm the first...' He holds his finger up before Taylor can get in a line about the fact that none of the others got pushed in front of a train, less than half an hour after having slept with the member of staff. 'And I'm not even married. So, I don't see the problem here, I really don't.'

'She was pregnant,' says Taylor. Voice low, calm. Great tone. 'It may not have been illegal, but it would have been very bad for your career.'

'You think I was the only one she was sleeping with?' says the desperate Dr Ferguson. 'Have you learned anything about Tandy in the last day and a half?'

'We'll know soon enough, when we get the results of the lab work back on the foetus.'

'Fine, but I say it again, I wasn't the only one.'

'You weren't the only member of staff?'

'I don't know. Jesus.'

'Why are you so sure there were others?'

'Oh, just look at her. She was gorgeous, she was confident. Girls like her... they're always the same.'

Go on, you idiot, keep digging.

Taylor maintains the cold stare across the desk. I already told him Ferguson doesn't like it. Can't handle the silence.

'I can prove I was on the train, on my way to Partick, when Tandy died.'

'We know,' says Taylor.

'What?'

46

That throws him. If this guy ends up in court, I hope for his sake he just tells the truth straight from the off, because otherwise it's going to be embarrassing.

'We have CCTV of you getting on the train in Cambuslang. We have CCTV of you getting off the same train in Partick. The person who pushed Miss Kramer onto the train tracks was smaller in stature than you.'

His face starts to relax, his shoulders are a little straighter.

'Well, why the fuck am I here then?' he says.

Manners. People just have no respect for the police. See the amount of this kind of shit we get?

'Because someone killed Miss Kramer. The only exceptional fact in her life we know so far is she was pregnant. The only person we know for a fact was sleeping with her is you. Therefore, the only person in the entire world so far we know had a motive for perhaps wanting her dead, extreme though I admit that is just because she was pregnant, is you. That's why you're here. And the fact you had a perfect alibi, and had quite possibly arranged to go ahead of Miss Kramer to the university so you wouldn't be seen together, does not mean you didn't arrange for someone else to push her in front of the train.'

'But...'

Words dry up. You could see his emotions come and go. Taylor had him when he said about them going on separate trains so no one could see them together. That's absolutely what happened, and no doubt he got to go first, because his job as a lecturer was more important than her position as a student. Great kicker when Taylor mentioned the possibility of him hiring someone to kill her. There's nothing to suggest it, but it's always good to put it out there and see what happens.

'You couldn't even let her get on the same train, three carriages apart, could you?' says Taylor. 'You made her wait in Cambuslang.'

Not something you'd wish on anyone in itself.

'Right, Dr Ferguson, I need to go to the airport to meet

the girl's father. You're going to stay here with Sgt Hutton and tell him everything about you and Miss Kramer. The first time you noticed her in class, the first flirtatious glance, the first time you slept together. I want it all. And when I get back, and if the Sergeant's happy with the information you've given him, then we can talk about what happens next. At the moment, all that's happening next is you're talking. And talking.'

Taylor pushes his chair back, gives him a final stare and then leaves.

Great speech, beautifully delivered. Just leaves the place feeling a bit flat afterwards. Now it's going to be like trying to pick the room up again after Oor Andy has just beaten Djokovic 17-15 in the fifth.

* * *

Sitting at my desk a few hours later. Dr Ferguson is gone. We've got everything we need for now, and I doubt he's about to flee the country. You get a feel for these people, and this fellow isn't the kind to get anyone too worried. Yes, he's in his forties and he was sleeping with a nineteen year-old, but we've all done that, right? Or, at least, some of us have.

I told him to prepare for it all getting out. It's going to happen. People are going to know, if they didn't already. The two of them seemed to have done a decent job of keeping it under wraps, but too late to worry about that now.

Taylor came back, looking as miserable as you're going to feel having spent two hours with the deceased's father, and authorized the release of the lecturer. Happy to go on my say.

Now we're sitting separately, at our own desks, trying to tie things together, seeing if anything matches, if any piece of information sparks off any other. Back in the ops room at seven this evening.

Morrow returns to the room, having been gone for a

while, and takes a seat opposite.

'How's it going?'

I lift and drop a couple of pieces of paper.

'Don't know we've got much beyond our lecturer. For all his apparent presumption he wasn't the only one, seems he was. At least, if there were any others, she was keeping them a good secret 'n' all. We really only stumbled upon this guy because he happened to live where she died and he's absolutely shite under interrogation. Not sure we'd have got him otherwise.'

Look around the papers and notes hoping something else might jump off a page at me.

'Little else. We've looked through her stuff. She was pretty regular in her Facebook, Twitter and Tumblr posts. Mostly Fall Out Boy and Chris Hemsworth.'

'I like Fall Out Boy,' Morrow contributes to the conversation.

'You just want me to know you've heard of them,' I say.

He laughs, finally sits down.

'Hey, did you hear about the thing in Clarkston this afternoon?'

'Clarkston?'

'Fucking gruesome.'

Morrow never used to swear. Must be my bad influence. At least I'll leave some legacy around here.

'Gruesome?'

'Double beheading. Go on, put it up on BBC News.'

'In Clarkston?'

'That is just some freaky, weird shit man. Two white folks in a Muslim community centre. Used to be a church. The place was locked up. The guy who runs it was opening it up for this AA meeting they have on Wednesday afternoons...'

'An Islamic AA meeting in what used to be a church?'

'Yep.'

'Isn't there so much irony in that itself, it could explode?'

'I don't know if it's irony,' he says.

'Suppose.'

'Anyway, he opens up, nothing untoward about the locks or the doors or the windows or anything, then goes into the main hall, and boom. There they are, tied upright in chairs in the middle of the hall, back-to-back, heads in their laps. In red paint on the wooden floor was scrawled, *Unbelievers*. Oh, they got the *i* and the *e* the wrong way round.'

'Holy fuck,' I say.

'Yes,' he says, 'holy fuck. You've got a church, you've got beheadings and you've got Islam.'

'A perfect shitstorm.'

'Exactamundo,' he says. 'It looks like a fun case, but kind of glad it's not ours.'

Well, I'll just have to disagree with him there. I don't think it looks fun at all, but I do have absolutely no doubt I'm delighted it's not ours.

'I'm disappointed for you, but you'll just need to crack on with our mundane, old pushing in front of the train.'

'Yep, I'm on it.'

'Sit. room at seven.'

'Right.'

And even though I dismissed the conversation, there's no way I'm getting that image out of my head. Two decapitated bodies tied back-to-back. More extreme and instant than the Plague of Crows, but it's certainly reminiscent. Not that what the Plague of Crows did wasn't extreme.

'Maybe it's a Highlander type gig,' says Morrow.

I'm still thinking about it and I don't want to be, so I don't respond.

'Perhaps we should be checking out the whereabouts of Christopher Lambert.'

'You can have that one,' I say.

He manages to focus for about a minute and a half, and then says, 'You know *Highlander 2* is like, I don't know, the worst sequel of all time. I mean, what were they–'

'Constable!'

Finally he shuts up, looks back down at the pile of papers I'd placed on his desk. He looks at his, and I look at mine, but I still can't concentrate. Not now.

11

'Well, I don't know. I never do.'

Clayton stares at a vague spot on the wall in front of him. Not looking at the still life this time.

'I just blocked it out,' he says, making another of his affected hand gestures. Under other circumstances, Dr Brady might have been making notes on the hand gestures, and what they meant. She didn't think, though, given the current set-up, he would appreciate it. 'I mean, it was like it hadn't happened. I created in my mind – oh, this is good, you probably want to write this down – I created in my mind a character. A beastly character. I never saw him again, I never held him responsible for anything again, but in my head I knew he was to blame for poor Adam's death. So when they asked, when they came asking – oh, and they did – I knew who did it, and I wasn't saying. That was my secret. So, I wasn't lying when I said I had nothing to do with it, I really wasn't. Adam's killer was this other character who, I admit, I was protecting. But that was all. Who was I to judge?'

Dr Brady realises more and more, as the sessions continue, she will be writing less and less of what she actually thinks.

'Did you have an alibi for the time the murder was committed?'

'Mother,' he says, throwing the word across the room. 'Not that she thought she was protecting me, or lying for me. I said I was in my room, and she backed me up. Elaborated, of course, just to make sure. Said she'd brought me a cup of coffee and some cake at almost the precise time Adam died.'

He laughs, a high, curious, ugly sound, which somehow crawls right inside her.

'I don't even like coffee,' he says, laughing some more. 'Well, if they'd got us in separate rooms at the same time and asked us questions, I dare say they could have found us out on that particular lie, but what do the police know? Stupid.'

'Perhaps they just didn't suspect you at all,' she says.

'Probably not. There was so little to suspect. Just an anonymous, fat, little kid, sitting at the back of the class.'

He laughs again, rueful this time, completely different in tone. Contemplative.

Brady has a question for him, but doesn't really want to ask. She takes a deep breath, watches him. Expecting his eyes on her, but he seems quite focused on whatever indistinct point he's staring at on the wall, a smile on his face.

'Have you killed anyone else?' she asks finally.

His eyebrows shoot up and he turns and looks at her, his expression amused rather than annoyed.

'Why, yes! Of course!'

She manages to hold his stare, but doesn't ask him to elaborate. Again the fanciful wave of the hand, then he turns back to his current spot on the wall.

'Took a while, of course. I mean, really, I'm not some, I don't know, I'm not an uncontrollable psychopath. I took my time, I really did. There were others there, others in the class that year, who really... well, it was almost remiss of me not to do it, it really was. But I'm not stupid. If another member of the class had gone, well, really... The police would never have been away. And I know what you're thinking. You probably see it all the time, you're thinking I'd somehow scared myself. I was frightened by my own power, my own ability to be so cruel. Well, you're having none of it. It was just a matter of common sense.'

'You said yesterday you were crying while you were hitting him in the head.'

She wonders if he's going to turn on her, but you have

to point these things out. The room is completely silent, not a sound entering from outside. She can hear herself swallow. Some people, most people, don't like the contradictions being pointed out. Especially people like Michael Clayton.

'So, I waited,' he says eventually. His voice low, the tone the same, having addressed her words internally and having decided to completely ignore them. 'Waited so long I quite forgot about poor young Adam. That may sound... I don't know, how does it sound? Heartless? That I forgot Adam was dead? Anyway, there you are, you can't decide what your brain remembers and what it doesn't. And then it was university, and I stayed at home of course, because mother didn't really want me staying in student digs. That would have been too... vulgar...'

'Which university did you attend?'

'Glasgow, of course. Good grief, I wasn't going to go to Strathclyde. And all those other so-called universities around here, well they were just some fool's pipe dream back then.'

'What did you study?'

'Oh, maths and eh... maths and computing. I was good. Had little trouble. A very smooth path. Well, academically. Otherwise... I thought, I really thought, you know, it's time for a change. I can be a different person. Why not? People change. There was no one there from school, no one who was going to judge me. No one to tell other people I was this strange little boy sitting in the corner, not speaking to anyone. I could be an entirely new character. I could reinvent myself. Isn't it just perfect? So, there I was. The talker. The debater. Joined the Conservative party, joined the debating club. Ha!'

Having given the plan and the set up, he stops when it comes to explaining what went wrong. She waits for him to talk this time. In truth, she wishes he wouldn't. She doesn't want to know. The story that's coming won't be a pleasant one.

'Really, they just... can you believe it?' he says finally,

the tone of voice now low. The bitterness has flowed through him, and has gone. Sorrow remains. The regret is at his rejection, however, not at the way he handled it.

'Perhaps I wasn't so good at the part. I don't know.'

'You didn't… did you get on a debating team? Did you g–'

'No! God no. I mean… There was Phil. I remember Phil. He was good, I admit it. And there were a couple of others, I had to give them that too. But Bethany…'

Another burst of near-hysterical laughter.

'She was a piece of work, she really was. The debating skills of a wildebeest fleeing from a lion. My God… No, no, it wouldn't do at all.'

Another pause. He stares at his vague spot.

'Why did they pick Bethany over you?'

'Because of her tits,' he says, his voice level. 'Her tits. She would go around, Jesus, she would wear these thin V-neck jumpers and no bra. I mean, don't get me wrong, she had great tits. But tits don't make the debater, believe me, they really don't.'

Brady has a sudden thought.

'You didn't kill Bethany?' she says. 'You killed someone who chose Bethany over you.'

'No,' he says, matter-of-factly, 'it was Bethany.'

She lowers her eyes. She can't read him. She's not sure her insights at the end of all this are really going to be of any use to anyone.

'I left it over a year. I waited. I'm good at waiting. I can wait as long as it takes. I stayed in the club and in the party, making a gradual withdrawal. Soon enough I was the person I was at school, the quiet one sitting at the back. When I came for Bethany it was almost eighteen months later. When the police were asking who might have had a grudge against her, they'd all forgotten about me. It was so long in the past. And… and yes, it sticks in my throat to admit it, but they were all so, all so damned won over by her fucking tits it probably didn't even occur to them I had been slighted. So, you know what? No one came asking.

Not a single, fucking copper! Dear God.'

Another short silence. The details of the death are coming. She doesn't want to hear them.

'And you know what? You know what I found out? When I dragged her into the bush, when I stripped the clothes off her, when I finally removed the thin V-neck jumper she always wore?'

He turns and looks at Brady, his face hardening, a look of curious contempt.

'Her fucking tits weren't even that great. Jesus. I mean, they were all right, but not especially pert or anything, the nipples were kind of, I don't know, pale and non-descript. It wasn't me who was fooling anyone, it was her! She was the one playing a part. Playing the part of the girl with the great tits. Fucking hell.'

'What did you do to her?' she asks, the question burning in her throat.

'Oh, you know, just strangled her. Nothing, it was nothing. Didn't even rape her. Thought about it, but rape is so... Well, for one thing, it leaves behind some rather clear evidence of the perpetrator. You have to bring some element of calculation into these things.' He taps the side of his head, not looking at her. 'So, yes, that was Bethany.'

'And did you create another character? Someone else you could blame for Bethany's murder?'

'Yes, yes, oh yes. But, as I said, I didn't need him. So, the good thing was, he was still there. I had him in reserve. I mean, for the next time. Do you want to hear about the next time?'

He turns and stares at her with a look of expectation.

12

In the door at seven minutes after nine. Stopped at the shops on the way home, determined not to have another night of alcohol and no food, or of me standing in the kitchen making a couple of crappy pieces of toast and eating cheese from the fridge, more or less drinking wine from the bottle. Bought a salmon fillet, some salad and a wholemeal ciabatta.

So now I'm sitting at the table, place set, dinner on a plate. Listening to Bob. Been enjoying his albums of old American standards. Yeah, I know, they're excruciating, right? Got to be plenty of people thinking that. His voice is so up front, it's great. I love it. Everyone else, I don't give a shit what they think. My only complaint is they're too short. You put one of the CDs on to sit down to dinner, you eat your dinner, you're thinking about shit, and then, poof! it's over.

Shadows In The Night, the first one, is my favourite. Pretty bleak and melancholic, though. Slow, so full of sorrow. Perfect for a miserable, grieving misanthrope like myself.

Glass of wine, the usual Chilean Sauvignon. Stare at an indistinct spot on the wall in front of me. Mind near as empty as it's going to get. Bob drones on, occasionally holding the notes, frequently magnificently off-key. A beautiful sound. New York in the fall, autumn leaves and lonely cups of coffee in old cafés that have been on the same street corner since the '40s. Untouchable women walk by, too remote, too unapproachable.

Maybe those places don't exist anymore. Those cafés. Maybe all you see is Starbucks and Dunkin' Donuts and some coffee chain we've never heard of, serving the same stuff we get in the same cafés over here, and the women are just women, and the falling leaves are just dull and old and a sign of impending, gathering gloom.

June in Glasgow. Autumn in New York. Maybe I could take a few days off, head out there. Don't travel much. Don't get around much anymore... Bob doesn't do that one.

Don't feel like going online. Perhaps tomorrow I'll check out flights to New York in October. If I remember. And if I don't, well I guess I'm not bothered.

The album comes to an end. The silence, just for a second, seems crushing, and then I lift the bottle, pour the third glass of wine, look at the clock. Ten o'clock.

With an almost theatrical sigh, decide I'm going to stick the news on. I doubt our local rail death will have made any kind of impact, but I'll take a look anyway. Grab the remote, TV on, sit back at the table.

First up they've got the double beheading. Heart sinks. I don't know what I thought there was going to be. Some crappy English political story maybe. The kind of thing the BBC can get excited about, when they can have one of their correspondents standing happily in front of Number 10, looking like it's all terribly important, despite the fact we'll all have forgotten about it by tomorrow morning.

But no, despite having taken place in the complete independence-voting backwater of Glasgow, they've made the double beheading their main story.

And there, on the screen, is the story of our times. Two whites beheaded in an Islamic centre. Outside the building, there are demonstrations. Demonstrations against the Islamic community. Demonstrations against immigrants, all immigrants. And then here comes the Muslim community leader to say we can't blame Islam for this, and that they are appalled. And there's the government minister saying they'll clamp down on this kind of appalling extremist behavior. And then the expert predicting there will more to come, and the Tory backbencher saying the security services should have more power, and then there's the liberal saying we must respect the right of people with a grievance, whatever their religion, to behead people.

Maybe she doesn't quite go that far.

I turn it off. Don't want to know. It's all so fucking depressing.

I have a niggling doubt. It doesn't make sense, of course. Why would they do it in an Islamic centre? Wouldn't you do it in a church? And I know, it used to be a church, but wouldn't you do it in an actual, live, functioning church, or at least in one that's not been converted for Islamic use?

Fuck knows. Maybe they were also objecting to their own place hosting AA meetings.

Take a long swallow of wine. I had thought the third glass would be my last, but the fourth now looks likely. Once you've had the fourth, the end of the bottle is in sight, and there seems little point in putting it back in the fridge.

Get up, which in itself seems an effort, over to the CD player, start Bob off again from the beginning, and sit back down at the table. Back against the chair, eyes straight ahead at an indistinct point on the wall that seems to define my evening dining experience, glass of wine in my right hand, as the slow, wretched chords of *I'm A Fool To Want You* fill the room.

* * *

The crow's back again in the night. I remember I'm in the same position. I remember I can't move. I remember the feel of his beak against my skull. I remember the pain. When I wake in the morning, it's like I can still feel it. The pain is still there.

I take a couple of paracetamol with some toast and a cup of tea, and the pain leaves. I can't remember what the crow said though. Just his voice. Just the accent. Maybe the crow sounds like he comes from old New York because I've been listening to the Dylan CD every day.

They say that accent, the accent of old New York, is dying out. Like the voice of Pathé newsreels and 1940s cricket commentaries.

13

Called into Connor's room. Me and Taylor, and DCI Dorritt. I'm never sure why I get called into Connor's room, but particularly today, as we're not discussing the train death.

Taylor still seems pissed off, although it's not particularly directed at Connor. It's hardly his fault. If Connor had his way, he'd increase his budget by 800%, and be in charge of a station four times the size. He won't like the cuts any more than anyone else, although for different reasons. I doubt too much of the extra work that will have to get done will find itself his way.

'So, we're going to have to look at it all, right across the board. The recommendations are going bottom up, not top down. Of course, the decisions on what actually happens will go the other way, but we have to make proposals that suit us best, and meet the requirements of the organisation on all levels, and then staff those proposals appropriately up the chain of command with a view to things working out to our advantage.'

Still not sure why I'm here. Perhaps he's looking for some earthy commentary on everything he's saying. The occasional, *shut the fuck up* or *get to the point!*

'What kinds of things do you want us to look at?' asks Dorritt.

'Everything,' says Connor. 'No one's leaving, so that's fine. Can we move to a smaller building? Would it be cost effective, both in the short and long term, to sell this place, move in somewhere smaller? A different location in Cambuslang. A cheaper location. If we stay here, can we sell off some of the property? Can we move, for example, another government office onto the premises, rent the space out to them? Look gentlemen, everything's on the cards here. And don't think I'm immune. Even I'm looking at the real possibility of having to give up this office. We're looking at all of us, every one, being in a large open-plan. That may well be just how's it going to have to be.'

Maybe we could have a massage parlour. A pub. Sex shop. All three in one exciting, modern venue. I keep all that to myself. Taylor looks like he's ready to shout at someone, and it'd be foolish to provide him with an easy target.

'Can I ask why I'm here?' I say, because I seem to have too much urge to talk, yet not hungover enough to say anything that's going to have Taylor manhandling my testicles.

'Yes, of course. Like I said, this is going to be bottom up…'

'I'm not at the bottom.'

'Well… I'd like the views of the constables, and I thought you'd be a good man to go around, get them together, form, if you like, a task force. I'm not expecting… of course, I'm not expecting anything from them of the likes… you know, I'm not looking for the boots on the grounds men to come up with great, you know… what I'm looking for is nuts and bolts stuff. Penny-pinching we could call it. How we can save on the day-to-day stuff, but without it looking like… we need to not worry the public. We need the public to know the police are still here for them, that we're still capable of doing the job.'

What a dick.

'Should I give my task force a name?'

The question's just out there before I can stop it. Should have kept my mouth shut. For his part, Connor's mouth opens a little but he doesn't really know what to say to that. Don't look at Taylor, but can feel the death rays penetrating my head, more piercing and more painful than the beak of any crow.

And there's the crow. Back in my head. The stupidity of that last comment, and of the very idea of me heading up any kind of task force – a task force of lowly idiots, too stupid to think of big ideas – is gone. The crow is back, and he brings with him sorrow and fear.

I make a small gesture, dismissing the question and the room relaxes. I owned the room there for a moment, which doesn't happen very often. Of course, I owned it by being Jim Carrey in a room full of Angela Merkels.

* * *

Back into the office. Dorritt peels off. Taylor walks towards his office, me behind, and he indicates for Morrow to join us as we enter.

'I don't even want to talk about that,' he says, not looking at me, as he sits down. 'Any of it.'

He glances at his computer, without taking anything in, then indicates for Morrow to close the door. We wait, as Taylor places his hands on the desk, composes himself. I don't think he's trying to work out what to say. Just getting the ill feeling of sitting with Connor out of his head.

'Right, we've got a murder to solve, and we need to get somewhere today. I've had enough of this shit. 'Cause this… whatever we see, whatever any one of us thinks, when it comes down to it, it was a young girl getting hit by a train. And as time passes, and we don't find this guy, it's just another bullet in the ammunition of all those fuckers out there who think we don't do a decent job. And at some point there'll be an inquest, and we'll be standing up there saying we couldn't work it out. We had the guy caught on camera and we knew nothing.'

He says all this while staring straight ahead. Finally lifts his eyes, moves from me to Morrow and back.

'What have you got?'

'I think it's random,' says Morrow, straight off. I give

him a glance.

'Why?' asks Taylor.

'She was popular,' he begins. 'I mean, more than usual. She was a Californian amongst a bunch of pasty, white Scottish kids. She brought a bit of Hollywood. She had the looks, the accent, everyone liked her. And she wasn't stupid, they liked that as well. She'd slept with a couple of the boys, a few of them had a thing for her, but it was nothing serious. No one had any expectation. If there were any of them with a secret desire for her, someone who maybe knew about her and Dr Ferguson, then it was a damned good secret. The classes she was in were fairly small, they all seemed like a decent bunch of well-adjusted kids. The tutors, not just Ferguson, are all very positive about the students. The ones I've spoken to, at any rate.'

I nod in agreement.

'We've been all through her social media,' Morrow continues. 'There's nothing. She was bright, attractive, popular, and did what she said on the tin. She's your classic untimely death, front page of the newspaper, popular kid, why did she have to die?'

That should have been yesterday's newspapers, except Cambuslang isn't quite on the national radar. Maybe today they might have caught up, but then there's a double beheading and an outbreak of religious and racial disharmony to talk about.

'I really don't think somebody murdered her for who she was. She just happened to be standing in the wrong place at the wrong time. Or, the right place at the right time, if you're the guy in the beanie.'

Taylor accepts all of that, then turns to me.

'The CCTV footage from the half-hour prior to the killing shows our man loitering at the station. He passes up two trains. Now, it could be he was waiting specifically for her, but it was a very precise set of circumstances he needed. The victim had to be standing close to the edge, she had to be distracted so as not to be too concerned about the train and not notice the guy hanging around just

—

64

behind her, and it probably helped there weren't too many witnesses around. With the other two trains that passed through the station without stopping in the previous half hour, there was no one especially close to the platform edge. As a way to kill a specific person, it's not especially effective. What if they don't go anywhere near the platform edge? What are you going to do? Drag her kicking and screaming, and then look at everyone else and say, she jumped!'

'So you agree?'

'Yes. Definitely a random killing. Look, there's the possibility the seeming randomness comes from Ferguson, or someone, paying for this to be done to her, but I don't buy it. Really don't. This isn't about the girl, it's about the guy in the beanie.'

'So you think there's no point in pursuing any further inquiries at the University?'

Give myself a second to think.

'I don't want to say there's no point. But I think the things we started to find out, like Ferguson getting her pregnant... we shouldn't let them go, but I don't think that's our focus. This is a random guy, killing out of badness.'

'And pre-planning it,' says Taylor, 'as indicated by the disguise.'

'Yes.'

'Hmm, all right, that seems reasonable. Not good for us, not good for the possibility of getting a result, but reasonable. What next?'

'I'd like to broaden the CCTV search,' I say. 'Rope in film from every camera in the area, see if there's any further sign of him. From shops, cafés. Just the immediate aftermath...'

'We looked at a lot of it already,' says Morrow.

'I know. But this is it, this minute, the guy in a beanie. Ten minutes later, five minutes, whatever, he wasn't a guy in a beanie anymore. If we're going to get sight of him, it's then. We need to be looking at people and thinking, could it be him? Could this person be the beanie guy, two minutes after he'd taken the hat and coat off? Same trousers, perhaps, same build maybe. Anything. And we need to get the image of him from the CCTV out there. I know there's no face, but we've got to do it.'

'We already issued it,' says Taylor.

'And no one's paid any attention. We need to get them to pay attention. It's like Morrow said, she was American, she was smart, she was front page of the newspapers attractive. Let's get her on the front page of the newspapers, get people talking about her and interested in her. Let's get them interested in this random guy, who just chose a girl out of badness and pushed her in front of a fucking train.'

Taylor scratches his chin. Coming out of his funk, the funk that talking to Connor inevitably puts him in. Coming up for the air of a genuine investigation, some serious police work to get stuck in to.

'Yes,' he says. 'Let's spend the day in this direction. We'll leave the University be for now, at least. We'll not say anything to anyone about that, of course. If any of them are stewing, we'll let them stew. Dr Ferguson can stew. Haven't heard from Balingol, whether he's confirmed Ferguson as the father of the baby, but I don't suppose it matters. Still, we won't lose sight of it.'

He stares again at his desk, cheeks puffed out, the universal sign of a man in deep contemplation, and then indicates the door.

'Go to it. You don't need to bring every suggestion to me, just work on what you think is best. If you need me to authorize anything in particular, I'll be here.'

We turn, Morrow opens the door.

'And Sergeant, concentrate on this. I know you must be desperate to get your task force up and running, but not today.'

Decent gag, although Taylor's face does not crack, and then we're out the door.

Back to the desks, sit down. Morrow's looking at me,

questioning the task force remark.

'Above your pay grade,' I say, laughing.

He keeps the *bugger off* to himself and then starts moving paperwork around. We'll need to divvy up, get into the sit. room and get the others on board with what we're doing.

Move the mouse to bring the monitor back up, quick check of e-mails.

And there it is, right there. The thing to stop the morning in its tracks.

I can feel my stomach curling in on itself. Throat dry. It's not fear. It's not even dread. Just… it's just this. This shit. All this fucking shit.

I open the e-mail, but it's only got one line, the line I could see in my inbox, then I forward it to Taylor, get up, indicate for Morrow to follow me, and back into the boss's office.

14

The sender's e-mail address shows as: namewitheld@glasgow.ac.uk

There is no title in the e-mail.

The single line reads: **Have you worked it out yet?**

Taylor has the e-mail open already as we walk into the office. I stand back from his desk, let Morrow lean forward and look at it.

'That's from the university, right?' he says.

'Yep.'

'Fuck it,' says Taylor. 'I expect it's a pointless exercise, but just send a reply, a blank reply, from your account, Tom, see what happens. I presume...'

He lets the sentence go. I pass the instruction down the line, indicating for Morrow to go and do it. He turns, walks quickly from the room.

'Fuck, we had a plan, thirty fucking seconds ago,' says Taylor.

Swearing an awful lot these days. Very poor.

Taking it in turns, as one so often does in a partnership, I immediately have to be the positive one, to pick the investigation back up again, even though I walked in here with my stomach in my mouth under the crushing weight of pessimism.

'It's easily looked into,' I say. 'I'll get in there, establish who runs their tech, speak to them, see how it could have happened. It could be anything. Remote computer genius, right down to some first year kid just putting a week one lesson into action and pulling our chain.'

'Yes, but unless it's the latter, it ties this thing to the

university, which means it's quite possibly what we'd just decided it's not. i.e. they were targeting Tandy Kramer herself.'

'I don't think so. I don't think this alters the arguments we've just been making.'

I'm saying it. I really don't think it.

Footsteps, Morrow back in the room.

'Got the Mailer Daemon straight back,' he says.

'Fuck,' says Taylor.

'Right,' I say, taking a much tighter grip on the thing than I feel like I have, 'I'm going in there to speak to their IT. Rob, you just keep doing what we were going to be doing. If I'm not back by the time you're ready to move ahead, get some of the others in and get on with it.'

'Yep,' he says, and he's gone again.

Look at Taylor, shrug, not much else to say. Well, at least, I don't.

'It was sent to you, Tom,' he says. 'They know you're investigating Tandy Kramer. Who knows that? You've not been on TV, you've not been high profile...'

'I've been at the university, spoken to a lot of people,' I say.

He nods, turns away.

'Fuck,' he mutters again. 'Just be careful. You've had enough shit in the past couple of years.'

I wait for him to turn back, but he doesn't, so out the door, give Morrow a quick thumbs up and then off down the stairs, back out into the world.

* * *

'I'm not sure.'

In a small office with a woman in her late forties. She's squeezed into an emerald green top, showing every middle-aged bump and lump and bulge. Tell you what, it's unbelievably sexy.

I mean, I don't know where my head is, do I? I'm fucked up. I own my fucked-uppery. I've given into it, enabling myself. I allow it to excuse everything. Weirdly, since the time of Philo, it's not had to excuse much. I drink every night, but rarely get drunk. Sure, I'm regularly late for work, but it's the lack of sleep that's getting me rather than the alcohol. Haven't had sex, at all, which means, more to the point, I haven't had sex with anyone I deeply regret having had sex with. And let's face it, I usually exist in a permanent state of *what the fuck were you thinking?*

I know. The feeling's more than likely mutual.

Yet, I'm sitting side on to this woman, no desk between us. She's attractive, a large woman, great breasts, legs crossed, skirt just above knee-length, long dark hair, and I want to sweep all the crap and paperwork off the desk and bang her right here.

Seriously, where has that come from?

Ah, yes, of course. I'm fucked up. I have the wastrel's excuse. I don't have to feel bad about myself.

'You don't know?'

She sighs.

'I expect it's the same with you. Cuts, cuts, cuts. I was working in the accounts section. Been there for fifteen years, then they move me here.'

Lovely soft accent. Highlands somewhere, I reckon.

'But someone must oversee the e-mail system?'

She smiles. Great lips.

Focus!

'Off-site.'

'Off-site? Is it in Scotland?'

'No. Sorry, you didn't have to come in here, although I'm glad you did. Could have saved yourself the trouble with a phone call. Everything's run out of California somewhere. When we're talking about it, we always call it Silicon Valley, but I don't know if it actually is. We just call it that. Office joke. Could be in Los Angeles for all I know.'

'Do you have a contact there?'

'Yes, of course. Do you want me to speak to him, or would you–'

'It'd be best if you could just give me his number.'

Check the clock. California, eight hours behind, do the quick calculation.

'Probably won't be in work yet, anyway. Yes, just give me the number, I'll call him later. A couple of contacts, in fact, just in case.'

'Of course.'

She reaches over the desk, lifts a business card from a small holder. My eyes get stuck on her breasts, the stretching of the tight green top, as she moves. When I look back at her face, she's already looking at me.

Jesus, I need to get a grip. By the age of forty-seven one really ought to have mastered the skill of staring at a woman's breasts without her noticing. Or, more to the point, have stopped staring at women's breasts altogether.

Yeah, I know, it'll never happen.

'Sorry.'

She looks at me in a superior manner – and it is one of the ways in which women hold immense superiority over us – but accompanies the look with a straightening of the shoulders.

'This is my card, in case you need to get in touch again. I'll write the American numbers on the back.'

I watch her, leaning on the desk, copying numbers slowly from a sheet. Wedding ring. A bonus. Always better when they're married.

'What do you do all day?' I ask. 'I mean, if you're in technical support and the technical stuff is staffed out?'

She smiles, glances over at me, catches me looking at her breasts again. She raises her eyes, but she's still smiling.

'Are you going to stop that?' she says.

Manage to look slightly abashed. Just slightly.

'Maybe if I just got them out, you could have a good look and we'd be done with it.'

I have some glib comment to say to that, but it'd only get in the way. No words required.

She smiles again, there's a small movement of her

eyebrows.

* * *

'And then I fucked her on her desk.'

Eating pizza, eight in the evening, still in the office, with Eileen Harrison. She laughs.

We're sharing a 14" funghi with extra cheese. Eileen likes extra cheese, like there's never enough cheese on a pizza.

'You are unbelievable,' she says. 'I mean, seriously, did you make that story up when you were fifteen?'

'Look, it happened. These things just happen.'

'It happened this afternoon?'

'Yes.'

'You had sex on a desk with a large-breasted witness in the middle of a murder inquiry?'

'I think *witness* is a stretch. She was someone I just happened to be speaking to.'

She looks around. There's no one within earshot anyway. I had already checked. It wasn't as though it lasted very long, but even so, I don't want Taylor getting to hear about it, the mood he's in. And Eileen's right. I do feel like a naughty teenager, worried about getting caught with his pants down.

'OK, details,' she says.

'I gave you the details.'

'You gave me a little of the set up, which quickly jumped from the two of you chatting happily about you being a pervert, to the two of you fucking on the desk! Those weren't details.'

'How many details do you want?'

'Remember when, a few weeks ago, I told you about me and the fitness instructor at the gym, late evening, everyone else gone home?'

What a great story.

'That kind of detail.'

Take my last bite of pizza. Need to be getting back to

—

72

the grind.

'And don't give me the, I've finished, sorry, need to get on with it crap.'

'I have and I do,' I say, looking up, with what I'm afraid can only be described as a mischievous look on my face. 'Have to admit, there was a moment after she'd removed my trousers when I thought maybe she was going to avenge my staring by taking a photo and sticking it on Instagram, but no...' Close my eyes for a second. Shake my head, open my eyes again, look at Eileen. She's smiling. 'Wicked tongue on her.'

'Always a bonus.'

'And then...,' I begin, but really, I don't want to get into this now. Middle of a murder enquiry, bad enough doing what I did, just ridiculous getting turned on again in the office. 'Well, you'll just have to wait for the details, my old friend. Need to get on.'

She rolls her eyes.

'Charlatan,' she says, still smiling, as I get up and start walking away.

'Thanks for the pizza.'

'Leave me.'

A casually waved hand, and I'm across the office and back at my desk. Sit down, bring the e-mail in-box back up. Constantly checking for anything new. Of course, it could come from anywhere.

Look back at the short report I'm writing up for Taylor. The feeling of unease, that I have lurched back into my old ways, that I have been stupid and immature, a feeling I haven't had in months, suddenly comes sweeping over me, and I feel useless again.

Sex on a desk with a stranger. Giggling about it over pizza with my mate. *Grow the fuck up, man!*

And I force myself to think about California, and an e-mail coming from there, coupled with the fact that was where Tandy Kramer had lived, and that was where Mr Kramer arrived from this morning, and that maybe, rather than spending twenty minutes fucking whatever-her-name-was in the emerald top, I really ought to have been shooting back here to say to Taylor, *Hey there's this, and it might just mean something.*

Waste of fucking space.

15

Home just after eleven. With the sex, comes the darkness.

I feel guilty. Not just because of acting like some sort of sex-obsessed, teenage wanker while I should have been working, but because of Philo. In my head, which is the only place she exists for me anymore of course, she's not judgemental. She thinks it's funny. I can't get past her thinking it's funny. But she wouldn't have thought it funny when she'd left her husband and she and I were living together.

Into the kitchen, light on. There she is on the door of the fridge. The small black and white photograph I cut out of the Evening Times. Smiling back at me, every time I'm in here.

How pathetic.

Into the fridge, can barely look at her, other than some sort of apologetic glance, grab a bottle of wine, get the glass from the draining board, into the sitting room. Slump back on the couch, unscrew the bottle top, pour half a glass, take a drink, top back on, bottle on the floor.

Half a glass of wine at the end of a long day, investigating crime, working hard at the office, fucking women on a desk? Are you a pussy? I'm going to drink the whole fucking bottle, half a glass at a time. It's something about keeping the wine colder in the bottle than in the glass, but at the rate I'm drinking it, it really, really doesn't matter.

I put the television on, as ever BBC News pops up first. I don't know why I do it. Putting the TV on late at night never ends well.

First up, starving and burned Syrian children. Yes,

Hutton, on you go, you feel sorry for yourself because you had fucking sex on a desk, you stupid twat. Much worse than having your entire society destroyed, losing your family and getting half your face burned off.

Next half glass.

Sit through a report on trouble brewing in the Baltic states, the beginning of unrest amongst the Russian population in Estonia. The man from the BBC, standing at a safe distance from a demonstration that is shaping up to turn violent, discusses whether the unrest is genuine or is being orchestrated by Moscow. There's a brief interview with a commentator from Moscow denying all Russian involvement.

And then we're on to continuing unrest in certain parts of Glasgow after the double beheading. Today not as bad as yesterday. Well, there's some good news. Following that, a quick mention of another suspicious death in Glasgow, a twenty-seven year-old fuckwit badly beaten, and then drugged. Police are still in the initial stage of their enquiries; i.e. they haven't a fucking clue. That was a one-line item with three seconds of footage of a taped-off scene in a sink scheme somewhere on the south side, and then we're onto sport.

What a nice epitaph for the deceased. They can put it on his gravestone. *Here lies Malky Big Baws. Loving son and father of eight, he was the last item on the news before the Test Match.*

More wine. This time I don't bother putting the bottle back on the floor, leaving it sitting between my legs. It won't be good for the temperature, but it's not going to be in the bottle very long anyway.

16

Friday morning. Have been in since five to seven. Set the alarm for five forty-five. Forced myself up, ate breakfast, drank coffee, walked to work.

Suddenly I realise just how good I've been mentally the last few months. I would have said I was shitty, humourless, going nowhere, barely contributing to my own life, never mind anyone else's. Yet now I've plummeted back to pre-Philo levels of ill-humour and despair, I can see, by my own standard, the last few months have been pretty fucking good.

You don't know what you've got until you lose it, and I just lost some kind of peace of mind. It might have been mournful, but at least it wasn't catastrophic.

Roll on the end of the world, my feeble friends, it can't come soon enough.

Taylor sits down opposite and looks across.

'You're in early,' he says.

I acknowledge him, but don't really have any words. He looks like he might be about to say something along the *what's the matter with you?* line, or *who are you and what have you done with the real Hutton?* but decides not to bother. We're both men after all.

'Any more e-mails?'

'Nope. You speak to the father about it?'

'Yes, saw him last night. Asked him straight up. He looked… he's pretty dead. Think he's probably popping something. He's American after all, they have a pill for everything. But his daughter just got murdered, can't blame him. So, I don't know, I really don't think there's a connection between the university having their shit hosted in California, and Kramer coming in from California, but we'll see. Anyway, for now we're not looking to let the body go until Monday, and I told him it's not out of the question we keep it longer, so you know, we've got time to look into it.'

'He must be pissed off, having to wait around Cambuslang?'

'He's staying in the city, and he's got a cousin in Perth. I got the *my family left Scotland in 1792* line.'

'The year of the sheep,' I say.

'What?'

'There were sheep riots in Ross-shire. The government clamped down, fucked everybody up the arse. Lots of them emigrated.'

'There were sheep riots?'

'Riots about owners populating their land with sheep rather than people.'

'Oh.'

He stares blankly at the floor, probably considering his embarrassment at his complete lack of knowledge of Scottish history. Fucking listen to me, fucking Neil Oliver here.

'I'm not sure he actually said 1792. I think I just said that now, as a kind of, any given year.'

You know, 'whatever' as a word, phrase and social concept is overused, but sometimes there's just nothing else to say.

'Whatever.'

'Anyway, he's going to visit the cousin in Perth for the weekend. Some home comfort, he said. His ex-wife, Tandy's mother, lives in Brazil with her Zumba instructor, hadn't see Tandy since she was eleven.'

'Another happy family brought to its knees.'

'Yes, that would be it. Anyway, Kramer's coming back in on Monday morning. We should have a decision for him by then, either way. And we're getting a visit from the American consul in Edinburgh, or someone from their office, this afternoon, but Connor can handle it.'

'Let me,' I say, although my voice doesn't carry any enthusiasm for the joke.

He smiles, stands.

'Come in and see me when Morrow gets in and we'll discuss the day.'

'K.'

He taps the desk, is staring vaguely across the office.

'Another murder in Glasgow last night, d'you see that?'

'Heard it on the news,' I say.

'Four murders in three days,' he says. 'Seems kind of weird.'

I can't muster much enthusiasm for the conversation. I want to know about our murder, not anyone else's. All murders are shit. Sometimes life goes a while without springing one on you – unless, obviously, you live in America where people get murdered by the dozen on a daily basis, all in the name of one of the amendments or other – and sometimes it just dumps a shitload of them in your lap.

'Maybe Glasgow's just becoming that kind of place,' I say.

Catch his eye, then look back at my inbox. Slowly working my way through the crap as he talks to me. For example, there's one from HQ entitled Effective Use Of Arrest Statistics When Dealing With The Media. Straight in the bin without opening. They can probably look and see who reads, or at least, opens their shit. I'm happy for them to discover that as soon as I see anything with their fucking name in the title, I'm depositing it in Trash quicker than a professional cyclist flushing drugs down a toilet.

'Might let the day develop a little more, but I think I'll give the others a call, maybe get together, see if there's anything to join up.'

'Good luck,' I say.

'Yeah, right,' he says, although neither of us actually knows what I meant.

Did I mean a genuine, hope you find something? A sarcastic, do that if you want, but make sure you don't take me with you? An acknowledgement that the hardest part would be in getting three different Glasgow DCIs into the same room to talk to each other? And if Taylor is junior to the others, which he might well be, they're really not going to be interested.

'You look terrible,' he says, as he turns and walks away.

I look at his back, disappearing into his office. Mutter some expletive or other, much too quietly for him to hear.

* * *

Standing in Taylor's office with Morrow and a Detective Constable who's come along from Dalmarnock. We've spoken to him before on tech matters. Back at the height of the Plague of Crows, when that bastard was stringing us along. Detective Constable MacGregor.

Taylor's not here, we just wanted somewhere we could close the door and keep out the noise, and this was available.

MacGregor's the kind of kid who makes me feel at least double my age. Not good on a day like today. He'll probably even make Morrow feel long in the tooth. Maybe we can gang up and kick the shit out of him before he leaves.

'Can I be honest with you, Sergeant?' he says.

'I think that'd be best.'

Hands in his pockets. Jeans, collared t-shirt, unshaven. He's been watching *Serpico*. You can always tell.

'Didn't really need to come over, but there's a constable here... Tina, you know her?'

I catch Morrow's eye, and nod at McGregor. Everybody knows Tina. I mean, seriously, *everybody*. Wouldn't be surprised if even Connor had attempted to get his wizened old manhood some action there.

Worth knowing, though, I'll give her that.

—

'Met her a couple of weeks ago at Riverside. She was on a course we were running. I said I'd see her again, like to keep my word.'

'Very noble,' I say. 'And why didn't you need to come over here?'

'Because, TBH, this is just a piece of piss, man.'

'Why?'

'Honestly, Sergeant, if even *you* wanted to send that e-mail, you could. Remember the last time I came over here to help you guys out?'

I acknowledge it, but we're not thinking about it.

'That guy was awesome, seriously. But this, fuck, I mean, this is just a simple joe job. You could put *I want to send a bogus e-mail and pretend it came from Downing Street* into Google and it'll take you straight to a site that'll do it for you.'

'And the University aren't going to be able to tell it's happened or where it came from?'

For about the fifth time in the couple of minutes we've been in here, he glances through the glass door.

'They might, depends on what kind of protocols they've got set up. So, I know what you want, you want to know if we'd be able to trace it right to the terminal where some guy sat and sent the thing, right?'

He glances over his shoulder.

'She doesn't work in this office, Constable,' I say, 'so if you could concentrate for about another two minutes, then you can go downstairs and try to find her.'

He smiles and nods. Fucking lemon.

'You spoke to the University's people in San Jose?' he asks.

'Yes.'

'What'd they say?'

'I didn't understand them, so I thought I'd speak to you instead.'

'I'm glad I could be of help,' he says.

'You haven't been.'

This seems to surprise him.

'You want me to talk to them?'

'Yes, please, that probably makes sense.'

'Awesome sauce,' he says.

'I know, ultimately, you're not going to be able to tell us anything...'

'I'm glad I've been able to manage your expectations,' he says.

'... however, here's what I'd like to know. Is this just the work of someone with my level of ability, who went onto Google and followed a link to FakeAnE-Mail.com, or is there a greater level of technical ability at play here? And if it was straightforward, presumably you might be able to track down where it came from, yes?'

He purses his lips, head tilted to the side.

'Possibly,' he says. 'Give me the numbers in San Jose, I'll speak to some people, get everything I need, get back to you.'

'Thank you.'

'Awesome sauce,' he says again. Looks over his shoulder for the first time since I told him not to. 'Where do I find Tina, man?'

17

'Do you think I'm gay?'

He delivers the words with comedic flair. He's been acting the role ever since he started using her as his psychiatrist. There has been something in his tone. A touch of camp on his lips. Just a perfect suggestion of it. Enough to make someone wonder.

She doesn't answer, so eventually he looks round. She's staring at him, but today she doesn't seem to be playing her part.

Their eyes meet. She manages to hold his gaze for a second, but then looks away. Today she doesn't have the strength for it. Today those eyes seem to burrow right inside her. She could kill him some days. Hates him every day. The fear comes and goes.

She's a psychiatrist. She knows. The response is normal. She has to examine herself, try to keep her head right. The circumstances may be peculiar, but what she's going through, thousands of people have gone through before. Today, however, her head is not in the game. Beyond self-examination. Beyond help. Unable to remove herself from the situation, unable to convince herself all will be well.

She knows he's playing a game, and he's not the kind of person with whom anyone would want to play. Not, at least, when it is so completely on his terms.

He turns back to the wall in front. What is he looking at today? His eyes settle on the framed page from a 1920's Sherlock Holmes omnibus. He's always wondered who butchered the original book, to remove the page and put it in the frame.

It's from *The Five Orange Pips*, three-quarters of the page with text, and an illustration on the upper right of the page, although it isn't of Holmes. Five men, standing around a table, staring in horror at the pips that one holds in his hand.

'He thought I was gay,' he says. 'How funny. He did make me laugh.'

He laughs, as if to emphasise the point. Eyes on the illustration. He likes the illustration. It, itself, makes him laugh. As often seems to be the case, it is not particularly representative of the scene as it's described in the book.

'We worked in the same office, my first job after graduation. Yes, you can see it, can't you? School, university, first job. A natural progression. Very linear. Perhaps, however, I will go back some day. Go back in time. I mean, in my narrative. Obviously I can't actually go back in time. Where, where... where was I? Yes. Gay. He thought I was gay. I played along, what did it matter? We went out for dinner a few times, but always far away. Never in Perth. Never anywhere we were going to be seen. He didn't want people knowing. He was one of the bosses, you see. One of the suits. That was what was so perfect.'

He pauses, but doesn't look round at her. Curiosity crosses his brow. Is that the sound of her crying? He could confirm by looking at her – of course, he *knows* it's the sound of her crying – but this is more about him talking, getting the story out there. He doesn't want to tell the wall, he wants to tell an actual person. A psychiatrist had seemed perfect, though it's not like he thinks he needs help.

'It was hilarious. When we went out, even though it was in Dundee or Stirling, or some little pub in Perthshire somewhere, out in the country, I always wore a disguise. He thought it was perfect, he laughed so much. He thought I was doing it in case we were seen by someone from work. That, of course, wasn't why I was doing it at all. And then the fourth time, when we arranged it would be at his place, I wore a gimp suit.'

84

He giggles this time, a strange sound, a laugh such as she hasn't heard from him before. She bites her lip, tries not to sob, tries to keep everything under control. She's scared enough by him, but is even more terrified of the thought of him seeing her break down.

She wipes away a tear. Sniffs as quietly as possible.

'That was my character for this murder. The gimp. Not very original, and by God I looked dreadful. I arrived at his apartment in this absurd thing, wearing a coat, with the mask tucked around the neck. Hat and glasses, of course. There was someone who saw me leave, I think, and they gave a description to the police. Classic. Didn't sound anything like me.

'I get in, straight away, hat and spectacles off, pull the mask up. Me! Me in a rubber gimp suit. He looked so turned on, it was hilarious. Eyes lit up. God, he loved it, absolutely loved it. I mean, the main reason for the suit – and honestly, I found it really comfortable, but I'd never wear one again – was to throw him off his guard and, of course, the complete containment of me. Of me! You see? No hair, no fingerprints, no DNA left behind.'

Another pause. She stares at the carpet, the small area inside her cage, inside this bizarre room that has been her home for the past six days.

'I did wonder how far I'd let it go. I mean, God, he was on me like a wolf. Biting at the suit, his hand on my cock.'

He snorts.

'Yes, all right, my cock hardened. What was I going to do? When you're wearing rubber, and someone puts their hand on it, it doesn't know, does it? The cock doesn't know whether it's a man or a woman who's caressing it, does it? Jesus. Don't... don't look at me like that.'

She's not looking at him. He knows she's not looking at him.

'He kissed me on the mouth. Ugh... His man-breath. Horrible. So, I broke away, I grabbed his crotch as some sort of cover, and said, wine! Lots of wine! Your finest bottle! He laughed, red or white, he says. White, always, of course. I looked around the room, in case there was something useful, which there wasn't, and then he's back with a bottle of, you won't believe, Chardonnay. Anyway, we weren't about to drink it. He pours two glass, but of course, I couldn't possibly have put mine to my lips. We toast. I put the glass down on the table. I lift the bottle, I pour what's left in it over his head. He looks annoyed at first, but then he's laughing and licking at it as it spills over him. Then the bottle's empty. Much easier to use an empty bottle than one with liquid sploshing around inside, making the weight unbalanced. Then I jabbed him in the eye with the open end. Ha! He staggers back a little, confused, curious. Is this part of the game? He didn't say it, but I could see what he was thinking. Jabbed him in the Adam's apple, then as he grasped at his throat, brought the bottle quickly up into his erection. Now he's bent in half, still not sure if this is part of a game. I jump at him, he falls back, off balance of course, hurting, no idea what's going on, and then I'm on top of him as he's lying on the ground, and I put the neck of the bottle in his mouth and press down, pushing the opening right back against his throat. He can't scream, of course, mouth full of glass. Now, at last, the fucking pussy, he starts to fight. Too bad. Too late. I squeeze the bottle in there, pressing it down against his lower jaw, breaking teeth, pushing it back up against the top of his mouth. And then, I don't know, it was weird. The bottle broke. Would you think a wine bottle would break like that? Because of pressure against someone's jaw? Weird.'

He looks round at her, turns quickly away. *Useless bitch*, he thinks.

'Just the neck, just at the part that was inside his mouth. Lucky, really. Meant I didn't get cut, which was the main thing. So I lurched forward, of course, lost my balance a little bit, and the broken neck stabs into the back of his mouth. Oof! Messy. God he was thrashing now. Like a wild pig! It was hilarious, it really was. I thought, what are you doing? Settle the fuck down!'

He sighs heavily, suddenly bored with the story, mimicking the fact this was the point in the narrative when he had decided enough was enough.

'Well, I had to bring it to an end then, of course. He was becoming tiresome, and I couldn't risk him catching me with, I don't know, a stray blow. So I got off him and stood on his throat. I had control, you see. Stood on his throat. Got blood on my boots.'

He rolls his eyes at the inconvenience.

'Didn't take long. Then, I don't know, well he was dead, and I decided to enjoy myself. Stripped him naked...'

He pauses, has come to a part of the story he doesn't seem to enjoy so much.

'Didn't really know what I was doing,' he says eventually. 'No plan. You should always plan. I cut off his penis with a shard of glass. Sheesh. Don't know why I did that. Traced some random stuff on his stomach. Then I turned him over and made a pentagram on his back. I mean, what the fuck? Jesus, I didn't even know if it was a proper pentagram. Then I thought I'd insert the neck of the bottle into his anus... well, why not...? but, you know, I think I might have needed some lube to do it properly, and I was thinking, ugh, lube... Rather a half-hearted effort, so I left it there. Quite enough for one night.'

He turns, gives her another glance, then looks away again, back to the Five Orange Pips, clearly unimpressed with her performance.

'Stopped at Tesco on the way home and bought some Chardonnay. Had a taste for it that evening. And pizza. I bought a pizza, although I think I only ate half of it in the end.'

18

Taylor finds me across the road, on my own, drinking coffee. Stepped out of the office for half an hour. Half my morning on the railway station murder – proceeding like a slow-moving train, arriving late at every place it stops – and half on the other endless stream of crap that crosses the desk of every detective sergeant in the country.

Another aggravated assault? It's all yours, sunshine.

Sitting at a table on my own, stooped over a long-since finished flat white, shoulders hunched, terrible posture. Straighten up as Taylor enters, and he stops beside me.

'You want another?' he asks.

'I should be getting back.'

'It's all right. You want another?'

'Yeah, sure. Flat white. And one of those long chocolate croissant things.'

He gives me a look, then turns to the counter.

So it's back. My desire. My desire is back. And the thoughts that go with it. And the depression that goes with it too.

There are two women at a table by the window. They haven't noticed me at all, which is something. One of them... nah. There's nothing about her. Nothing to look at, nothing to get interested in. Nothing. She's someone's mum, and she gave up a long time ago. I can't hear what they're saying, but I imagine she's sitting there talking about the kids and the school and the TV and the garden and what the fuck Peter is really doing when he says he's working late for the third time this week and where the fuck they're going on holiday.

Her friend is a different kettle of potatoes. It doesn't

matter what she looks like. There's a light about her. An openness. She's not saying much, but when she speaks, the words will be more optimistic. She won't just talk about the average goings-on of an average day, the kids and the supermarket and the school gate politics, and if she does, her perspective will be completely different.

I like her. She doesn't even know it, and she wouldn't be interested in me even if she did. And already I've undressed her and, like my good friends the Hartwells, I've fucked her up against the window.

Shit. I was supposed to follow up on the Hartwell crap. Something else that's fallen through the cracks. Shouldn't mention cracks, not in relation to Mrs Hartwell at any rate.

Taylor places the coffee and pastry on the table for me, then goes back to get his own. Sits down, looks out of the window.

'Contemplating the end of your football management dream?' asks Taylor after a few seconds.

'Something like that,' I say.

Take some coffee, continue to follow Taylor's gaze out of the window. Slow day up this end of Cambuslang. Cars go by. A few pedestrians.

'How are you getting on pulling the three murder investigations together?' I ask.

His mouth full of chocolate croissant, he answers with a roll of his eyes. Dabs at his lips with the napkin.

'I mentioned it to Connor. Off the scale disinterest. Didn't tell me not to pursue it, but thought little of it and didn't care either way.'

'You can always count on him to care about completely the wrong things,' I say.

'Yes. Spoke to DCI Taylor in Springburn, the one from yesterday. He seemed interested. We compared notes. Didn't really get anywhere, but it's a start.'

'He's also called Taylor?'

'Yeah, I know, total mind fuck,' he says dryly. 'Then I spoke to DCI Waterbridge, who's leading the investigation into the double beheading. The one everyone's talking about. The poster child of this week's murders.'

'And he didn't want you anywhere near it?'

'Damn right. It's his investigation. It's a racially-motivated crime, and it very, very, very – and he really did use the word three times – clearly has nothing to do with either of our so-called murder investigations.'

'He said 'so-called'?'

'Yes.'

'What a dick.'

'Yes.'

Taylor takes another bite of his croissant, still looking out of the window.

'So, that's that for now. It was always a slim hope, and really the best chance of success was putting all three together and seeing if it got us somewhere.'

'Maybe there's nowhere to get.'

'Probably not.'

'Three days and we come to the desperately-clutching-at-straws part of the investigation.'

He laughs without any amusement.

'We started doing that long before now.'

We watch the day go by. Two middle-aged bastards sitting in a sad outpost of Glasgow, looking out on a grey summer's early afternoon. This is it. This is the real end of policing.

'She looks like your type,' says Taylor, voice low, indicating the woman at the window.

The fact he knows me this well depresses me still further and I don't reply. My chocolate croissant comes to an end, leaving, for the moment, a satisfying aftertaste.

'D'you mind if I give Tandy Kramer's father a call and speak to him?' I say.

'Might as well. Get another perspective. Maybe you'll have a nose for something. Anything from MacGregor?'

'Top of the list when I get back.'

'Right.'

Another drink of coffee, another couple of minutes pass, leading towards the end of the day. Time stagnates.

'Try to get an answer from MacGregor before you speak to Kramer,' says Taylor, bringing the latest melancholic silence to an end. 'One of the reasons we started getting suspicious about Kramer was because of the e-mail you received. If it turns out... if it didn't come from California, I don't know if we have any reason to suspect his involvement. And, of course, he wasn't even in California when it was sent anyway.'

'He might have been able to do a thing,' I say.

He gives me a raised eyebrow.

'A thing? You lost me there with your techno-babble.'

'If he's able to send an e-mail from California pretending it came from the University of Glasgow, doesn't it sound reasonable there'll be some thing, a thing he could do, to allow him to send a delayed e-mail?'

Taylor stares expressionlessly across the café. A while later he nods.

The woman at the window gets to her feet. Her friend is talking about how the last school her children were at was so much better. Another couple of women walk in the door, and stand surveying the café, wondering where to sit. They notice the two leaving from the window and decide to wait for them.

* * *

There are two e-mails waiting for me when I get back to my desk, an unexpectedly long fifty-seven minutes after I left. Well, there are in fact thirty-seven e-mails waiting for me, but only two of any interest.

One from MacGregor stating that the original e-mail, asking if I had worked it out yet, was sent from a small café on Dumbarton Road, about ten minutes walk from the University. He had already been along there, identified the terminal from which it was sent, established it was paid for with cash, and had had a look at CCTV footage to see the identity of the person sitting in the seat. The man had a moustache, and was wearing thick-rimmed glasses and one of those '60s leather hats, like the Beatles had in *Help*. He didn't know the name for that kind of hat, and neither do I.

In short, however, the guy was in disguise. They could also make out from the footage he was wearing gloves. Nowhere on the keyboard, regardless of how many times it had been used since, and it might not have been many, would there be any fingerprints worth collecting.

The guy came and he went, leaving nothing behind.

A decent job, the query followed down to the final detail, as far as it could go. My opinion of MacGregor rises a little.

The other e-mail is a follow-up to the previous one, which has caused us so much consternation. Same e-mail address, the same blank e-mail title, and again a single line of text.

If you work it out, I'll stop.

I stare at it for a while, running through the implications. Morrow is at the desk opposite, but as usual, he has his head down. Good lad.

It doesn't freak me out or anything, the way the last one did. No shock value this time. In fact, I'd been expecting it. I just sit there, reading it over and over, trying to decide everything it means.

Eventually I forward it to Taylor and, same as last time, summon Morrow to come with me as I walk into the office.

'I think you're going to have to get in touch with your fellow DCIs again,' I say.

19

I have a real and unexpected sense of sadness I don't quite understand. It comes from what I did yesterday afternoon, that at least I know.

It was as though I had a chance to redeem myself. Whoever is in charge, whatever force there is out there, I'd been given, or I'd given myself, the opportunity to atone. I'd wasted so many lives before, my own included, but finally I had found someone to believe in. I'd found Philo, and it didn't matter it only lasted a few days. Maybe, in fact, it could only have lasted a few days. But it was enough, and it had given me the chance of a life again. All I had to do was stay true to her. True to that life.

It didn't even mean I couldn't ever be with another woman, fall for another woman, love another woman. But it had to mean something, and that something was most definitely not jumping on the first woman I came across whose clothes were a little too tight, and who was as interested as I was.

The woman in the office, and seriously I can't even remember her name, was a test. That was why she was so easy. She wasn't a teenager's fantasy. She was a test. And I failed.

Someone out there is unhappy with me. I don't know who it is. I don't even think it's Philo. But whoever or whatever they are, they have turned their back, and no longer do their hopeful eyes look upon me. I've taken the hope and I've washed it away.

That's why I was sitting staring forlornly out of the window of the café across the road. That's why I didn't react the same way when the second message came in.

That's why I'm sitting here now with Taylor, in Connor's office, barely interested in the conversation taking place, even though I'm at the centre of it.

Connor is shaking his head. Doesn't like this kind of thing, obviously. Reasonable, however, to say nobody does. No one wants one of their detectives to be part of the story, other than the part that solves the crime.

Taylor had already told him about the first e-mail, which he'd been happy to pay not too much attention to, happy to believe it was aimed at the station rather than me, and happy to see it as confirmation of the story having something to do with the University.

'Is it possible there's something else going on at the University? A wider scandal, of which Tandy Kramer's murder was just one part?' asks Connor.

I lift my head. I think that's the first time I've ever heard him make a good point. He is, as usual, ignoring me.

'We need to check,' says Taylor. 'The sergeant can go along there.'

'It's possible this act of murder is just one thing among many,' says Connor. Of course, having made a good point he now feels it necessary to labour it. 'If there are other incidents taking place, not interesting enough for the news media, but that have been getting reported to the police, we wouldn't necessarily have heard about them.'

'Yes,' says Taylor.

'I'd like you to check it out before I go off on some wild tangent, roping in other forces, and trying to weasel in on the Clarkston investigation where, I have to tell you, we would not be popular.'

'Yes.'

'I accept that if, in some way, this has anything specifically to do with the Sergeant, and I think it's far too early to make that presumption, then we will look at moving forward—'

'I'll call the University now,' I say.

I get a glance from Taylor, and the usual who-the-fuck-are-you and I-didn't-realise-you-could-even-talk look from

Connor.

'But I've been up there a couple of times already and no one's said anything. It's a good point and we should have checked before we came in here, but I don't think there's going to be anything. Either way, it won't take long to establish. So I'll go and make the call now, while you discuss the way forward. That is, if we're going to look at the possibility this last e-mail was referring to the other Glasgow murders.'

I don't wait for any approval. I think I've shocked the meeting by making a decision above my pay grade, so will just leave them to talk about me in quiet tones of general astonishment.

Walk out, close the door behind me. The last thing I hear is Taylor saying, 'The sergeant has a point...'

* * *

By the time I've got an answer, there must be thirty minutes have gone by. Having been so fucking bold, I don't want to get it wrong. Speak to five people from different administrative areas at the university, another couple of calls, then wrap it up by making a quick call to the Partick plods.

Nothing. There is nothing for anyone to stop, not in relation to someone getting pushed in front of a train. We know there's not been a spate of weird crime around the streets of Cambuslang, so it can't be that. I wonder, perhaps, if there have been other issues on the rail network, so put a call through to the transport police office and to Network Rail, and again there's been nothing out of the ordinary.

Should have thought of all this before we went in there, obviously. Taylor is going to be kicking himself for not going in with all the facts. Neither of us is thinking straight. Wonder what his excuse is.

Nevertheless, he hasn't emerged in all that time. I knock on the door, enter. Connor is on the phone and indicates with his usual superior air for me to sit down. Glance at Taylor.

'We're good,' I say, quietly. 'Sorry, should have thought of it bef–'

'It's fine. He just had to have his moment,' says Taylor, voice low, as Connor is talking and wrapping up the conversation.

Phone down, he looks across the desk.

'The DCI and I are going into Riverside,' he says. 'Managed to pull it together without mentioning this second e-mail of yours. Is there anything?'

'Looks pretty clear across the board,' I say. 'If we consider the various aspects of our case... Cambuslang, the rail network, the University connection, they all check out as having nothing particularly unusual happening crime-wise the last few days.'

'You called Network Rail?'

'And our Transport guys.'

'Good good,' he says. 'I'll save it for the meeting this evening, then. It should add weight.'

He's nodding, but not at me. Persuading himself he's done the right thing.

'We've just been discussing...,' he continues, speaking slowly, sorting out his thoughts. 'This could be directed at the station, or those e-mails could have been directed at you personally. If it's the latter, and I'm really not keen to make that kind of assumption at this stage, but if it is the latter, is there anyone–'

'Clayton,' I butt in, not letting him complete the sentence.

His lips purse, his face hardens. Taylor glances round, gives me a bit of an eyebrow, then turns back to Connor. The storm clouds continue to gather above Connor's head.

'No. Fucking. Way,' he says.

Curious. The Superintendent never swears at home.

'Clayton,' I repeat.

'We are not going there again, gentlemen,' he says. 'We were burned once, we got our man, or woman, I should say, and we found nothing on Mr Clayton. You found nothing on him. The officers we had through from Edinburgh found nothing, and believe me, they looked. We're bloody lucky he didn't pursue it through the courts or we would have been absolutely screwed. Fucked beyond the wildest imaginings of any of us. All of us, all three of us in this room, barely got out of that mess with our—'

'The crows are back.'

He stops. He wasn't expecting that. There's a lovely silence in the room. You could cling to it, cling to it for as long as possible. Get lost in it.

Under other circumstances, perhaps.

'What?'

He decently leaves the 'the fuck' off the end of the question. I can feel Taylor's eyebrow on me again, but I don't turn.

'I've been dreaming about crows. For a couple of weeks now. I wondered what was going on, why they were back...'

'Ah.'

The tension in his face goes, and he looks almost relieved.

'Sergeant, I've seen this kind of thing before. You, clearly, are suffering some version of PTSD from your experiences in the wood. And the fact that somehow you managed to keep the crows in your head, the dreams of crows, at bay for this long... well, is remarkable in itself. But this, this now... Well, I don't know why they're back now, at this particular point, but it was inevitable.'

I don't say anything. Said too much already, of course. There will be words exchanged with the boss when we leave, I expect.

'I think perhaps we need to get you back in touch with a doctor. That is of a higher priority to going back for Mr Clayton. I don't want to say the man has a clear run at doing anything he pleases, but seriously,' and now he turns to Taylor, 'before we go after him again for so much as a parking ticket, I want to see absolute, irrefutable evidence. I don't think a dream about crows quite covers it.'

He looks back at me, and fuck me, but he actually looks sympathetic. He's playing a blinder today.

'I'm concerned for you Sergeant, and I want you to see a police psychologist within the next week. I need to know you're still cleared for duty.'

He looks back at Taylor.

'Get everything you can together on our crime, and anything from our end to suggest there might be a connection with the others.' Check of the watch. 'Thirty-five minutes.'

Taylor stands, walks to the door, and then I'm out after him and the door is closed on what, it's safe to say, was a meeting with Connor Taylor didn't see coming. He walks to his office, me a pace behind, knowing he'll want me to follow him. Inside, close the door. He goes and stands at the window, hands in pockets. I go and stand beside him.

Outside it's grey and warm. The car park is quiet. I can see Gostkowski down there having a smoke. White blouse, unbuttoned at the neck, pencil skirt below the knee. Haven't seen her around much the last couple of weeks. Not sure what she's working on.

'Can we talk about what just happened?' he says.

I smile, although he's not looking at me. A sad smile. It goes quickly.

'You dreamt about crows.'

'Every night,' I say.

'And it started a couple of weeks ago?'

'Think so. Not sure exactly. I think it had been going on a few nights before it really clicked. I wasn't remembering at first.'

'What happens in the dreams?'

Don't really want to think about it, but then I was the fool who just went and put it out there.

'I'm in the forest. On the ground. Can't move. I can hear the crows, and then one of them is on the ground beside me, tapping at the side of my head. Stabbing its

---

98

beak into my skull.'

'You think that's a metaphor for something?' he says, a rueful smile in his voice.

I smile with him, the same, old sad smile. The Smile of the Fucked.

'Then it speaks to me.'

We're both looking straight ahead.

'Is there any point in asking what it says?'

'Don't remember.'

'It doesn't, for example, mention Clayton? Because, you know if it did, if you had a crow in your dreams specifically implicating Clayton in the girl's death at the train station, I think it's the kind of proof Connor's looking for.'

Can't help laughing.

'I don't know what it says,' I say eventually.

'And you think this is a sign of Clayton being back, because you still think he's responsible for the crows business? Somehow your subconscious is tuned in to all this. Tuned in to Clayton in some way.'

'Bang on.'

I say the words *bang on*, but not in the way they're supposed to be said. Not with any enthusiasm.

'Connor knows Clayton came to see me in hospital, right? He knows he more or less confessed?'

I know what Taylor's going to say. The same thing I would say if someone was saying that stuff to me.

'He knows what you said. But we all came to speak to you. We all know what you were like, the level of drugs you were on, the state your head was in. And you know no one else saw Clayton at the hospital. If Clayton did come to see you…'

And he pauses, waiting for me to insist he did. I stay quiet.

'… he did so in the certain knowledge he could say anything he damn well pleased. And even if you'd been recording everything he said, he could just say he was messing with you, to get back at you for messing with him.

The worst we could have got him on was wasting police time, and there's no way Connor's going after the guy for that. And I'd agree with him.'

'You know where he is now?'

'Clayton? Right this minute?'

'Is he still in the same house?'

'I don't know. But whatever you do next, Sergeant, don't go round there. Don't go anywhere near him. Connor can be an absolute arse, we all know, but this time... this time he's right. We can't go near Clayton on the back of a dream crow.'

'I know.'

He finally looks at me. I keep my eyes out the window. Gostkowski has gone. The car park is deserted. Across the way there's an old couple, the man walking ten yards ahead of the woman. We see them coming along that road all the time, the man always a few yards ahead of his wife, both of them with walking sticks.

'I'll get you an appointment with a psych.'

We stand and stare out of the window. The day passes before us. The silence in the room is of a similar quality to the silence in Connor's room.

'A male one,' he adds, a short while later. 'Just in case.'

20

Things change so quickly. Investigations fly by, pieces of information here and there, slotting in perfectly, or hanging around on the periphery, waiting to be picked up, waiting to find their place. As so often seems to be the case, I feel like a passenger. I'm just there, while things happen around me. Bad things. Pointless things. Things that sometimes lead to results. What do I ever contribute?

I said to Taylor I'd go and speak to Kramer to confirm his assessment. Then the next e-mail came in, and off we went on another tangent. I thought, there's little point in seeing Kramer now. So that sparked the next thought, the one that said, maybe that's what he's expecting you to do. This might be the moment when you miss the thing. The breakthrough. You were going to do it. Regardless of what's happened, you need to follow it through.

So here I am, sitting in the bar of the Holiday Inn in the centre of town. Kramer's getting the drinks. I thought I oughtn't to drink alcohol while interviewing on a case, and then he said he was getting himself a gin and tonic and I crumbled and asked for vodka tonic. Just like that, the weak, pathetic wretch surrendered to one of his many vices.

'You got a daughter, Sergeant?' he says, after we've been sitting in silence for a second or two.

'Don't see her much.'

'Too bad.'

'Don't deserve to,' I say. At least it forces me to get going, because we're certainly not here to talk about me. 'Tell me about Tandy.'

'I think you people have heard it all by now,' he says.

'Tell me something I haven't heard. There's always something.'

I hold his gaze. I thought, coming here, it was going to be like looking in the mirror, looking into the same miserable depths I find myself in. Perhaps, even, it would be worse.

Regardless of all my crap, self-inflicted and otherwise, there can be nothing like losing a child. I don't know whether the newness of the event might make it worse or whether the real torment will take longer to kick in. Maybe there hasn't been the time yet, for him to live every day, getting up, having the first thought of the day, day after wretched, shitty day, his daughter is dead and he'll never see her again.

But it's not there. The look isn't in his eyes. It's not that I see a lack of concern. I don't see guilt or fear, I don't see disinterest. But I also don't see heart-wrenching hurt and regret. The pain that ought to be there.

'What's there to say, Sergeant?' he says. 'She's dead. Someone killed her. Maybe they knew who they were pushing in front of the train, I don't know…'

'When was the last time you spoke to her?'

'Your boss asked me already, Sergeant,' he says. 'Are you reading off the same cheat sheet? Is that all you've got?'

And he's right. It is pretty much all I've got.

'You're not here to ask any more questions,' he says, 'or any different questions. You're just here to see what he's like, scope out the Californian guy. That it? Look me over, see what you think? Is it possible I was nailing my daughter? Huh?'

'You lied to DCI Taylor,' I say.

'I don't believe I did,' he says, 'but go on, Sherlock.'

Oh, for fuck's sake.

'You told him you spoke to Tandy at the weekend. You told him you spoke to her every weekend, sometimes during the week, too.'

'That's correct.'

Take a drink. God, it's good. Perfect amount of vodka, great mix, temperature colder than the kiss of a vampire lesbian.

Yeah, whatever.

'Well,' I say, having left him hanging, 'it's correct that's what you told him. It's not correct that's what you did.'

He's staring, trying to figure me out, trying to understand what I know, and where I'm coming from. Have I checked phone records? Have I spoken to anyone else in California? Have I, perhaps, spoken to Tandy's mother.

I've got nothing on him other than the look in his eyes. Tandy may have lived with him, but there was no great relationship there. Probably explains why she was studying in Scotland and not in California, or anywhere else in the US.

'You have a daughter,' he says, and his eyes are dropping.

Is this all he's been waiting for, I wonder. Another father to talk to?

He goes quiet for a while. Stares at the floor. Holds his drink, but doesn't lift it. Now there's real feeling in those eyes, real thoughts rather than evasive thoughts running through his head, but there's no need to push him further. It's coming. Just need to wait until he decides the time is right.

Wonder why he never talked to Taylor? Natural defence against the first line of attack, perhaps. Eventually the weight of lies start to kick in, take their toll.

Finally he lifts his drink again, lifts his eyes at the same time, takes about a third of the glass in one go then places it back on the table.

'We all want to be thought reasonable men, Sergeant. I'm a reasonable man. Decent. Tandy was... she was wild. After her mother left, I couldn't do anything with her. She needed a mother. She was...' The gaze drifts away over the hotel bar, coming to rest on the lower leg of a woman sitting at a nearby table. I'll give the guy the benefit of the doubt and say he's staring into space, not really focused on anything. 'Always bringing boys home, always much older than her. I mean, when she was twelve, thirteen. She didn't care what I thought. Wild... like I said.'

Not the Tandy Kramer we've come to know from her lecturers and fellow students, but how often do you see that? The daughter, a completely different person from the friend.

'Did you sleep with her?'

He doesn't look at me. A doleful smile on his lips, another drink.

'No, Sergeant, I did not. I did not sleep with her. I did not understand her, and if I'm honest, I gave up on her, and she gave up on me, a long time ago. I don't know what her plans were, but I'm pretty sure she wasn't coming back to California. Not to cross my front door, any road. California's a big place. More than big enough for the two of us.'

He drains the drink, turns back to face me.

'About a year ago,' he says, 'to answer your question. The last time I spoke to her was about a year ago.'

And that, I think, might just be that for Mr Kramer and this particular line of inquiry.

* * *

End up talking to the guy for an hour, albeit mostly on his part in dress-up battle re-enactments. You hear about people doing that kind of thing. In the UK, it's usually going to be Civil War, or Bannockburn, some kind of shit like that. In the US, you'd think Civil War and Little Big Horn. This guy does *Game of Thrones*. He dresses up as characters from *Game of Thrones* and plays out battle scenes. Because that's not weird.

Fuck it, who knows? Could be the master tactic of the murdering father, engaging in chitchat with the investigating detective, and making him think you're a sad, simpleton loser because you like to dress up as Stannis Baratheon.

I suppose there are some of those *Game Of Thrones* prostitute sex scenes I might have inadvertently re-enacted.

Get home some time just before ten. Nothing, I think, to report in the end, other than that Kramer should be allowed to return home with his daughter's body, whenever we're ready to release it. Could go back into the office, but decide against.

Tomorrow might be Saturday, but it's just going to be a regular working day. Get in early, find out how it went for Taylor and Connor. Perhaps the boss will expect me there now, but I've had enough for today. Enough of all this shit and death and of thinking that somehow someone is targeting me.

To the fridge, bottle of wine, get a tumbler, stand in the middle of the kitchen turning the screw. If only I could remember what the crows said. I don't believe, whatever powers he has, I don't believe Clayton has the ability to put crows in my head. The crows are making that decision. They must be there to warn me. Or help me.

First taste of the wine. Dry. Probably something about gooseberries and citrus fruits.

The doorbell goes. I stand for a moment, not really sure about the sound. The doorbell? Not the buzzer from down on the street. The doorbell. Someone in the building ringing my bell. One of my neighbours come to speak to me, which is weird. My neighbours never speak to me.

Set the glass down on the table, go to the door, don't bother with the peep hole. And there's the explanation right there. A guy with a beard, in green Lycra, holding a clipboard with his green cycling gloves, wearing a political rosette with matching cycling helmet for the FSN.

Who the fuck are the FSN?

'Good evening, how are you?' he says.

Politics. Jesus.

In fact, I think I'd prefer it if the guy was selling Jesus.

And right there I think of sitting in the church at the top end of Cambuslang, the peace and quiet it afforded, and wonder if it might be worthwhile going back there some time.

'I wonder if you've decided how to vote in next month's council by-election, my friend?'

Oh, for crying out loud. I haven't decided what I'm going to do in the next five fucking minutes.

Oh, wait. Start getting drunk. I have made that decision.

'There's a council by-election?'

'Yes, there is. The councilor won last month's Holyrood by-election. Did you vote then?'

'I don't vote,' I say.

He looks taken aback. Like, whoever heard of such a thing?

'Why not? People died so you could vote,' he says, although he doesn't quite have the conviction of his words, like it's a learned response. Like it's what you're supposed to say.

'Who the fuck are the FSN?' I ask.

Possibly could have chosen words that were slightly less aggressive, but he started it. He rang the bell.

'The Federal Scottish Nationalists,' he says. 'We're an alternative to the SNP, for those who want independence but... well, who want an alternative to the SNP.'

I stare at him from four feet away. There's a silence, but it's not an engaging silence. I think he's waiting for me to be impressed. Or perhaps he's guarded, in case I turn out to be one of those bulldog Nats, the walls of my bedroom covered in pictures of the Dear Leader with her Bay City Rollers hair, and I'm about to chib him for daring to suggest there should be another option.

'What does that even mean?' I say eventually.

'What?'

'Federal Scottish Nationalist?'

'We want independence,' he says.

He suddenly doesn't sound sure.

'So what's federal about it exactly? You want Scotland itself to be a collection of states in a federation? Millport and Orkney and Glasgow and Edinburgh, with little centralised power?'

'What?' he says.

'How many of there are you?'

'What d'you mean?'

'In the party? How many of there are you in the party?'

He swallows, looks a bit lost. It's not getting to me though. I'm not about to feel bad for picking on him. If you're going to go around sticking your noses into people's lives at ten o'clock on a fucking Friday evening, at least know what the fuck you're talking about.

'I'm not sure,' he says.

'Jesus…'

'Take a leaflet,' he says, holding it forward.

'No.'

'Please.'

Holy crap. Seriously, I could have drunk a glass of wine in the time I've spoken to this fucktard.

Snatch it off him, don't look him in the eye again, close the door quickly in his face. Fuck me. Stand there for a second, then walk through to the kitchen.

Jesus. What a dick. And I mean me, not him.

He's just doing what he wants to do. Some harmless conviction, and it's not like the independence movement doesn't need an alternative. And what the fuck do I know about federalism?

Glass in hand, my phone pings. Mutter grimly, for all the world like my life is plagued by interruptions, take a drink, phone out my pocket, read the message.

No Sender. That's who it's from. It says No Sender, as though I have the name No Sender in my phone as a contact.

You seem stressed. Relax. Maybe turn on the news. Something I prepared earlier.

Close my eyes. Fuck. Immediately it seems obvious it's from the same person who's been sending the e-mails. An anonymous communication. That makes sense. And straight away, I think of Kramer, stupidly Kramer, the last person who I spoke to in relation to the investigation.

Except, I wasn't stressed. How would he know I was stressed? I sat in a fucking hotel bar, drinking vodka, talking about *Game of Thrones*.

The FSN guy? What? Close my eyes. Picture him. The cycling helmet, the beard. The glasses. He was wearing glasses, so inconspicuous I barely noticed. And the bad teeth. He had noticeably bad teeth. And the gloves. He was wearing gloves.

Straight back to the door, look out onto the landing. No sign of him, no sign of him having been here. Stand still, listening for the sound of footsteps, or laughter.

He's gone.

Maybe turn on the news. Crap.

Close the door, back inside. The glass of wine still in my hand, I down the rest of it in one, and turn on the TV.

21

Back into the station.

Have you ever noticed how your life is like a sitcom? Sitcoms are low-budget TV, generally filmed in front of an audience. Therefore they mostly take place on a restricted number of sets. The work place. The bar. The trench in *Blackadder Goes Forth*, the sitting room in *Big Bang Theory*.

And here's my sitcom life. The sitting room. The station. The café. The bar. Other short, vague parts of it conducted on the street or in the bathroom or on the doorstep, pre-filmed and shown to the studio audience on a monitor.

Taylor is sitting at my desk, talking to Morrow. He stands when he sees me approach. I'm tired and I don't want to be here, but thought I'd better. I didn't call in or anything, just came back as soon as I saw the news. I expect some sarcasm from him, but he just nods.

'You saw it, then?'

A body found in a basement in Milton of Campsie, as yet unidentified. Had been there for a week or so.

'What's the score?' I ask.

'On close inspection, this one seems a little different. I mean, Connor and me were with the suits in Riverside, and not really getting anywhere, when news of this came in. Fourth day in a row with a murder in the Glasgow area. That turned the tide in our favour at least. But looking at it, I'm not so sure. The other three were all murders in the last three days. This one... the victim has been dead at least a week. Haven't got all the details yet. So, it could be... fuck, who knows, it certainly doesn't seem to fit the bill.'

I take out my phone, the text is still up there. Hand it over. He reads it, his expression hardens, he passes it on to Morrow.

'What does it mean, you seem stressed?'

I've been giving it thought on the way in here. Had to walk, after all, couldn't bring the car with this much alcohol in me. Very circumspect. Would happily have done it in the past.

'Three options,' I say. 'It's someone who just happens to follow me, day to day, on the job. They're going to know I'm stressed. Second, earlier tonight I had a drink with Kramer, so it would make sense. Except... I really wasn't stressed. I know I wasn't. I don't think I would have come across that way to him, and it's the only time I've seen him. And, of course, how would any of these people know I hadn't already seen the news? Which leaves the third option. Thirty seconds before I got this text I'd had some political canvasser at the door.'

'On a Friday night? SNP?'

A reasonable assumption. They're the only ones putting people out on the streets anymore.

'Said he was from the Federal Scottish Nationalists.'

'The who?'

I shrug, having not already checked. We look at Morrow, Morrow turns to the go-to guy in anybody's room, Google.

'So what happened with the guy?' asks Taylor.

'I got annoyed at him. Didn't want to take any of his shit, eventually closed the door in his face.'

'You looked stressed?'

'I dare say.'

'And when did you get the text?'

'Pretty quickly afterwards. Within a minute. I was standing at the door – you know the front door opens straight into the sitting room – and he would've heard there was no TV playing.'

'What'd he look like?'

'That's the thing. Everything about him said disguise. Middle-aged man in Lycra, ostensibly. Lime green, like one of those sad fuckers you see out on his bike. Wearing gloves, bit of a beard, glasses, still wearing his cycling helmet. If you were expecting someone in disguise, he looked like it. But I wasn't. Brain was switched off. Seems really obvious now, but at the time, well he just looked like a sad fucker, doing sad political shit at ten on a Friday night. Yet remove all that shit, am I going to recognise him?'

Of course, I've been thinking about that as well.

'Well, are you?' asks Taylor, and we both know what he's asking.

'I don't know.'

'No such party,' says Morrow.

Taylor looks back at the phone message, puts his hands in his pockets, walks off a little way, turns back, head down.

'*Something I prepared earlier…*,' he says.

'What about the house where the body was found? The owners?' I ask.

'They say they know nothing about it, and you know… well, at the moment we're inclined to believe them. A couple in their 80s. The man looked confused, the woman looked like she's ready to sue someone. The police, if need be, like it's our fault.'

'And the victim?'

'They claim no knowledge of her.'

'How'd she die?'

'She'd been bound with duct tape, but the duct tape equivalent of the girl getting painted gold in *Goldfinger*. Completely bound, completely covered, head to foot. They're presuming she'll have suffocated at some point, but we'll see.'

'I guess it wouldn't have taken very long. I mean, to die.'

'Possibly not. Waiting on that as well.'

Taylor starts tapping the desk.

'So, are we losing the case, anyway?' I ask. 'I mean, if it's being centralised?'

'No decision, but it's likely. The Clarkston guys are super-reluctant to give up their racial hatred, double beheading, despite not having got anywhere. Everybody's the same, Connor too, really, but we're the little guys. Ultimately, I think we'll find by tomorrow afternoon it's off our hands. As usual, with one of these things, we just have to do as good a job as possible, hand over as much as we can, and hope we haven't missed something glaringly obvious they discover in the first ten minutes.'

'And what if...,' I begin. The words fail. Taylor's looking at me, waiting for me to say it. Morrow's staring too, although he doesn't know what's coming.

Fuck it.

'What if it's Clayton and it's aimed at us?' I say. 'Me... aimed at me. Jesus, really, what if it's *not* Clayton and it's aimed at me?'

'Did you think your political guy looked like Clayton?'

And there's the question.

He looked like a door-to-door saddo in a cap with a beard. Any guy could look like that. Look at the Groucho mirror scene in *Duck Soup*.

All right, they were brothers, but the principle's the same.

'I don't know,' is all I've got.

* * *

'Who sent you?'

The last syllable emerges as a high-pitched ejaculation, as the beak of the crow stabs into the side of my head.

I can't see it – I can never see it – but I can sense he's looking at me, his head tilted to the side.

'What?'

Take a breath. At least I've managed to get him to stop. Maybe if I can keep him in conversation, I'll recover my strength, be able to get up off the forest floor, before he can do it again.

'Who sent you?'

'What d'you mean, who sent us? Get outta here! You some kinda schmuck or what?'

I stare at the trees above, the leaves moving in the wind. Unattractive trees. Vague trees. Impossible to tell what kind they are. Maybe if I close my eyes again it will all go away. The damp. The trees. The crows.

'Fuck!' I blurt out, as the beak stabs into me again. The same spot. Is it my imagination, or is the crow starting to get somewhere? Can I actually feel my skull weakening in that area? Is my brain beginning to feel the cold, right there, through the thinning skull?

'Jesus,' says the crow, 'will you just relax?'

'How can I relax? You're stabbing my skull!'

'We've been over this,' says the crow. 'Every goddam night. I really don't know why I keep coming back here. Why don't you just wake the fuck up and we can all get on with our lives?'

'It's not that easy.'

'Jesus,' he mutters.

He grabs my ear with his beak, bites and pulls, and I yelp at the pain.

I wake up. Eyes open, staring at the ceiling. Sweating and uncomfortable. My ear hurts, like it's been bitten, and my hand goes straight to it. I feel sick.

22

Saturday morning. I'm heading into the office, but have decided to stop off at the church at the top of Cambuslang. The Old Kirk. Haven't been back here since last year. I realise I've missed it.

Woke up at 06.30. Headache, the dull throb right bang where the crow has been pecking away at me. I know it doesn't make sense. I mean, you get hit in your dreams, why should you be in pain once you wake up?

Yet, where's the crow coming from? It must be coming from inside me, inside my head, my imagination, my guilt, my something. He's there for a reason, and he's causing me pain. Pain in my head, inside and out.

Mundanely, I take two paracetamol and the pain fades by the time I've finished eating breakfast.

Drive the car into work, taking the five-minute detour to the Old Kirk on the way. It's only 07:45, but somehow it doesn't seem surprising the gate to the church is not chained up, and the front door is open. Must be something going on, which seems strange, given the church is no longer in use for regular services.

Wedding or a funeral.

Park the car, then stand in the car park for a few seconds, looking up at the old building. A nice morning. Summer. A freshness still in the air, but the day will be warm and not too muggy. The steeple is etched against a hazy blue sky.

Through the gate and up the path to the front door. Look over at the two graves that caused all the fuss the previous November. The grave I dug up with the body of the young girl, and the new grave, where the body of church member Maureen Henderson was buried in a hasty ceremony to make sure the graveyard did not slip into obsolescence.

I've followed the story, presumed that once the fuss had died down, the church in Cambuslang would make sure the body was reburied elsewhere. Instead, the matter has become buried in the courts, and Maureen's body remains where she was interred. The longer she stays there, one feels, the greater the chance she stays there for good.

I open the door and enter. Immediately feels cooler in here. Take a moment, listen for any sound, and then walk through the short hall, open the door on the right and into the nave.

She's there at the far end of the church, arranging flowers at the altar. She turns at the sound of the door, a scowl on her face, which immediately relaxes when she sees me. She turns back to what she's doing, rather than watch me walk towards her.

The old place looks emptier than before, although the same quiet calm remains. Hands in pockets, I stop when I get to the front of the church, and Mary Buttler turns and smiles.

'Hey.'

'I thought you'd be back eventually,' she says, 'although I was beginning to wonder. What brings you here today?'

Reply with my shoulders.

'Not sure. I guess some part of me knew instinctively you'd be open. Wedding or funeral?'

She gives me a bit of an eyebrow, glances at the flowers and then looks back.

'You can't tell?'

'No idea,' I say.

'Funeral,' she says.

'An old parish member?'

'Jean,' she says. 'Lovely woman. Been in a home for the past ten years, hadn't been here in a long time.'

We hold the gaze for a second, then she turns away and continues to work with the flowers. I watch her for a short while, and then walk further towards the back of the church, up the steps, to where the choir used to sit.

'The place looks... I don't know, seems emptier than before.'

I look up at Jesus in blue as I say it. Jesus, whose name I mention so often. I expect he doesn't mind. He's the forgiving sort...

She tuts, and when I look round she's shaking her head.

'The St Stephen's lot have been up here. Take what they like, move it down to their dreadful building. They're like... they're like ISIS. No respect. They won the war, they won the peace, and now they just do what they like. I'm sick to death...'

Another loud tut, she takes a moment from what she's doing – probably not a great idea to work with flowers when you're thinking about strangling someone – deep breath, then returns to the job.

'Won't be my problem for much longer,' she says.

'Why not?'

She doesn't answer immediately. Funny, I came here for peace, and thought I'd get it, but not unsurprisingly walk straight into the continuing bitterness of the old church merger.

The peace really only comes from an empty building. As soon as people are involved, there it goes...

'They said all combined posts in the church had to be advertised. Due process they called it. It's the law, they said. So my job was opened up to everyone, not just in the church, of course. Thirty-seven people applied, but only two of those were from within the church community. Myself, and one person from amongst the St Stephen's crowd. Guess who got the job.'

'Ah.'

She looks up. Eyes a little red. Seems like a reasonably open wound onto which I've just poured salt. Crap. Had to ask. Well, she wanted me to, I suppose.

'How long have you got left?'

'This is my last duty. I hand over the keys on Monday morning. I need to move out of the house by the end of June. Not that she's getting the house, she doesn't need it. Lord knows what they're going to do with it, but whatever it is, we can guarantee it'll be to their benefit and no one else's.'

She straightens up, a pair of scissors in her right hand.

'I could bury these in someone's head,' she says, 'and the only thing stopping me is not knowing who to do it to first.'

'I think there might have been enough murder over these churches,' I say, but there's no condemnation in my voice. I find myself on her side, completely.

I walk back down towards her. There's a tear on her cheek. Jesus, how stupid do I continue to be? How self-centred. I came here for me, that's all. If the place was open, what was I expecting? Peace and quiet? Solitude?

Yet, naturally, I walk into someone else's problems, and they seem so much more intimately significant than mine.

I walk over beside her and take her into my arms. And it's not the asshole me who's holding her. It's the not the dickhead who would, under other circumstances, be happily banging her over the back of a pew while Jesus watched, looking somewhat perturbed.

I just hold her, she presses her cheek into my chest.

I'm comforting her, but she's comforting me too. It feels safe and warm. And fleeting.

Over her shoulder I look up at Jesus. He's looking sceptical. He knows me after all, but I give him the nod. We're good here, I say. He relaxes.

There's just the three of us, and we're all joined by the same melancholy. The passing of the years, the changing of the guard. The things you need to do to get by.

23

The politics have arrived.

Summoned into Riverside. Me, Taylor, Connor. Morrow left behind to work the case. No one in particular in charge, not that there generally needs to be.

There are thirty-three people in the room. The Chief Constable of Scotland standing before us. An Edinburgh man through and through, and there will be plenty here wishing he'd fuck off back where he came from.

This really is turning into the Crows business all over again. Fuck, what do I care? Don't care about the politics, don't care about who's in charge. At some point it will all be over, and I'll be back on the domestic violence and pub violence and petty theft that makes up a majority of what we do.

I remain haunted by my stupidity. Still feel the absurd embarrassment and wretchedness from having sex on a desk. Still feels like I stepped over a line, or through a portal, stepped onto another path.

Have barely thought of Philo since then. It feels wrong to. I have this sense she doesn't want me thinking about her. Maybe at first she was amused by my sexual tomfoolery, but not now. Not now that the dust has settled and she's had a chance to think about it.

Now she's dead, she only lives on when people think about her. That makes sense, right? When someone thinks of her, she survives, she's there, she exists through the thoughts in that person's head. Yet now, for the first time since she died, it feels like she doesn't want me to be thinking of her. She doesn't want to exist in my head, or exist because of my head. Her husband, the weak cuckold, he'll be thinking about her today, and she won't be torn. She'll be there, with him, continuing to exist because of him.

Jesus in blue didn't really help. I had a brief respite of a few minutes, Mary in my arms, feeling some comfort. But she had to get on with her preparations, and I had to get to work, and it was over. And once she's gone, the chances of me going by the Old Kirk and finding it open are virtually nil. It wasn't just Mary who was going into that old church for the last time.

Thirty-three people in a room. How many of those are men? Thirty-three. It's pretty fucking funny, isn't it? How shit an organisation is this? It's a surprise we're not here to discuss women's issues.

Yes, I know, they've intentionally made sure there are no women in the room so I can concentrate.

'Look, gentlemen, we all know how this could go,' says the man at the front. The Chief Constable of All Scotland. Jefferson. The highest officer in the land. First time I've sat in the same room as him. I wonder if I'm actually legally entitled to even open my mouth in his presence.

Itching to say something, although I'm not even sure what yet.

Concentrate!

'We're still some way off making a significant advance on any one of these investigations. They seem so disparate, so otherworldly in some ways, I can well understand why there are reservations about their interconnectedness. But perhaps, within this inherent contradiction, we see their true similarity. Their very diversity, and the fact they seem so unsolvable, perhaps points to the correlation between them.'

He's boring me. Maybe because he's just saying what I already think. Only, in a more long-winded way.

'Each of you, the teams working the four individual murders, will continue to pursue your investigations. However, management at superintendent level of each of the cases within your regular chain of command will be removed, and you will report to a single officer here in Dalmarnock. Chief Constable Tobin will take overall responsibility for the umbrella operation, with you feeding every piece of knowledge gained in your investigations into his office. I don't need to tell you...' But you will anyway... 'that as you do not have sight of what the other investigations are involved in, and cannot necessarily know what is relevant and what is not, we request you feed everything back to the centre, regardless of how trivial or irrelevant it may seem. It may well be such a piece of information that finally leads to the breakthrough in this case. If at any time...'

On and on. Finally zone out. I'll tune back in if people start laughing.

Not sure why I'm here. Under strict instructions from Connor to keep my mouth shut. Under even stricter instructions to make sure that should, for some obscure reason no one could possibly understand, I do somehow open my mouth, the name Clayton does not emerge.

Naturally, of course, I'm now sitting here trying to stop myself saying Clayton. The little boy in me. The part of me that's just the same as it's always been.

When you're young, you think somehow it'll be different being an adult. You'll feel different, and you'll think differently. Yet it never happens. Perhaps you grow up a little, you don't laugh at Monty Python so much, and you become a little more aware of the feelings of others and how you impact on them – although, of course, awareness need not necessarily lead to decency – but the real you, who you are and how you think, you're stuck with it from about the age of three. That's just how it is.

And now, while the grown up part of me knows I should keep my mouth shut, the other part, the part that's always been happy to stick my hand into a bunch of nettles, even better if I'm taking someone else's hand with me, is itching to let rip. Connor be damned.

Uh-oh. Get the sudden feeling everyone is looking at

me. And yes, everyone *is* looking at me. Thirty-two men. Or, thirty-one men and the demi-god at the head of the table. All looking my way.

Must have switched off at the wrong moment.

I look the big man at the front in the eye. Of all those other bastards looking at me, I can feel Taylor's eyes the most. He's the one who's disappointed, the one who knows I drifted away.

'Sergeant?' says the beak at the front.

Now, I would normally be predisposed to think ill of this guy. It's just how it is. He's in a position of authority, and by the very dint of wanting to be there, and conducting his career in such a manner as to reach that position, then he must be a dick. Weirdly, though, I like the cut of his jib. And here, right now, I can see him looking at me, and he knows I wasn't listening, and I can tell he's going to be cool about it.

'I was saying that really, the reason we're all here is because of the e-mail messages and the text you received.'

'Yes.'

'Do you have any insight into why someone might have chosen you? I know Superintendent Connor said you were reviewing all your old cases.'

The name is right there. In my mouth, the tip of my tongue, on my lips, and by God I can't stop it, and boom! here it comes, spewed out onto the table in amongst the thirty-three bold and brave men of the Scottish Police Service.

'Clayton,' I say. Doesn't come out quite right, so I repeat the name.

There follows a murmuration of raised eyebrows. I can sense Taylor's deep breath, and the jagged stare of Connor, stabbing into my head. The poor man must be silently screaming, *don't mention the fucking crows!*

'That would be Michael Clayton,' says the beak.

'Yes,' I say, my estimation raised further by the fact he knows who I'm talking about. He's done his research.

He glances around the room, gauging the reaction of

those present who know the story, and then comes back to me.

'You never established anything on this man before. Indeed, the Police Service was fortunate not to end up in court. Do you suppose he's continuing the murderous ways we were unable to previously prove, or do you think he might have seen these murders are taking place and is taunting you? Taunting the police. Trying, perhaps, to lure us into further acts of indiscretion.'

That there is a good point. It could well be, despite his position, this man is really not a complete idiot.

Don't mention the crows!

'He's a very clever man,' I say. 'I don't doubt it's him who's contacting me. There's no one else, no one else who would care enough. We know he's got the technical computer ability to carry it off–'

'You suspect it,' begins Connor, 'and have absolutely–'

He's silenced by a move of the beak's hand. Jesus, there's authority. Also, to be fair to Connor, someone with respect for it. I think I'd just keep talking all the more if someone did that to me.

All right, I'm not mentioning the crows, but everything else is on the table.

'He was suspected by a predecessor of ours, DCI Lynch, in a murder/rape case a few years ago. He couldn't pin him down, Clayton managed to sue the police...' The beak looks like he knows what I'm talking about, but I keep going anyway. '... and then he came to Lynch afterwards, a few months after it was all done and dusted and we'd basically had to shelve the case and place it in the Unsolved column, and told him he'd done it.'

The beak lifts his head. Hadn't heard that part before.

'Now maybe he was just blowing smoke up Lynch's arse. Maybe. But Lynch was convinced he had him, and the guy was always just that little bit ahead of the game. Just enough, like he knew exactly what he was doing. Which is what happened with us. He played us all along, always one step ahead, set us up the whole way, and at the end of it walked into my hospital room and laughed in my face.

'I know, I know it proves nothing. And all it does is put us in the same position as the previous two times. If we think he's the one sending the e-mails, then he's taunting us and we're going to have to go after him if we want to prove it.'

Jefferson's hands are on the table, fingers steady. He looks at Connor.

'Does he have any sort of police harassment case against us, or anything specifically against the Sergeant that would interfere with us tackling this?'

Glance at Connor. He looks concerned, but then, if it goes tits up this time it's not going to be on him, so he could probably do with taking the poker out his arse.

'Nothing specific,' he says. 'But then, that might well be because he wants us to blunder in and make total fools of ourselves again.'

He looks at Taylor and me as he says it.

'Well, gentlemen,' says Jefferson, 'when you go and see him later today, you'd better make sure you don't blunder.'

24

We drive back to Cambuslang in silence. Since I'm the one at the lowest pay grade, I'm driving. Connor sits sternly in the back, his presence a succubus to the atmosphere. At one point Taylor can see me contemplating sticking Bob on the CD, catches my eye and gives me a *just don't* look.

Bob remains silent. Given my balls out performance in there, casually tossing Clayton into the mix for all the world like he was a teaspoonful of cinnamon and the investigation was one of those pumpkin pies people talk about, I consider just sticking Bob on anyway. On this occasion, however, it would be Taylor I'd be pissing off, not Connor, so I don't bother.

Do we know what kind of music Connor listens to? I don't think so. I don't remember ever knowing. Jim Reeves, probably, or some other funeral-music-loving miserablist.

We get back to the office, and as we walk into the open plan Taylor indicates for me to follow him into his room, indicating to Morrow, as he passes his desk, for him to join us. We are aware, as we walk in, that Connor, clinging to us like a ringwraith intent on crushing every last living spark in our bodies, has not been shaken off.

He closes the door and stares daggers at Taylor and me. Morrow might as well not be here. I expect he's got something of an *oh Jesus, what the fuck have I done?* look on his face.

Connor looks like he's having to do some major composing of himself, before letting rip. You can see various sentences and words formulating in his mouth and not quite making it out. Perhaps he's imagining the puritanical Mrs Connor looking censoriously at him from behind his shoulder.

'Don't fuck this up,' finally shoots from his lips, like evil, black sperm ejaculated from Sauron's wizened old penis.

Jesus, where did *that* come from? Not a great image.

He turns and leaves, slamming the door behind him.

We stand in silence for a few seconds, as the atmosphere lightens. Morrow has both eyebrows raised, which is fair enough. It is, without question, a double eyebrow moment.

'What'd I miss?' he says, unsure whether or not he ought to be smiling.

'Detective Sgt Hutton couldn't keep his mouth shut,' says Taylor. 'Fortunately, at least, there were no women in the room, so he managed to keep his trousers on.'

Morrow smiles fully now. I don't have a lot to say to that.

'We need to go and speak to Michael Clayton,' says Taylor. 'Boss's orders. The Chief Constable, not him,' indicating Connor with a dismissive thumb. 'So, before that happens, the three of us are going to sit here and think of things to say to Clayton so we don't sound like the *fucking Muppets*, although I'm pretty sure that's what's going to end up happening.'

'Do we really want to be going anywhere near Clayton?' asks Morrow. 'I mean, why are we even thinking about it?'

Taylor looks at me, to allow me to explain myself. I give Taylor the official *bugger off* look of disapproval, and then turn to Morrow.

'My dreams are being haunted by crows. I think they're telling me something.'

Morrow holds my gaze, then looks at Taylor to see what his face is doing – nothing – and then turns back.

'You said that to the Chief Constable? And you still have a job?'

'No, I didn't. Nevertheless, whatever it was I did say, and I can't exactly remember what that was, it was enough to convince the old man we should be allowed to pursue Clayton in the course of our enquiries. So, it's happening, and as our good friend Connor said, we better not fuck it up.'

The old man? Ferguson can't be more than five years older than me. Perhaps the confident man, or the non-wastrel, would be a better nickname for him.

Morrow gives another glance to Taylor, who confirms the fact this is a real thing and not a crappy leftover from April Fools Day.

'So, sit down, and let's start going over it,' says Taylor.

He gives us a moment, the sound of the chairs being dragged across the floor, and then the three of us are around the desk.

'Right, we've got four murders, one of which was a double. All in the Glasgow area, which basically is the only thing to connect them. Which means, of course, they may not be connected at all. We also have to be wary of the possibility that two or three of them are connected, but one of them isn't. One of them could be completely unrelated, but just happened to fall within the same timespan. Right, Sergeant, first up...'

Standard practice police work. Going over everything you know.

'Tandy Kramer, pushed in front of the train. We have CCTV, there's no doubt it wasn't an accident. We've been unable to identify the person who pushed her, just as we've been unable to identify any person who might have held a grudge against her. A genuine, straight up mystery.'

Taylor stares blankly at the desk while I talk, then makes a small gesture towards Morrow.

'Double beheading in a converted church. Looks like a terrorist, or at least, racially-motivated, murder. First victim, Reginald Silvers, forty-seven, unemployed. Second, Claire Hanlon, forty-three, three kids, worked as a phlebotomist at Monklands General, no idea what she was doing in Clarkston. She had a tattoo on her left forearm that exercised the squad for a while. A couple of detectives got quite excited about it. Turned out it was a Radiohead symbol.'

He smiles, Taylor just looks pissed off.

'*Unbelievers* written next to the two bodies. They've been searching for a connection between the two victims, or a connection between them and the Islamic Centre or the old church as it was. Nothing. The CCTV outside the centre was switched off, which is obviously different from what we have at the train station. As far as we're aware, there had been no previous threat against either the victims, or the centre itself.'

He pauses, can't think of anything else.

'Personally, I'd say if any of the four are unconnected, it's this one,' he adds.

'If it was an act of radical Islam, you'd think at least the killer would have been able to write unbelievers in Arabic,' I say.

'And spell it correctly,' adds Taylor. 'There's the thing that makes it look like it wasn't Clayton. It's sloppy. That's what makes it look less like a terrorist, and more like a couple of fuckwits trying to stir up trouble.'

'Unless that's what Clayton wants us to think,' I say.

He gives me a doubtful look.

'You can ask him,' he says.

'Third guy had been at a party. Billy Thomas, regular bloke, twenty-seven, father of eight by six different women. Lived with one of the women and three of the kids. He left the party to walk home on his own – reportedly very drunk – and never made it. Got accosted, beaten to a pulp. First indications are he wasn't dead at this point. He was then killed by having a massive dose of heroin injected into him. Shit quality too. Here, it's definitely the latter that makes it suspicious. He was unemployed, moved in an extensive social circle, a lot of interconnections, a lot of rivalry, a lot of small-time hoodlum stuff. Black market fags from Eastern Europe, dope, extortion on various levels. Looks like there might be a queue of people quite happy he's dead.'

'The Treasury,' throws in Morrow.

'Unfortunately, it's too late for the gene pool,' says Taylor.

'The thing to set this one apart,' I continue, struggling against my glib colleagues who refuse to take this seriously, 'is the heroin. The guy was unconscious. If someone had wanted him dead, then why not stand on his throat or cover his nose and mouth for thirty seconds? These people, the ones the plods over in Springburn are lining up as the potential suspects, they wouldn't waste that amount of heroin. Not even shit stuff. Very weird. It's like… this is the one, despite it looking like a petty, ugly little gangland-type hit, this is the one that says there's something else happening.'

Taylor has the same look on his face as before, taking it in, thinking it through, trying to remember if there's anything I might have missed.

'Maybe it is significant the heroin was lousy,' says Morrow. 'Maybe that was one of his things, maybe that's why he was killed. Selling crappy shit for too much money. This was someone's way of getting him back.'

'They're looking at it,' says Taylor. 'It's a possibility. There's a lot of argument going on between the various stations, but it's not like any of them are doing a shit job within their own area. Still, I'm inclined to agree. It's a good point for someone to make, but who exactly is it aimed at, since the victim himself would never get to see the point?' He starts nodding, as if someone, somewhere is pulling him up on the statement. 'Course, it's completely out of our patch, it might well be aimed at someone over there. But however lousy this stuff was, it was still of a standard that would've been getting sold on the street, so someone was happy flushing several hundred pounds worth of shit away when they could've made the same point, with the same result, with a lot, lot less.'

He ends this part of the conversation with a small,

dismissive hand movement.

'We don't know, but we've got the basics... Rob?'

'Lastly, we've got a woman, still unidentified, left lying in a basement, bound and suffocated.' He pauses. 'Actually, I'm the wrong guy here, I don't really know too much more, sorry.'

Taylor looks at me.

'She was killed by the tape strapped around her head,' I say. 'Suffocated. This happened before the body was dumped. Since we don't know who she is, we can't begin to say where she was picked up, where she came from, when she disappeared etcetera. She'd been dead over a week, but not much over. The couple who live in the house... they don't even register on the scale of suspicion.'

Taylor pushes his chair back, gets up and stands at the window. Hands in his pockets, looking down on the car park.

'Train; religious beheading; petty thuggery and drugs; bound, suffocated and placed in a basement...'

His words drift off. And the words of that first e-mail drift into my head. Have you worked it out yet? Well, it's a couple of days later, and no, no we haven't. Haven't the faintest idea. Not even entirely sure there's anything to work out.

Normally I'd get up and join Taylor at the window, but the presence of Morrow keeps me in my seat. I mean, if I do that, what's poor Morrow going to do? Would he feel awkward sitting there, the last one at the desk, or would he feel the need to get up and join us, so there would be three of us standing at the window, looking down on a warm, bright day, three superheroes whose powers don't extend much beyond being able to light more than one fag with the same match.

Mind's drifting.

'Who's going to see Clayton?' asks Morrow.

Taylor straightens his shoulders a little at the return of conversation.

'I had thought about it being you,' he says, 'but best not to bring you into it. So the Sergeant is going, which unfortunately means I have to go with him, to make sure he doesn't make a complete arse of everything, leaving the Police Service open to such an enormous law suit the entire operation has to shut down and go out of business.'

He turns round, looking at me and not Morrow.

'The very future of policing in Scotland depends on me not fucking up?' I say.

'Pretty much.'

There's a lovely pause in the conversation, as we all think about the consequences. We haven't even talked about what we're going to say to Clayton yet, which is probably because none of us has the faintest idea what that's going to be.

'Meet you at the Job Centre,' says Morrow.

25

We have some further discussion about how this is going to go, but most of the conversation is Taylor stopping himself saying 'and you keep your mouth shut.' Into the car, sit in silence for a few minutes, and then I stick Bob on as we hit the M74 to drive to the other side of Glasgow.

Bob's Christmas album is a gem. No, seriously. This year, if you buy one Christmas album, make it *Christmas In The Heart* by Mr Dylan. All your Christmas favourites are there. *The First Noel, Silver Bells, Winter Wonderland, Must Be Santa*, and many more. With a backing track and angelic choir straight out of Bing Crosby, and the sixty-eight year-old Bob croaking his way through a total of fifteen yuletide classics, you can't go wrong.

Questionable choice in early June, I admit, but sometimes these festive CDs just find their way onto the player.

Bob is rasping his way through *Hark! The Herald Angels Sing* when Taylor finally voices his vague displeasure at the choice of listening material.

'What... the fuck?' he says.

Taylor's as big a Bob fiend as I am, so I don't know what his problem is.

'What?'

'It's June.'

I leave it a second as I cut inside one of those bloody women sitting at fifty miles an hour in the middle lane, glance over at her in annoyance, see it's actually a bloody man and feel a fleeting moment of embarrassment at my prejudice, before moving out in front of him.

'Bob transcends the months.'

'Seriously, Sergeant... I know you've got fifty Dylan CDs in the car, why the fuck are you listening to this one?'

'Rebecca was in the car last weekend. Took her to a chess competition.'

'You said.'

'She doesn't like Bob.'

'I know. No one does. It's only you and me left.'

'She agreed I could put him on if it was this, and we just listened to *Must Be Santa* on continuous loop. So, that happened. And I haven't removed the CD. On the plus side, I took *Must Be Santa* off continuous loop.'

He glances at me. Mentioning Rebecca, and the unstated fact I rarely see her, is enough to soften any argument. Nevertheless, it doesn't quite get him to back off the anti-Christmas music crusade.

He looks in the pocket of the passenger door, digs out *Planet Waves*, removes the offending Christmas CD from the player, puts it away, and within fifteen seconds *On A Night Like This* is filling the car.

I let it play for a while then say, 'This album always makes me sad because of *Forever Young*. Reminds me how I little I have to do with my kids.'

He looks at me, wondering whether or not I'm taking the piss. He can't decide, but leaves it on anyway.

* * *

Standing on the doorstep. The front gate was open, the car parked at the top of the driveway. A big old Victorian house out past Bearsden. Doesn't seem so long since we were last here.

We checked to make sure Clayton hadn't moved, but didn't alert him to our arrival. For all the conversation and the tension in the car on the way down here, it's entirely possible he won't be in, it's entirely possible the guy's in Australia or China on holiday. Could be anywhere. But the front gate is open, and the Lexus in which he raced away from us over a year ago, the only car he had at the time, is sitting in the driveway.

The fact he hasn't moved is something that worries me. If these e-mails and the text have come from him, then this could be exactly what he wants to happen. He sits in his big, old fucking house, waiting for us to turn up and walk into his trap. The suits are all scared of him, and he'll know it.

Standing with my back to the door, looking out at the well-tended garden and the trees bursting forth. Summer sun, that whole thing going on, one moment in the neverending cycle. Leaves grow, they look nice, they die, branches are bare, leaves grow back again.

'Great metaphor for the circle of life,' I say.

Taylor gives me a quick, impatient glance.

'What?' he says, the question not asking what I meant, but asking why I'm saying anything at all.

'Leaves. Growing, flourishing, dying, growing again...'

He catches my eye. He looks pretty pissed off. I get that it's with the general worry of being about to talk to the walking Venus Feds Trap, rather than at my metaphor.

'That's not a fucking metaphor,' he says. 'That literally *is* the circle of life. Fuck's sake, Hutton. Get your head out your arse.'

He looks away. My head is so far up my arse the rebuke bounces harmlessly away, like someone firing a Nerf pellet at a Klingon War Bird.

The door opens. Michael Clayton. Dressed like Roger Moore in a 70's Bond movie. Sports jacket and slacks. Only the collar of the white shirt is smaller, along with the knot in the tie. My eyes travel all the way down to his shoes, not unlike the way, I'm afraid to say, I have looked at many a woman in the past.

Those look like expensive shoes. Smart, brown Oxfords. Continuing with my head being detached from the game, I contemplate my own shoes, scuffed and a couple of years old, given the benefit of a clean once every six or seven months.

The three of us stand and look at each other. Hard to read the look on Clayton's face.

'Mr Clayton…,' says Taylor.

Clayton smiles, broadly, cutting Taylor off.

'I'm not sure I would entirely say I've been expecting you, gentlemen, but somehow I'm not surprised. A few unexplained murders in Glasgow, must be time to round up the usual suspects… Is that it?'

'We'd just like a word,' says Taylor.

Clayton holds his gaze for a few seconds, and then turns to me. The familiar detached amusement.

'Have you the slightest, the remotest, the tinniest excuse for coming to talk to me?' he asks. 'At what point did one of you turn to the other and say, I know, some poor girl was pushed in front of a train in Cambuslang, let's go and speak to Michael Clayton, he simply must be involved?'

All this with his eyes trained on me. Like he knows the crows are in my head. Like he knows it's the only damned reason we're here. Like he knows Taylor and I had the conversation.

'We're pursuing several lines of inquiry, Mr Clayton,' says Taylor, 'we'd just like a word.'

Clayton slowly shifts his gaze back to Taylor, and then with a theatrical movement, steps back and ushers us into the house.

'You may as well come in, then,' he says. 'I'd hate to disappoint.'

* * *

He's behind a desk in a small office, Taylor and me in chairs opposite. We'd examined this room before, back during the Plague of Crows business, but we didn't interview him in here.

An expensive office, two walls of old books, a large globe, paintings of battle scenes on the walls, an old desk lamp, heavy wooden furniture. The window is north facing, the light dim, the room cool. There's no computer on the desk, the only device a retro dial phone. One could expect the place to be dusty, but unsurprisingly with Clayton, it's immaculate.

Tea has been offered and turned down. Nevertheless, he left us sitting in here and took the opportunity to go and make himself a small pot. While he was out the room, we didn't move. We sat here, not wanting to be caught looking through papers and books and files and drawers.

He slowly pours tea into a cup through a strainer, his movements precise. The pouring liquid is the only sound. The moment could almost be elegiac, one of those you want to capture and stop, stay in for as long as possible, except the guy pouring the tea is a psychopath.

He places one sugar cube in the cup, using tongs to lift it from the bowl, stirs slowly, and then adds a little milk. He is being so particular and meticulous he could be performing some ancient Asian tea ceremony.

'Can you tell us what you've been doing this past week, Mr Clayton?' asks Taylor.

Clayton continues as though he hasn't heard the question, lays down the spoon, lifts the cup with the fingers of both hands, takes a silent sip, pauses for a second with the tea just beneath his mouth, then places it back in the saucer.

'Almost perfect,' he says. 'Just needs another minute or two to cool down.'

Finally he engages Taylor, clasping his hands together, then resting his chin in them, his elbows on the table.

'I've been here,' he says.

'Can anyone verify that?' I ask.

His eyes move between Taylor and me, then he says, 'I hardly think so.'

'What have you been doing?' asks Taylor.

'Writing,' he says. 'A memoir.'

He leaves that comment in the air for a few seconds, and then continues, 'And yes, both of you gentlemen are in it. How nice of you to come back and potentially add another chapter.'

I don't look at Taylor, but I bet he's thinking the same thing I am. The suits back in Dalmarnock will be pishing themselves when they learn this bastard is writing a book.

'It's called *There's Always A Reason And It's Usually Stupidity*. Just a working title of course, but my agent loves it. We'll see. These books go through so many processes along the way, so many drafts. I've never done it before, feels quite tiresome now I've actually started.'

'You've got an agent?' asks Taylor.

'Yes, of course.'

'I thought they were quite hard to come by?' I say.

What the fuck do I know?

'With the story I've got to tell, there was practically a queue.'

'Who's your agent?' asks Taylor. 'And has he found you a publisher yet?'

'Davina,' he says, 'my agent is called Davina. Lovely girl. Works for Cooper, Baylor and Reibach in Clerkenwell.'

'London?'

'Of course.'

'We'll speak to her,' says Taylor.

'I'm sure you will.'

'Has she found you a publisher?'

'She hasn't officially gone out yet. We're perfecting the first few chapters. There was some talk of a ghostwriter, but I really did want to take care of it myself. When we're settled on the first, I don't know, five chapters I think, then she will go to auction. She's already put out some feelers. She's very confident. She thinks we could be looking at a six-figure deal.'

He makes a dismissive hand movement, the very idea of talking about money being so vulgar.

'Have you seen anyone this week?' I ask. 'Have you played golf, been to the shops, out for dinner?'

His eyes rest on me. I get the feeling, like he's thinking it through on the spot, that just for a second there's something going on in there that hasn't been calculated.

Everything about him seems premeditated, like he's reading from a script he's already written. Now, though, it looks as though he's contemplating going off-message, like the politician goaded into a rogue moment, with his advisors covering their eyes and groaning. Except, Clayton makes every politician you ever watched look like a rank amateur.

'I've seen my psychiatrist,' he says. 'If you must know.'

Taylor recognises the departure too.

'How long have you been seeing a psychiatrist?'

'Ha! Provided with that piece of information, I wondered how long it would take you to blunder into doctor/patient confidentiality. Three seconds, was it? Longer than I thought.'

'Can you tell us the name of your psychiatrist?' I ask.

'You people...' he says.

We get the look again, the eyes drifting between us, then he opens the drawer at his right hand, lifts out a business card, and tosses it across the desk.

'You can call her, if you like. I rather presume she won't tell you anything.'

Taylor lifts the card, glances at it, then slips it into his pocket.

'Which day did you see her?' he asks.

Another pause. Feels like Clayton's back on script, which would be odd if he'd never intended telling us about the psychiatrist in the first place. Perhaps he writes these scripts in seconds in his head. Perhaps that's one of his talents, one of the things to separate him from regular, everyday murdering scumbags.

'I see her every day,' he says.

'Have you seen her today?' asks Taylor.

Clayton flicks the switch to impatience, as it must suit whatever plan he has.

'I just said I see her every day, didn't I? Today was a day, wasn't it? An actual day? So, yes, I saw her. Why don't you call her and ask?'

'I will,' says Taylor.

There he goes, pushing the buttons. What a bastard. It's one thing being quietly weird and smug, it's what we expect; another thing altogether getting annoyed at us, when he knows fine well we have every reason to be here.

Mouth shut, I think to myself. Keep your mouth shut.

* * *

Driving away, the light of early evening beginning to dim a little further. Taylor looks thunderously angry. Bob remains silent. This is no time for Bob.

'Pain in the arse it's a Saturday evening,' he says, eventually. 'Nevertheless, we need to try to get these two people, at least before Monday morning. You take the agent, I'll try to get the psychiatrist.'

I can feel the darkness descending – the deep dark of the long, drawn-out nighttime – as a result of seeing that bastard again. It all comes flooding back, despite my pathetic attempts to keep it at bay with glib, dry humour. Never likely to cut it.

Need a cigarette. Not smoking so much these days, but right now, I could use the whole packet. Will stand outside, in the carpark, when we get back to the station. I'll stand out there and hope no fucker joins me.

I stare ahead into the evening and wonder how much alcohol it'll take to get me through the night. Jesus, do I even care if I get through the night?

* * *

Clayton stands at the window, looking out on the warmth of a grey evening, the ends of his fingers tapping together, a pastiche of a comedy villain in this year's big animated feature.

He's asking himself questions, carrying out a conversation in his head. There is someone else in the room for him to speak to, but these questions aren't for her. They might point to some interesting psychology, of course, but the fact that he's asking himself the questions rather than the psychiatrist, is probably indicative of the fact he's not particularly interested in hearing what she has to say anyway, regardless of the effort he's made in getting her here.

It all seems so easy. Perhaps he should be doing something to make it a little more difficult. Create a problem of his own design, which he will then have to work to sort out.

Perhaps introducing the psychiatrist into the mix might bring something of a frisson to the game. He would wait to see how that played out, and then decide if he would toss any more alligators into the pit.

The police had already tried Dr Brady's phone, it having rung within twenty minutes of Taylor and Hutton leaving his house. They would already be trying to track her down. Either way, it would be a mildly interesting spanner in the works for the next day or two. Nevertheless, all part of the plan.

The ends of his fingers tap slowly together, the clockwork wheels click round in his head.

26

And so 11:03pm finds me at home, drinking wine. Couldn't even be bothered stopping off at the bar on the way back here. Felt like drinking vodka, but there's none in the house. There's wine, and it'll do.

Couldn't get hold of the agent, so I e-mailed. Left it at that. Not surprisingly, Taylor couldn't get the psychiatrist either. The rest of the evening dribbled away in a descent into the old, familiar oblivion. Fucking hated being there by the end, but didn't want to leave to come home.

Yet what else is there? Go out? Sit in amongst people? Listen to them talking, laughing, arguing, whatever the fuck else they were going to be saying?

And so here I am home, fuelling my descent. I don't want anything else. I don't want anyone else. There have been plenty of times when this would have had me trawling the streets, picking up someone, regardless of whether or not I had to pay for it. Hey, you always have to pay, one way or another.

Philo, that was as good and as healthy as it was ever going to be, and I'm sure as fuck paying now.

But no matter how shit I feel, and no matter how shit I want to feel, I don't want any piece-of-fucking-shit woman who I'm going to hate the absolute fuck out of, lying in my bed.

So, no drugs – there are never drugs – and no one else. Just wine, and my favourite lesbian porn DVD. Haven't watched it in, fuck, I don't know... Haven't watched any porn in God knows how long. Haven't needed to. Haven't cared.

You want to judge me? On any of it? Who gives a shit?

Who gives a damned shit? Judge away, you bloody fools, then hide in your own corruptions.

Still drinking wine from the glass – soon enough it'll be straight from the bottle – and flicking between scenes trying to find one that really gets me going, because I'm sitting here naked from the waist down, thinking I'd be spending my evening drinking and masturbating, but my cock is just like, 'oh for God's sake Hutton, you fucking arsehole, are you seriously doing *this*?' when my front door buzzer goes from out on the street.

Down the rest of the glass, pour some more from the bottle, take another drink.

He knows where I live. That's my first thought. There's a peculiar moment of fear, because I don't want him coming up here now, seeing me like this. Defences are down – yeah, as well as my trousers – and I'm no match for him. Not now. But he'll know. He'll know I'm here. He's a sly fucker who knows things. That's who he is.

The buzzer goes again.

Another slurp of wine, some of it splashing on my chin, wipe it away with my sleeve, stand up, trousers back on, leaving those M&S briefs that are made with, God I don't know, some sort of NASA technology, lying on the floor, and go to the door. Pause, my head resting on the wall.

Maybe I could just let him kill me. That would be easy. *You win. On you fucking go!*

He doesn't want to kill me yet, though, does he? Too much sport still to be had.

The buzzer goes again, and I angrily jab the button.

'What?'

'Hey,' says the unexpected voice of Eileen Harrison. 'Thought I'd come and check up on you.'

The tension floods out of me. Great waves of it. It could bring tears if I let it. Where was I ten seconds ago? Getting ready to die, right? Yep, that was it. Ready to stand before that fucker and let him do whatever he wanted.

'Tom?'

'Still here.'

'You all right?'

'No.'

'What are you doing up there?'

I laugh, a wretched, contrived, desperate, stupid laugh.

'Tom?'

'Drinking wine and watching lesbian porn,' I say.

A small pause, then she says, 'And you didn't invite me?'

I put my head back against the wall as I buzz open the door from the street, then I open the door to the flat and stand there, like the fucking wasted loser I am, listening to her footfalls on the steps.

Have a brief thought Clayton will be beside her, a gun at her head, but he'd hardly need the cover of Harrison to get in.

I stand away from the door as she comes up, she pushes it further open, looks at me, then closes the door and walks into the flat. She surveys the situation.

Nearly empty bottle of wine on the carpet beside the settee. A single glass. NASA technology M&S briefs on the floor. She looks at the television. It's your classic scene of the older woman and the neophyte, played out in porn movies around the world and, I'm guessing, virtually never in real life.

'Mum and the babysitter?' she says.

I smile. You know, one of those black humour, everything's fucking shit smiles.

'I think it might be a stepmum and her son's girlfriend, or something,' I say. 'The dialogue was a little complex. I got lost.'

She watches it for a few seconds, then bends down and lifts both the NASA pants and my wine glass. She tastes the wine, approves – you can't go wrong with a Sauvignon Blanc – and feels the texture of the underwear.

'Hmm, that's nice, what kind of material *is* that?'

'I don't know. I think it might be from space... Maybe we're getting a little too personal here, Sergeant.'

'You think? Hey, we're about to watch lesbian porn together, and I rarely do that with my underwear on either, so you know… I'll get myself a glass.'

She throws the NASA pants at me, gives me a look that is understanding and compassionate, just a glance, just a if-this-is-what-gets-you-through-the-night look, then turns in to the kitchen, returning a few moments later with a glass, another bottle of wine and the bag of Doritos I'd neglected to bring through in the first place.

She opens the bottle, fills her own drink, settles into the sofa beside me and clinks my glass.

'So, what are we watching?'

'*Lesbian Bonanza*,' I say.

'Hmm… I thought I'd seen it, but I don't remember this.'

'This is *Lesbian Bonanza 6*.'

'Ah.'

She opens the Doritos and offers me the bag. We both take a handful, stick them in our laps and then settle back. Wine, Doritos and porn.

The stepmum is lying back on the sofa, her clothes hanging off, her breasts glorious, and also oiled for some reason that is not entirely clear, while the babysitter or the son's girlfriend or the plumber or the accountant or whoever the young lady is, is on her knees, completely naked, teasing the mum, her tongue running over the older woman's thighs.

'Fuck me with your tongue,' gasps the mum.

'I know it's wrong,' says Harrison, 'but if I had to choose, I'd go for the twenty year-old.'

It's a small sofa, her leg is unavoidably touching mine. At long last my penis starts to wake up to the fact there's porn on the TV and a woman beside me.

27

Into the office just after eight. Wouldn't have predicted that ten hours earlier. Weirdly feel all right, despite the three and a half bottles of wine we got through. Even managed to stumble into bed before falling asleep.

There was some recovery done, although it was from a long way back, so let's not get excited about how switched on I'm going to be today, right bang smack in the middle of something this big. And I say we're in the middle, but really, fuck knows where we are. If this is Clayton, God knows how long we could be here. He certainly played the long game with the Crows business. What was that in the end? Nine months maybe. Spun it out, kept us hanging, toyed with us perfectly.

Maybe he does the same again.

Maybe I need to take matters into my own hands. Go round there, put a bullet in his stupid fat head. I couldn't be doing with a murder trial, any of that shit, I wouldn't want the Police Service as a whole to take the brunt of it, as it would, so I'd probably have to also kill myself in the process.

There's rarely a day when it sounds like a bad idea. At the moment I don't feel horribly depressed. Just dead. Just like it wouldn't matter.

I wonder if I can go back and see Philo today. Will she have forgiven me yet?

Probably not. And she might not have approved of last night either.

Run into Sgt Harrison at the coffee machine. We smile.

'You look better than anticipated,' she says.

'I shaved and drank three flagons of water.'

'That'll be it.'

'You managed to put yourself together all right too.'

'Same routine,' she says. 'Minus the shaving.'

The coffee machine spurts and coughs and gargles. It's kind of a pain in the arse listening to it sometimes when it's other people standing here getting a drink, but I like it when it's me. I suspect everyone feels like that.

'Thank you,' I say.

I wondered if there'd be some awkwardness this morning. I mean, it was made for awkward, after all. Eight hours ago we were sitting together on a sofa, legs touching, naked from the waste down, masturbating together to lesbian porn. That's not the kind of thing one generally does with one's best bud. I don't think. Anyway, it was a first for me.

It was an innately tough situation, of course. Because there was Eileen, naked, turned on, very horny, and right next to me. At that point, I wasn't caring she was a lesbian. I was drunk, and I'd have given anything to be able to fuck her. Eileen, though… Well, she's a lesbian. The thought of having sex with me would be on a par with the idea of me having sex with Morrow or Taylor. And that, my friends, is something no one wants to think about.

So I did my thing, and Eileen did her thing, and beyond the pressing together of the legs, nothing else happened. Which was weird, right enough, but on the other hand, it means we're standing having a nice chat this morning over the coffee machine, and I like her even more than I did yesterday, rather than the alternative, which would have been the two of us barely speaking to each other again, which is the case with me and virtually every other woman in this place.

'That's all right,' she says. She knows what I'm thanking her for. 'You too.'

The coffee machine spits and gurgles. We stand in companionable silence.

The warm feeling of early morning coffee machine good humour lasts all the way back to my desk, and then, as I sit down, I see the next e-mail in the series.

He brought you *Have you worked it out yet?* He followed that with the record-breaking *If you work it out, I'll stop,* and the one the critics loved, *You seem stressed. Relax. Maybe turn on the news. Something I prepared earlier.* Now, in conjunction with Microsoft and whichever fucking server he's using this time, the cunt who's messing with your shit brings you:

The first one didn't quite work out the way I intended, so I had to do it over. That's all.

That's all.

The boss is in his office, but that's not my first move. Lift the phone, straight on to the transport police. I have the number sitting there from having called them the previous day.

I get the same guy in the same office in Glasgow.

'It's Detective Sgt Hutton, Cambuslang...'

That's as far as I get.

'I was just about to call you,' says the constable whose name I don't recall, the same sense of urgency in his voice.

* * *

The freshness of morning has yet to disappear. The sky is grey, but the clouds high. The sun will appear at some point, and soon enough this freshness will vanish, and the day will be just another mild to warm miserable, crappy day in the west of Scotland. With a chance of rain.

Victim number six of the week lies dead on the tracks, in a small siding near Dalmarnock, train tracks all around, but most of them obviously no longer in use.

Head severed.

She'd been dressed in black, and tied to the tracks. Interestingly, though, not in the traditional old western movie way. Her body had been pinned down, perpendicular to the track, with her head placed in between the two rails, her neck tied down onto a single rail. When the train came slowly along, as it would have done so close to the end of the line, the wheels ran over her neck, but not the rest of her body. She would have died instantly, and then the repeated running of sets of wheels over her neck eventually decapitated her.

She looks no more than twelve years old, which makes this even more shit and, of course, even more newsworthy.

'So what happened,' says Morrison, the guy who seems to be in charge around here, 'is that Big Mac would have run over the girl's neck—'

'Big Mac being the driver of the train?' asks Taylor.

The guy gives him a bit of a, *well it's not a fucking burger, mate*, look.

'Obviously he's going slowly at this stage, so he's like that, notices something, notices, you know, like a blip on the line. But it's late, he hasn't seen anything. And it's... you know, this is the kind of thing that happens, you know. Branches on the line, you know. People just use train tracks as fucking dumping grounds, man. We get all sorts, man, all sorts of shit on the lines. Those people, you know the jokes they make, leaves on the line, the wrong kind of rain...' Shakes his head, spits. 'They should fucking see it, man, see the shit we have to put up with. Fucking tampons, fucking everything, man.'

'And Big Mac's over in the office?'

Morrison turns and looks over at the small grey building, the windows dirty and cracked, paint peeling on the frames.

'Aye. The other guy's talking to him at the moment.'

The transport police are all over the place, including the inspector who's going to be in charge of the investigation. He's already spoken to Morrison, before passing him onto us. Now he gets Big Mac before we do.

Morrison looks like the kind of guy who's going to be happy speaking to anyone. The television crews will be along shortly, and he'll speak to them too. He's probably already thinking about how this will play on Facebook.

'So, as a murder, it was intended to cause minimum disruption,' I say. Not asking any questions, just trying to keep focused. 'Middle of the night, no rail services affected, she was tied in such a way the train driver would barely notice he'd run over anything...'

'Never seen that done to a young girl,' Morrison throws in, as if that's going to help anyone, as if he's seen it done to adults and pet dogs. Just never a child.

'Thanks,' says Taylor, 'we've got everything we need now.'

Morrison looks surprised, grunts, glances at me, then turns and walks away. He pauses, wondering how he can possibly regain the initiative of the situation – he is supposed to be the one in charge, after all – and then decides it can best be done by sticking his nose into the Big Mac interview.

Taylor and I look back down at the scene, as officers start to place the tent around the victim. Last look at the sad, bloody, mangled face, and then she's gone. We step away from the edge of the track and look around.

'Tell me what the e-mail said again,' he says.

'*The first one didn't quite work out the way I intended, so I had to do it over. That's all.* The 'that's all' was his.'

Taylor lets out a long sigh, hands are thrust into his pockets. The tent continues to go up, and he turns away, looks up at the sky. Head back down, stares around the grim surroundings of post-Commonwealth Games Dalmarnock.

'You know the worst thing about this,' he says. 'We've been here twenty minutes already, and we haven't asked if anyone knows who she is. She's a young girl, she's dead, and her identity barely even matters. She's just another victim, we presume, of whoever's been killing people this week. Does it matter if she's a runaway, whether she's a kid on the game, a junky, a Ukrainian refugee, or the daughter of some stockbroker living in Bearsden? We won't care, will we? It won't be us telling her parents. She's just another victim along the way, like the unidentified woman in the basement, like the victims of the Plague of Crows...'

Another mumbled curse.

'Fuck it, let's get back to the station. Get Morrow in, get our heads together, try and sort out where this fucking thing is going.'

We stare down, one last time, at the scene of the crime, now covered by a white tent. For a moment one of the SOCOs holds the entrance to the tent to the side, and we get a final look inside at the girl, her head bloody and crushed, lying detached in between the two rails. A single eyeball, slightly removed from its socket, looks up at us.

28

We're sitting in the small room we've set up for the investigation. Just Taylor, Morrow and me. Taylor has cleared the whiteboard on the middle of the front wall and written simply: *The first one didn't quite work out the way I intended, so I had to do it over. That's all.*

None of us are sitting down, we're not in a teacher/pupil formation.

'So what could it have been that didn't quite work the first time round?' he says. 'What's different this time?'

Well, we may not be sitting in your classic teacher/pupil formation, but clearly our business is going to be conducted along those lines, except in this case the teacher doesn't know any more than the pupils.

Maybe that's usually the case. I certainly thought it often enough. Especially with that prick Herring.

Concentrate!

'On Tuesday he shut down the line,' says Morrow. 'Caused massive disruption, all day. This time it looks like he went out his way to make sure that didn't happen.'

'Yep,' says Taylor.

He writes *disruption* on the board.

'However,' says Morrow, just before either Taylor or I say it, 'he would surely have known on Tuesday it was going to cause disruption when he pushed someone onto the line in the first place. It was never not going to cause disruption.'

Taylor adds a question mark.

'The same goes for the driver knowing what happened,' I say. 'This time the driver didn't realise he'd killed anyone, but again, when our guy pushed someone in front of the train, the driver was always going to see it.'

Taylor writes *driver unaware*, again adding the question mark.

'This victim is a young girl,' says Morrow, 'but again, the previous one obviously wasn't, so that surely wasn't an example of it not working out right.'

Taylor writes *young girl*, again without comment and again adding the question mark.

He clips the lid back on the marker pen, taps it against the fingers of his left hand.

'This one was much more visceral,' I say. 'I mean, there was a lot more blood, if not the actual viscera.'

Taylor unclips the lid again, writes *blood* on the board. This time there's no immediate question mark.

'That could be it,' Morrow says straight away. 'I mean, he would have expected there to be blood the first time, wouldn't he? Someone pushed in front of a train, you'd think that's going to be pretty grotesque, yet she kind of bounced off.'

'She did,' says Taylor.

Another moment, then he looks at the two of us, away from the board. A small, hopeless movement of the shoulders.

'Why would he want there to be blood? Why would it be a problem if there wasn't any blood? Enough of a problem he'd need to go to all the trouble of killing someone else?'

Morrow doesn't have anything. I immediately start thinking of Clayton. Could this really have been him? Taylor and I were with him yesterday evening. While we came back to work, and I ended up slinking home and drowning myself in wine and porn, did Clayton immediately head out and arrange this? Did he already have the girl locked up somewhere?

For those kinds of questions, we really need to find out who she was and establish how long she'd been missing.

'You're thinking about Clayton,' says Taylor. 'Don't worry about that.'

Morrow glances at me then looks back at the board.

'Whoever this is,' says Taylor, 'he's given us a clue to what's going on, and we need to work it out. He said he'd stop if we did. And yes, it sounds like Clayton, I know, just the kind of fucked up shit he'd come up with. But whoever it is, maybe they're playing to some sort of code. Maybe they really do stop if we work it out.'

'But there wasn't blood with all of the others,' says Morrow, 'that's the odd thing. Obviously there was with the double beheading, but the guy who was knocked out and pumped full of crap? I mean, there might have been a little blood, I don't remember. But there definitely wasn't with the woman left in the basement. And it's not as though that one looked like it might not have gone to plan. It was... meticulous in its planning.'

Taylor turns back to the board. We all look at the single word up there, the one without a question mark against it. Blood.

'Could be he wants to see blood, but the woman in the basement wasn't one of his,' says Morrow.

'He sent me the *here's one I prepared earlier* text,' I say.

Morrow grunts.

Taylor thrusts his hands further into his pockets. Takes a pace or two to the side.

'I feel like it's right there,' he says.

Taps himself on the side of the head, hand goes back into his pocket.

Knock at the door, Constable Ablett sticks her nose into the room.

'Call for you, Sir. A Dr Brady?'

Taylor snaps his fingers.

'The shrink,' he says. 'Right, I need to speak to her, so we'll just leave this for now. But don't... just, you know, keep this in mind, let's think of something.'

He leaves the room, Morrow and I follow.

Back out into the open plan, the usual hum of activity. Morrow goes straight to his desk, I stand looking around.

Sunday morning, most of us still clearing up the remnants of whatever business came our way the night before, ninety-seven per cent of which will have been alcohol-related.

On the far side of the room DI Gostkowski is talking to Constable Adams, leaning across the desk pointing something out on an image on the computer screen. I watch her, not really thinking anything in particular. Mind wanders. Finally manage to shake myself out of it.

Back to the desk, look around at the paperwork, stare blankly at the screen, an almost unconscious check to see if there are any more anonymous e-mails, and then I pick up the phone to this agent of Clayton's.

Sunday morning, not really expecting to get anywhere, but the phone is answered immediately.

'Hey.'

She's young. Everybody's getting to sound too bloody young.

'I'm looking for Davina Rockwell.'

'You've found her!'

Jesus, she sounds enthusiastic about just being who she is. How utterly depressing. Immediately I know my voice will plummet several points on the enthusiasm scale to compensate.

'This is Detective Sgt Hutton, Police Scotland...'

'Right. Thought you sounded Scottish. Cool... Wait! Yes, yes, of course, you sent me an e-mail. I meant to call you, just totally snowed just now off the back of London.'

'London?'

'The Book Fair.'

'Ah.'

'Complete bedlam as always, and I don't just mean the amount of work. And this year it seemed even more bonkers than usual. I mean, God, it was like seven weeks ago now, and we're still chasing our tails. Seven weeks! Anyway... let's see, I'm just bringing up your e-mail. Wait for it, wait for it...'

Fuck. It would be nice if everyone on the planet was in

their forties and sensible. That's probably asking too much.

'Ah, yes, of course, you wanted to talk about Michael Clayton's memoir. Awesome. Did you want to make an offer, because we haven't actually gone out yet?'

'What?'

I'm looking down the phone at her like she's an idiot.

'I wondered if you wanted to make a publishing offer?'

'Of course not,' I say, feeling rather good about myself for not peppering that very short sentence with the word fuck. 'I'm from the police. Why would I make an offer?'

'Well, that's what the police usually do.'

To be fair to the girl Davina, she sounds like she's looking down the phone at me like I'm the idiot.

'What is?'

'When someone who's been the victim of police harassment is writing a book about it, the police often offer alongside publishing companies. Obviously they're looking to tie up the rights to the book to prevent publication.'

'No they don't!'

'Sure they do. Happens all the time. The police bid is always included. Usually serves to push the price up too. We love it.'

'Police Scotland doesn't have that kind of money,' I argue. She's got me believing her, though, even as I argue the point.

I can see the shrug at the other end of the phone.

'Far as I know it was brought in as a money-saving measure,' she says.

'Jesus, what? I don't understand.'

'If someone, some innocent victim of police harassment, and let's be honest, they are, frankly, legion, is about to publish a memoir, frequently you'll find the police going to court to stop publication. Invariably they'll a) lose, and b) end up with an enormous legal bill. Somebody, at some point, no idea who, decided it was more cost effective to buy up the book, put in some clause about the author being unable to publish his story in any other form anywhere else on the planet, then they stick the manuscript in the same warehouse they put the Ark of the Covenant at the end of the first Indiana Jones.'

I let the phone drop a little, and stare across the desk at Morrow. He gives me a inquisitively raised eyebrow, then realises I'm more just idly staring into space, and once more bows his head to whichever part of our business he's currently working on. Phone back up to my ear, elbow on the desk, forehead planted into the palm of my hand.

I hate the police sometimes. I hate the fact this shit happens, and not for a moment do I think she's pulling my chain.

'That's all very depressing,' I say.

She giggles. Yep, that's it. A giggle.

'It works for us,' she says.

'I bet.'

'Anyway, if you're not on to bid, why are you on…?'

The voice drifts off, I decide to wait until the thought process has worked its way through her brain.

'Wait… Sgt Hutton? *The* Sgt Hutton?'

'Not entirely sure how you mean that,' I say.

'The Sgt Hutton who's all over Michael's book?'

'He's mentioned me by name?'

She laughs.

'You're going to be the star of the show, Sergeant! Gosh, I was sleeping on the job this morning, wasn't I?'

Another giggle.

A minute ago, despite everything, I was beginning to think she sounded quite nice. Attractive, in that way people can be as attractive as you want them to be when you're just talking to them on the phone.

Now I just want her to shut the fuck up. Fucking giggling.

'Would it be possible to see some of what Mr Clayton has been writing, to talk perhaps about the process of–'

She cuts me off with the laugh.

'I can't do that, Sergeant. I shouldn't be talking to you

at all, but you know, hashtag-YOLO, you've got a lovely voice, that whole Scottish thing, so I don't mind. But really, client-agent confidentiality at this stage, so we have to keep it, you know, low-key. So we can talk, just not about what you want to talk about.'

She giggles again.

I take a second, during which I contemplate just hanging up without speaking, then quickly say, 'Thanks for everything, we'll be in touch,' and hang up just as she's sounding disappointed and sending a metaphorical sad face emoji down the phone.

Push the handset away from me, place my head in both hands.

I hate speaking to young people. Adds decades to your life.

'Come on,' grumbles Taylor, as he walks past my desk, 'get your head out your arse, we're going to talk to the psychiatrist.'

29

Taylor and me and the psychiatrist, sitting outside a café on the edge of Glasgow Green. Sun starting to break through, shirt sleeve weather. Not really the place to be conducting an interview with anyone, as the café is busy, and there are a lot of children around. The law of all things dictates it won't be long before one of the weans is crying.

The park is bustling, people hanging out, topless guys with beer bellies kicking balls around, mothers with prams, kids on the charge, a couple of old yins on mobility scooters. A guy speeds by on his racing bike, attired in bright yellow and turquoise Lycra, looking like a total dick.

Coffees placed on the table by the waitress, the psychiatrist already on her second cigarette. She's wearing a neck-high blouse, which most people in Scotland would probably think too warm for this kind of weather, but which would be getting worn beneath another three layers in this temperature in the rest of Europe. Whatever, it hugs her body, making her breasts look sensational.

Yeah, so I'm back. Bite me.

She's also wearing sunglasses, which isn't great, but I'm leaving it to Taylor to ask her to remove them. No thought, however, she might be wearing them to obscure the look in her eyes. It really has turned bright, the glare exaggerated by the white paintwork of the café exterior.

'How long has he been seeing you?'

She has a small smile on her lips. Her hair is blonde, her lipstick bright red, her blouse dazzling white in the sun. What a look. Total vamp. And that smile...

'Can't answer that,' she says.

'Are we going to get anything out of you?' I ask.

'You never know,' she says, this time turning to me. 'If you ask the right the thing.'

'Can we ask how often you've seen Mr Clayton this past week?'

She pauses, takes the opportunity to lift the cup and take a sip of coffee. The cup gets placed back in the saucer with a red lipstick mark on the rim. Fuck, that's sexy.

Jesus, I'm so in the wrong job. I mean, I'm not saying there's an actual job where it would be a prerequisite to get turned on by vampy women leaving lipstick marks on a coffee cup, but it does point to me being completely shit at what I'm supposed to be doing.

'I see Mr Clayton most days,' she says.

'And this week?'

'I've seen Mr Clayton every day this week.'

This time Taylor is the one to take a pause, lifting his cup. He slurps, and is nothing like as hot as the psychiatrist.

'Is that normal?' I ask. 'I mean, it sounds like some pretty serious shit, to be seeing a patient every day, doesn't it? You're going to have to be pretty fucked up, right?'

She smiles again, puts the cigarette in her mouth, draws it in while I imagine her eyes are on me, her cheeks sucking in, then blows the smoke out to the side.

Dunhill reds. Nice. She offered us one, and I said no, out of some sort of sense of duty or something. You know, thought I shouldn't be smoking on the job, some shit like that. Desperate for one now.

'I'm not going to get into how fucked up Mr Clayton may, or may not, be. He likes to see me most days. I will have a set number of appointments every week, and if he wants any extra, I'll do it if I have time.'

'And how did it go this week?' asks Taylor.

Another sip of coffee, another aloof glance cast away over the park. What the fuck is this woman doing on Glasgow Green? She should be in Monte Carlo.

You know, I'm not even sure she's that great looking, I

mean, underneath it all, but she's got poise and style and oozes fucking sex. Holy shit…

'We had three appointments booked between Monday and yesterday. I also saw Mr Clayton on the days when we had nothing booked.'

'And was he particularly bad this week? Was there something…'

Taylor lets the question go, as the femme fatale is shaking her head.

'Nuh-huh,' she says, before taking another draw, then holding the cigarette out to the side, perfectly poised between her fingers.

I reckon, and I think it could be do-able, she might be the right psychiatrist for me. Taylor and Connor both want me to start seeing one, she *is* one, so why wouldn't it work? I would happily lie down on a couch for her any day. I'd tell her everything, 'n' all.

'Are you aware Mr Clayton is writing a book?' I ask.

'Yes.'

'Has he told you much about it?'

Hesitation, the sunglasses turned my way, then she says, 'He's read me parts of it.'

'Are you prepared to discuss it?'

She smiles. Fuck, man, those lips.

'He has a nice style. Captivates the reader right from the off.'

The sunglasses move from one to the other of us, along with the lips. The smile goes, the sunglasses stay on Taylor.

'Could you take the glasses off, please?' he asks finally.

She doesn't rush to it, as I presume she does not rush to anything, then slowly she removes them. Closes her eyes, possibly against the brightness, then opens them, still looking at Taylor.

'You want to look deep into my eyes and check I'm not lying, Chief Inspector?' she says.

Yeah, OK, her eyes are terrific. I wondered if the dark

glasses were covering up something bland, that perhaps the eyes would detract from the mystery and the allure. But no. Straight up, gorgeous eyes. Deep, powerful, drawing you in.

I know, I know. Mood I'm in, one of the female Muppets would draw me in.

Taylor holds her gaze, pretty damn tight too. Doesn't let go. Much better at not giving in to these women the way I do. Much better police officer on all sorts of levels.

'We're investigating a series of murders in this city,' he says slowly. Great edge to his voice. You could get chills listening to this shit. 'Some of them have been horrific. All of them, whichever way you look at it, as murders do, have left someone dead. Someone's wife, someone's husband, someone's son or daughter, someone's mum or dad. That's what happens when somebody dies. Every death leaves someone else scarred. Now you can hide behind your confidentiality all you like, and I completely appreciate your right and your need to do so, but we too know things we can't tell you, and we have reason to suspect Michael Clayton might be involved in these murders. Whatever else you think, Dr Brady, I'm sure you don't want to protect a serial murderer. So please, within whatever bounds of confidentiality you are constrained, tell us everything you can, and will you please stop with the fucking 1940s Hollywood vamp shtick.'

Cool. Calling her out on the cover. Very bold. I mean, she might be like this all the time. This could be her, who she is. She's a blonde fucking Uma Thurman in *Pulp Fiction*. She's been like this since 1994. That's a long time to be someone, then to have somebody else see through you and tell you to cut it out.

The look you take as an adult, any look, even if it's the most understated, dull-as-shitwater look of the invisible shadow, is still a conscious decision, and it's pretty major when someone says, stop being you. Stop being who you think you are, or want to be.

Unless, of course, he's better at this than I am – fucking

ha! – and he sees through her. He recognises she's been like this for all of ten minutes. Or she's like this when she's speaking to people she doesn't want to be speaking to.

She holds the gaze. Maybe there's a marginal shake of the carefully held cigarette.

She puts it to her mouth, last suck, then grinds it out in the ashtray, the final movement allowing her to break eye contact, as she blows the smoke away to the side.

'I've seen Mr Clayton six times in the last six days,' she says. Voice steady. If she's been rocked by being called out, it's not showing. 'I wouldn't say there's been anything different about his behavior during this time. He's a troubled man, and I'm not openly going to speculate on the cause of that trouble.'

'Can you tell us at what time your appointments have been?' asks Taylor.

'Four o'clock every afternoon,' she says.

'*Every* day?'

'Yes.'

The smile again. Looks like he hasn't dented the veneer even a little, and I like her all the more.

'He comes to your place or you go to his?'

Slight pause. There we are. Right there.

'I go to him.'

That pause. What was that?

'You went to him every day?'

'Yes.'

Why'd you have to think about it then, Mia Wallace?

'Was that just the case this week, or do you always go to his home?'

'Not always, no. He has been a regular visitor to my office.'

'So, what was so–'

'He asked me to,' she says quickly. For the first time she seems troubled by the direction of the conversation. 'And more to the point, he paid me, paid me rather well, actually.'

She's been holding Taylor's gaze, then she glances at me before turning back to him.

'So, I need to make money, Chief Inspector. Are you going to hold it against me?'

'How did Mr Clayton come to you in the first place?' he asks.

Another pause. A more reasonable one, I suppose. That's one question she might well have to think over before deciding what to tell us.

She lifts the packet of cigarettes again, flips the lid and removes a smoke one handed, puts it in her mouth, lights up, long draw, and blows out the smoke as she settles back into her seat.

'I was recommended by his GP.'

'When was this?'

'A certain amount of time ago.'

'Is there anything else you *can* tell us?'

Another long draw, smoke held in the mouth and then exhaled to the side.

'I know quite a lot about you two.'

* * *

Driving back to the station. Less than ten minutes. Taylor doesn't speak for the first half of the drive. Got the feeling she really did piss him off. Face set, lips tight.

'No,' he says eventually, just as we're driving into Cambuslang.

His voice is as firm and unyielding as the look on his face.

'No, what?'

'No, she can't be your psychiatrist.'

I glance back at him, and then turn and look out of the passenger door window. The grey buildings of the town flit by. Not many pedestrians down this way, down the hill, before you get to Main Street.

I think about saying that I wasn't going to ask, but I don't feel like talking, and it would be a lie anyway.

30

The day is playing a blinder so far. Another anonymous, untraceable e-mail, a dead girl on the train tracks, a barely post-pubescent literary agent who seems to know more about Police Scotland than I do, and then the unspeakably cool psychiatrist, who is probably in a position to help us, and who gives us absolutely nothing.

There's always the possibility, of course, that there's nothing to tell. That, regardless of Clayton's involvement in the Plague of Crows grotesquery, and whatever he told DCI Lynch about the previous murder charge on which he was acquitted, he really does have nothing to do with this.

Still, I was the genius who brought it up and made sure it came to the attention of the senior suits in the service, so there's no backing away from it now.

Four in the afternoon, warm day, a quiet Sunday afternoon kind of buzz around the place. Morrow out somewhere, Taylor in his office, on and off the phone, me at my desk. Trawling through the details of the lives of all the victims so far.

That, of course, is regularly the most depressing part of any of this kind of work. The poor old victims, about whom we so often forget. Or, in my case, try to not give a shit about right from the off.

This is why, right here. You start looking into their lives, and you start to care. How can you not? How can you not care anything about them?

Today's victim was eleven years old and had been missing from her home in Kilmarnock since last Sunday afternoon. Her mother was a staunch supporter of letting her daughter roam free, playing in the street or in the park, walking to school, playing in the nearby woods. She didn't want to over-protect, she didn't want her kid watching TV for eight hours a day, while playing Two Dots on an iPod the rest of the time. She wanted to instill in her the kind of independence she'd had as a child, she wanted her to have the imagination to build a fort in the woods, and to go exploring and to make dams in any stream she could find. She wanted her daughter to be everything that children in our generation were, and which has now been lost through technology and fear.

And this is what she got for her trouble. Her kid snatched from a wood, a week of worry, followed by a lifetime of regret and self-loathing.

From what we've heard already, her husband is letting her take all the blame; indeed, has been doing so since the first moment they started worrying about where the kid had gone.

Kid dead, marriage over, you sue me and I'll sue you. Pass the pretzels.

Always worse, of course, when the victim is a child, but it's not like the rest of the dead leave behind stories that deserve to end in bloodshed and an early grave.

I read on, sucked further into the mire of misery, and getting nowhere nearer any kind of answer or connection.

Taylor pulls out Morrow's seat and sits down opposite.

'How are you getting on?' he asks.

'Got nothing so far. Nothing to suggest it's not the worst case scenario for us that we've been assuming all along; an entirely random selection of individuals.'

He stares idly at the papers lying around Morrow's desk. Glad to see that as Morrow becomes more experienced and his workload inevitably increases, he's becoming a lot less organised. By the time he gets to my age he'll be filing documents in the bin by the hundred-load like the rest of us.

'We should be talking to Connor,' says Taylor. 'I was hoping he'd have gone by now, and it could wait until tomorrow, but it doesn't look like that's happening.

Anyway, doesn't really matter. We are definitely presenting to the Chief tomorrow morning, so we need something, even if it's a *mea culpa* and some sort of retraction.'

I stare blankly into space, same as he is. Beginning to feel a little hopeless. Beginning to feel, absurdly, that Clayton has total dominion over us. Like he can do what he wants. Like we're the Thistle and he's PSG, and we can imagine for a few fleeting moments we have some sort of chance, but in reality, and ultimately, we're just going to get our arses handed to us, even if it takes a penalty box dive by that little bastard Neymar in the last minute.

'I want you to go back and speak to the psychiatrist,' he says.

I look up.

'Seriously?'

'Oh, no, I'm just sitting here making shit up,' he says, with instant anger.

I hold up an apologetic hand, and he waves it away with some element of apology at his outburst.

'Talk to her. I don't know what that was earlier, and maybe it's the real thing.' He shakes his head at the thought. 'I mean, seriously... If that's who she is, then fine. But try and get beneath it, if you can. Maybe you'll have more luck on your own. You can do, you know, whatever it is you usually do.'

'I usually sleep with them,' I say.

'I know.'

I give him a questioning look.

'I don't give a shit,' he says. 'Just get in touch with her, try whatever you think is necessary. It would be better.... It would be for the best if you didn't get her into bed, but actually, like I said, I don't care. Just try and get anything you can.'

He stands up, looks somewhat troubled about having instructed one of his officers to go out and prostitute himself for information – at least on that front he picked the right guy – taps Morrow's desk a couple of times, and then turns back to his own office.

Stops, looks round, comes back to stand at the desk.

'That moment, the second when I asked if she saw him at his house or her office... What was that?'

'I know, it was weird.'

'It was a straightforward enough question. And even allowing for her thinking everything over, deciding what questions were to be answered and what was encroaching on her damned confidentiality...'

'Yep.'

Holds my gaze briefly, and then turns away.

He gets to return to his desk, I get to go and see the vamp. Sadly, just at the thought, I can feel myself getting turned on.

What a dick. I mean, that's the point of a fucking vamp, isn't it? It's the tease, it's the style. They're vamps, they're not slappers. And really, this thing I've got going, where somehow I get women to sleep with me... it never happens on command. It just happens. Sometimes. And sometimes it doesn't.

Highly unlikely to be happening with Dr Brady, and if it did, how the fuck would I know she wasn't playing me on Clayton's command?

Note to self: exercise extreme caution and try not to think with your dick.

* * *

As it is, even my dick doesn't get to do any thinking. She answers neither her mobile nor her work phone. I sit at my desk, the phone still in my hand, the anticipation fading, and then decide that I'm going to go round to her office. Sunday afternoon, chances are there will be no one there, but I have to give it a go. Everything's open on a Sunday these secular days.

Stick my head into the boss's office, let him know what's happening so he can pass it on to Connor if the knob comes looking, and off out the door, armed with both her office and home address.

Her office is just off Kelvingrove Park, up behind, close to the statue of Field Marshall Lord Roberts, great hero of the Indian wars and others, who one day will no doubt find himself torn down, as righteous rage continues to grow against the old Empire.

A large Victorian detached house, converted into a series of offices and surgeries. I get buzzed in, where a man sits behind a desk, the downstairs hall off the front door having been converted into a reception area. A few chairs, pictures on the wall. It oozes money.

The guy glances at his watch as I approach the desk, then straightens his shoulders a little as I hold out my ID, steady before him for a few seconds, so that he can read the details.

'Sgt Hutton?' he says, looking up. 'I'm afraid there's no one here anymore.'

I glance around. The place is deathly quiet, and even though you might not expect there to be any particular sound coming from a medical practice reception area, there's a sense of the emptiness in the building.

'This is a private doctor's practice?' I ask.

'The facility is run by EmMed International, a subsidiary of Viathol. There are offices here covering various streams across the health spectrum, including dentistry, pediatrics, psychiatry, orthopedic... and many more,' he adds, as though advertising a K-Tel best-of-the-60s compilation.

'So why is no one here?'

'It's Sunday afternoon,' he answers, in a tone suggesting I'm the idiot.

'Why are *you* here?'

'To field enquiries until five pm. Such as this one. What can I do for you, Sgt Hutton?'

I glance up the stairs, then take a quick look around the room. There are two cameras trained on us.

'You like getting watched at work?' I ask.

'I doubt anyone's actually watching,' he says. 'They're

only there in case of any incidents. What can I help you with today?'

'I'm looking for Dr Brady,' I say quickly, ditching the vague conversational style.

'She's on holiday,' he says.

'We saw her today.'

'Where?'

'How d'you mean she's on holiday? Since when?'

'She's been off all week.'

'You know where she went? If she went abroad, England…?'

He's shaking his head, long before I get to the end of the question.

'I don't really know the practitioners particularly well. Only been here four weeks. Was previously working for the Forestry Commission. I'll probably move on again in a couple of months. This is pretty boring to be honest.'

Jesus, enough with the fucking commentary. It's not about you.

'When was the last time you saw Dr Brady?'

'That would have been a week past on Friday.'

'Can you describe Dr Brady to me?' I ask.

'What?'

'Can you de…'

'I heard you, it's just, you said you saw her today. You presumably know what she looks like.'

'Just describe her, please.'

'What's this about?'

'This is about me, a police officer, asking you, a member of the public, some questions, coupled with you answering them.'

'I do work for a private medical practice,' he says, and as he talks, that thing you get where the tone lifts slightly at the end of a sentence or statement becomes more pronounced, 'so I am bound by issues of confidentiality.'

'I'm not asking anything confi-fucking-dential, I'd just like you to describe what one of your doctors looks like.'

Nice, Hutton, you dick.

'All I'm asking is why?'

'So I know that the woman we interviewed today is the same woman you see in the office every day.'

'Why wouldn't she be the same? Why would someone be pretending to be Dr Brady?'

'Can you just describe her for me, please?'

He holds my gaze, then says, 'No,' swallowing noisily as soon as the syllable is out his mouth.

I manage to refrain from blurting out the work *fuck* too loudly, hands on hips, turn away. And there it is, the thing that was so natural in this setting, and so obvious, it hadn't even registered with me it was there. The large board listing every practice in the establishment, with photographs of each of the doctors and other practitioners in house.

I stare at it, turn and give the receptionist a glance, then walk over to the board.

'You can't look at that,' he says, although the conviction in his voice has vanished even before he gets to the end of the sentence. I ignore him anyway.

There she is. Dr Veronica Brady. Bobbed brown hair, fringe a little too long. No spectacles, barely any make up. Attractive, recognisably the same person we saw earlier today, but with none of the artifice.

'Is this a recent photograph? I mean, is this how she looked the last time you spoke to her?'

He doesn't answer. I give him a second, then turn round. He's looking at me, his face resolutely blank. Give him another second or two, then walk back over.

'Just fucking tell me if this is how she looked the last time you saw her.'

'We're on camera, you know. Sound too.'

'Good. We'll have evidence when we charge you with obstructing the police.'

'You can't do that!'

'Is that what Dr Brady looked like the last time you saw her?'

'Yes,' he says quickly.

'Thank you. You know when she booked this week off on leave?'

'She e-mailed it in,' he says. 'First thing last Monday morning. Asked me to cancel all her patients.'

'How many patients did she have this week?'

A short pause, and then, 'A full slate.'

'Did it include a Mr Michael Clayton?'

He stares at me, the look on his face hardening. At least, the look he was attempting to put on his face hardens. There's nothing hard about him, but I'm not going to push it.

My eyes move to the monitor beside him, he follows my look, then quickly presses a couple of keys on the keyboard to log himself out. Now there'd be no point in me going over there and manhandling him off his computer, which is obviously what a police officer such as myself would usually do.

He blinks beneath my stare.

'In your limited experience, have you known Dr Brady to take time off before at such short notice?'

'No.'

'Did she say where she was going?'

'No.'

'Just that she was going on holiday?'

He pauses again, before nodding at his own thought.

'I'm going to say she just wrote she was taking the week off,' he says, 'that's pretty much all. I don't know that she actually used the word holiday.'

'Is it possible she'll have seen any of her patients at her own home or at their home?'

Blank look, finally, 'I don't know.'

'Would there be a reason why she might not have wanted to work here all week?'

My tone is getting harsher, and I'm quite pleased to see he's wilting before it, his pusillanimity beginning to show. Unfortunately, he's not hiding anything. Just scared of the police.

'I don't know.'

I let out one of those long, exasperated, tired sighs and turn away. Look back at Brady's photograph. Quite ordinary. Nothing there to stir the contents of a pair of finest M&S NASA-technology pants.

'Would you tell me her home address, please?' I ask.

'Couldn't possibly,' he answers quickly.

I turn and look at him, just give him the menacing police glare, and then smile.

'I already know it. I'm going round there now. You want to call it in, see if you can get the cops to head me off at the pass?'

'What pass?'

It seems everybody on earth is now twenty years younger than me, which is bloody depressing.

'Thanks for your help,' I say. 'I'll see myself out.'

31

Grabbed by Taylor, just as I get back to my desk. The place is quieter than before I went out. Have just sat down, had time to look at my inbox to make sure there are no further mocking missives. Contemplating getting a cup of coffee. Beginning to think it might be Sunday evening alcohol time. Taylor arrives to get my mind back on work.

'How'd it go?' he asks, standing by Morrow's empty desk. 'You don't look flushed.'

I wonder what he means for a second, then remember he sent me off with strict instructions to have sex with the witness.

'Weird,' I say. 'Went to her office, the guy there says she e-mailed on Monday morning and cancelled all her appointments for the week. I went round to her house, no one in. Spoke to a couple of neighbours, no one had seen her for a while. They didn't sound like that was necessarily odd, because it's not like they were living on top of each other in a tenement, but even so... I broke into the house. Mail hadn't been lifted all week.'

'Bollocks,' he mutters. 'Did you try calling her again?'

'Her phone is switched off or she's gone somewhere with no signal.'

He mutters some other curse under his breath, stares away off to the side.

'Fuck it. Shouldn't have let her go.'

'We couldn't really bring her in, could we?'

'I don't know, Sergeant,' he says. 'Maybe. But this, now, having let her go... it's just weird, and we have absolutely no idea why. Fuck... Come on, we need to go in and see Connor.'

I get up, start walking a step behind him.

'You didn't leave any trace of your break in, did you?' he asks.

'I was the Pink Panther.'

He stops just outside Connor's door and gives me the look.

'You left a white glove with your initial on it?'

'I was discreet.'

'You?'

'Let's leave it at that.'

He turns, knocks once, and then we walk into Connor's office.

* * *

'I'm thinking of taking early retirement.'

The words ease their way out into the middle of a brief silence. Taylor has been giving him the rundown on where we haven't got to. Connor appeared at least to be paying attention, before turning away and staring off into a corner.

Taylor gives me something of an eyebrow, then says, 'I thought there didn't have to be any staff cuts, sir?'

Connor turns back, the momentary wistfulness having passed.

'No, no there aren't. But I'm done, I might as well admit it. My time here has been plagued, we all know that.'

I don't think it's about you, to be honest, but if that's how you want to paint it. I mean, it was pretty damn fucking shit before you arrived.

'We just seem to lurch from one disaster to another. And now we've got this. I mean, we could potentially have been completely under the radar on this one. Even if someone else had pulled all these bloody murders together, we're still the smallest, the least interesting. There have been six deaths now, and only one on our patch. We could have... yes, under the radar, we could have sailed under the radar, if it hadn't been for those damn e-mails.' He waves his hand, gives me a reassuring look, for which I'm obviously exceptionally grateful. 'I'm not blaming you, Sergeant. I'm sure you no more wanted them sent to you than I wanted you getting them, and you did entirely the right thing bringing it to everyone's attention.'

Well, thank you for saying so, I feel vindicated.

'But it promotes us into the Premier Division and suddenly everyone's looking at us, and what do we have...?'

And he waves a pathetic hand in Taylor's direction.

'I'm an organiser, I put things in order. That's my superpower.' What a dick. 'I came here to sort things out, and the place has been cursed since the day I arrived. *I've* been cursed. Whatever God intended for me here, it wasn't an easy ride, that's for sure. I think perhaps, when all this is over, it might be time for someone more suited to the task to take over.'

He laughs ruefully, sharing the smile with both of us. Neither of us smiles back.

'No doubt as soon as I'm gone, things will settle down. That'd be just like the thing...'

Palms of his hands on the desk, he looks between the two of us. Time to wrap it up. Thank God.

'So, basically gentlemen, we have nothing to take to the boss tomorrow? Having made our pitch... if Mr Clayton is not involved, well, we have nothing to add, and if he is, he continues to run rings around us.'

Taylor nods, looking extremely pissed off at that assessment.

'We need to find Dr Brady again,' he says.

'You had her a few hours ago.'

'We had no reason at the time–'

Connor cuts him off with a wave.

'And you're no nearer working out what he meant today, this morning. What was it, his last e-mail?'

'The first one didn't quite work out the way I intended, so I had to do it over, that's all,' I say.

'That's what he said, or that's what you're saying to me

now?'

'That's what he said,' I say, trying to keep the impatience out of my voice. We might as well be back out in the office getting on with this shit, rather than sitting here listening to him.

'And you've got nothing?'

It's almost not even a question. More of a taunt. He's owning the hopelessness of the investigation. He wants us to be shit. He wants us to not have a clue. He's that miserable cunt Denethor in *The Return Of The King*. He wants to be able to take nothing to the Chief Constable, so we can disappear back into the shadows, and he can blame his detectives while he's doing it.

'There was blood,' says Taylor. 'That's all we can think. The murder down at Cambuslang station had no blood, when one might well have expected some. For some reason, who knows why, he wanted there to be blood, so he staged another murder on the railway line where blood was guaranteed.'

Connor looks mournfully at his desk.

'Huh,' he mutters. 'He wanted blood on the tracks. Maybe he's a Dylan fan.'

'What?' escapes my lips. Not at the words *blood on the tracks*, just at the fact Connor mentioned Dylan.

Connor waves away the question, and the wave more or less turns into a dismissal in the direction of the door.

'Just a stupid comment. Goodbye gentlemen. I'll need you both here in the morning and we can go over our lines for the Chief Constable.'

'Didn't know you liked Dylan,' says Taylor, getting to his feet. Introducing a more conversational tone, even though I suspect he wants to boot Connor in the face just as much as I do.

'He lost me in the '80s, but I do sometimes enjoy his earlier work,' says Connor, but he's already lost interest, looking back down at some paperwork on his desk. Probably his pension plan.

Taylor looks at me, the same thing running through his

head – and it's not about Connor – and we walk from the room, then wordlessly through the station, and together into Taylor's office, closing the door behind us.

He goes to stand by the window, looking out on the early Sunday evening. A bland, mild to warm, crappy day.

'What the fuck?' he says. 'You thinking what I'm–'

'Blood on the tracks…'

'Blood on the tracks. That's what he wanted to be different. He wanted blood on the tracks. Is it a thing, other than a Dylan album title? I don't know, can't be Shakespeare, can it? I guess they wouldn't have had, I don't know… did they call roads tracks back then. Or is it a Holocaust thing? The train tracks.'

'Dylan didn't mean train tracks, though, did he? He meant the songs. The tracks on the album are bitter, bloody, angry. I always presumed he just meant the songs.'

'Jesus,' mutters Taylor. 'But there's something, and it's still what our killer meant, wasn't it? The first murder didn't work because there was no blood. And the second murder…? Lots of blood.'

'Unbelievers. He wrote *unbelievers* next to the decapitated bodies.'

'*Infidels*,' says Taylor.

'Yeah, I thought that before. But… yes, he could have used the word infidels, but he chose to use unbelievers. And spell it wrong.'

'Which doesn't sound like Clayton.'

'Unless he was trying not to make it too easy for us,' I say. 'If he'd written *infidels*, we'd at least, you know, maybe it would have struck us Dylan fans, the name would have stuck out. This way, didn't occur to us at all. Not until now.'

Taylor lets out a long sigh.

'So he wants to give us murders suggested by two Bob Dylan album titles. Apart from the obvious question – which is why the fuck would he even do that – there's the question of why just two? What about the other two?'

'*The Basement Tapes*!' I say. Mind whirring, suddenly got some sort of weird buzz. I mean, from just doing my job. Getting a buzz from doing my job! It's like all those years of listening to fucking Bob finally paid off.

'The girl in the basement, killed with tape,' says Taylor, thinking aloud.

'Exactly. Basement tapes.'

'Hmm, okay...' he says. 'This is beginning to sound like us stretching the balloon into the shape of the animal we want it to be, but let's keep going...'

'The only other one is the guy. Knocked unconscious, killed with drugs.'

The answer was bound to come quickly, and inevitably I get it first, as I'm buzzing and Taylor is riffing on scepticism.

'*Knocked Out Loaded*,' I say, and start laughing at the thought.

'Jesus,' he says. 'Well, it fits, I suppose. Or, at least, the balloon stretches that far.'

'Fucking Clayton,' I say.

'What d'you mean?'

'He's going after us. I mean seriously, the guy is coming after us, and he's taking the fucking piss. He knows we're Dylan fans. Or, God, I don't know, maybe he doesn't know about you, but he knows about me. He's coming after me. He's taunting me with Bob!'

Laughing out loud now. Coming off the work rush. Seriously. What a dick!

Taylor's shaking his head, not looking at me, not sharing my enthusiasm for the absurdity of it.

'I can't take that to the Chief Constable.'

I suppose it's not really funny, is it? *How fucking hilarious? A decapitated eleven year-old girl on the train tracks!*

'We need to think it through,' I say eventually, after I've brought myself back and silence has crept through the room. 'I mean, try to pin it down. Yes, it sounds stupid. Unbelievable. But then, if it's Clayton, we're dealing with a guy who orchestrated mass killing by crow. This seems tame by comparison. And if he's specifically setting out to taunt us, or taunt me, then fucking good on him. He's done his research. Taunt me with Dylan. Do these fucking awful murders, in some really obvious way, and yet it's not obvious... it's stupid, it's contrived, it's batshit crazy.'

Taylor's head has bowed a little further, hands go into his pockets. I give him the space to think it over. Do I really believe it myself?

'So, what do we do now?' he asks. 'Wait to see what tomorrow brings? See if he murders two blondes on top of each other, or, fuck, I don't know, kills someone in front of a slow train...' Voice tails off.

'Did that already,' I say. 'He got two for the price of one this morning.'

'Fuck,' mutters Taylor. 'All right, put something together for me. Think of a way where we can present this to the boss tomorrow without sounding like we're the fucking jokers.'

I put my hand on the door, then stop, turn back.

'Then there's the other thing,' I say. 'He said work it out and I'll stop. So, let's say we're right, and that's us worked it out. What now?'

Taylor turns at last and looks at me.

'That simple, you think?'

Open my hands. How the fuck should I know?

'You can't reply to the e-mails?'

'No, no point,' I say.

'So how are we supposed to let him know?'

'Go on TV. We know he watches.'

'Go on TV? Go on, I don't know, Reporting Scotland, and start calling them the Bob Dylan Murders. Are you serious?'

Don't have an answer. He's damn right though, so I'm not going to argue.

'Go,' he says. 'Pull something together, and I'll try to work out how we're going to communicate to the fucker without looking like clowns.'

I open the door, walk back into the office. Seems even quieter out here than it was previously. Back to my desk, the usual check of the e-mails. And there it is. The latest one waiting for me.

Did you like it? Two for the price of one.

32

'We could give a press conference where everything we say is a line from a Bob Dylan song.'

'What if he doesn't know Dylan well,' says Taylor.

'He sounds like he knows Dylan.'

'I'm not sure. You could do five seconds of research, go onto Wikipedia, and you'd get the list of Dylan albums. As far as we can work out, he hasn't even bothered learning any of the songs. The lines could easily mean nothing to him.'

'So, we do the press conference in Dylan album titles then.'

'Seriously? *Ladies and gentlemen of the press, welcome to the empire burlesque...*'

'Well, there are a tonne of albums to choose from. Let's go through them, discard the obviously useless ones like *Another Side of Bob Dylan* and *Nashville Skyline*, and see what else we've got we could use. I mean, I know there's no album entitled *We've Detained A Man Who's Helping Us With Our Enquiries*, but it wouldn't be much use if there was, because it would hardly be code. We need something that's out of place enough he's going to know we said it as a message to him, but not so out of place people are saying *who the fuck is John Wesley Harding and why do they want to interview him?*'

He smiles. We're sitting across the road in the café. The place is pretty quiet. Would much rather have gone to a pub, but Taylor thought we should a) stay nearer the office and b) not go out drinking.

We're here because the tech guys are currently checking his room to see if it's bugged. We've also handed over our phones. Now, the phrase *two for the price of one* is enough of a cliché that the e-mail I received could have been a total coincidence. In fact, it's a pretty dull platitude to say, and depressingly anyone would have said it. I'm inclined to suppose I'm dull enough for it, but that Clayton has too much wit for such banality, thereby pointing to the fact he, by whatever means, heard me say it.

'OK,' he says, 'we might as well talk about it, but I don't want to go anywhere near the possibility of anyone else picking up on it, because we'd either have to explain what we're thinking, in which case we're going to look unbelievably stupid, or else we're going to have to say we stuck Dylan titles in there for a laugh.'

'That wouldn't be a good look.'

'No, Sergeant, it wouldn't. And, of course, if he *has* bugged the place he'll already know we've worked it out. Presumably, though, he'll want us to do something public anyway. All part of the game. So... what have we got?'

'Album titles?'

'Go for it.'

I take the notebook out of my pocket, pen out, ready to jot some down.

'How about *Bringing It All Back Home?*'

Look up, waiting to see his reaction. I mean, none of them are going to be great, but we've got to try something.

'Keep going,' he says. 'Just write down what you think is best.'

'You know the album titles too,' I say.

'I'm thinking,' he says glibly.

I start scribbling, reading them out as I go.

'*Self Portrait... New Morning... Before The Flood... Hard Rain... Street-Legal... Under The Red Sky... World Gone Wrong... Modern Times... Tell Tale Signs...*'

Look up at that one, as it's the only really obvious one to be able to use. He indicates for me to continue.

'*Shadows In The Night. Fallen Angels.*' Shrug. Think on in silence for a while. 'That might be it. All the others are too basic or too completely inappropriate for you to be saying in a news conference.'

'Not me,' he says. 'You.'

'Thanks.'

'This whole thing is aimed at you. You've been getting the e-mails, it's you who needs to bring it to an end.'

He's got me there.

'So, yes, some of them would be ridiculous,' he says, 'but there are one or two that might be do-able. Work on something, show me in the morning. We can work out what else you're going to say and how we're going to play it.'

Take my first drink of coffee, immediately realising I've left it too long and the heat has gone.

'Maybe we can also manage to work out his next means of murder,' I say.

Taylor takes a long drink of coffee.

'Counting on you to stop it before it happens,' he replies.

* * *

The tech guys came up empty. If Clayton really is pulling some shit, and knows everything we're saying, he's hiding it well.

Still sitting at my desk, a little after ten in the evening. Have a few words jotted down, but largely working on other things. More inclined to just stand in front of the press and wing it, a course of action that's unlikely to be popular with my many superiors.

For now I'm going for opening with the phrase *Before the flood of murders began...* and throwing in *tell tale signs* somewhere along the way. That ought to be enough for Clayton, but not quite enough to have *Drunk Copper In Dylan Outrage As Glasgow Put To The Sword* newspaper headlines on Tuesday morning.

Eileen stops by the desk. On her way out, out of uniform, jacket on.

'Hey,' she says.

'Sgt Harrison.'

'Good day?'

'Any day that starts with the decapitation of an eleven year-old girl seems set fair.'

'Yeah, Jesus,' she says. 'Any nearer anything?'

'Well... the boss and I came up with a theory. I don't think we're ready to go public yet.'

'Do I count as public?'

Hold her gaze, take a quick look around the station room, turn back. Might as well run it by a non-combatant, non-Dylan fan and see what she thinks.

'We think he's using Bob Dylan album titles as inspiration for methods of murder, which would tie in with the killer sending me, in particular, the e-mails, because he knows I'm such a big Dylan fan.'

She stares at the floor, and then walks round and sits down opposite. Leans forward, her elbows on the desk.

'I'm not terribly familiar with Bob's work.'

'I know.'

'Run it by me.'

I explain our theory, murder by murder, and how they tie in with the e-mails, in particular the killer *two for the price of one* which, whether by coincidence or listening device, seems another layer of confirmation of the theory.

'So the little girl this morning was a *Blood On The Tracks* reboot, plus *Slow Train Coming*?' she says, when I've gone through them all.

'That's right.'

'Hmm... you make a convincing case, but I wouldn't want to be the one telling... well, anyone else on Earth. The suits are going to be incredulous, and the media will rip the shit out of you.'

'Yes.'

'Is there any particular order in those albums? I mean, can you tell from the sequence what he's going to do next?'

'Seems pretty random. They all date from the mid-70s to the mid-80's, but...'

'Are they just the obvious album titles to use as means for murder?' she asks. 'Insomuch, obviously, as any album title can be suggestive of a means for murder.'

'Yep, that's what we thought. It's a push to know what he's going to do next.'

'Isn't *I Shot The Sherriff* one of his?'

'Bob Marley.'

'Oh. What am I thinking of?'

'*Knocking On Heaven's Door*?'

'That's it.'

'Anyway, it's not an album title.'

She sits back, stares at the desk, her cheeks puffed out, and then gets to her feet.

'Well, good luck presenting that to a credulous public.'

'We're hoping we can pull it off without anyone actually realising what we said.'

'Should be simple enough,' she says. 'Thank God there's no, like, social media apparatus whereby everything said in public is dissected a million times over, with every conceivable theory put forward, and where the craziest theory, or the one where the authorities look the worst, is suggested as the most likely…'

'Thanks.'

'Good night, Sergeant. I've got the day off tomorrow. I'll look out for you on the news.'

'Got any plans?'

Just asking. About to go home myself, just killing a few more seconds before I have to go back to the flat and sit alone, feeling shit.

'Lie in, lunch at Marco's, watch an old movie in the afternoon. *The Apartment* I think.'

'Nice.'

'You?'

'Working.'

'Too bad.' She waves, heads for the door. 'That's the way it crumbles, cookie-wise.'

33

Clayton stands at the window, hands behind his back, looking out at the late twilight. From where he stands he can see the rear of his own house. The house where he lives. The house where the police will never find anything. The house where his bland life is conducted in mediocrity, each day passing by with him playing the required part.

As the leaves of summer have flourished, the extent of the view has decreased. He makes a point of never even looking this way when he's over there.

He wonders how soon it will be before the police decide they need to get a warrant to search the house.

'You should eat.'

There's no reply from the cage. He continues to stare out of the window, and then eventually turns and looks at Dr Brady, sitting in silence in the same seat as always, the tray of food still on the floor.

'You don't like chicken? I thought everyone liked chicken. Don't pretend you're a vegetarian.'

'I'm not hungry,' she says, the words choking out her mouth.

He grunts in reply.

She really isn't hungry. Doesn't feel well, coming down off the tension of the afternoon. He'd made her take a cocktail of drugs to steady her hand and her nerves, and now the effects have worn off, the feeling in her stomach is horrible, twisted, sickening.

She'd had the chance to run away and she hadn't taken it. Of course she hadn't. She could have talked to Taylor and Hutton, but she had believed everything Clayton had told her. She'd believed he was listening to the conversation, she'd believed he was watching her, she'd believed what he said would happen if she didn't come back.

'The chips will be cold,' he says. 'I didn't have time to make them from scratch, I'm afraid. They're oven chips. They'll be awful now the heat's gone out of them. The chicken should be all right.'

'I want to see Chrissie,' she says.

Clayton has already turned away, once more staring out of the window. He doesn't turn back. He sighs and shoves his hands deep into his pockets.

He'd spent forty minutes making dinner, and she wasn't going to touch it. So ungrateful.

He is becoming more and more irritated by her, but she still has her uses, still has her part to play in the dismantling of Detective Sgt Hutton. So much so, in fact, that he hasn't even decided how her part in the drama will end. It isn't entirely out of the question she might come out of it alive.

Unlike Detective Sgt Hutton.

* * *

'Hey, asshole.'

Open my eyes. Immediately aware of the damp of the ground, the cold leaves against my skin. Naked on the forest floor. Naked? Why am I naked? I don't even sleep naked. When did someone take my clothes off? When did they bring me here?

I try to get up, but can't move. Not an inch, not a muscle. Lying dead still, staring up at the canopy of trees. It's cold, and I want to cover myself, but there's nothing I can do.

'Hey, asshole,' says the voice again.

American. That doesn't make sense either. Maybe it's Tandy Kramer's father. He's American. He's the only American I've spoken to recently. It doesn't sound like him, though. An older accent. The kind of accent you don't hear much anymore, not even on TV.

Wait. How the fuck do I know what kind of accents you hear in America, if not from TV?

'You awake, asshole?'

'I'm cold,' I say.

'Sure you're cold. You're butt-ass naked, for crying out loud.'

'I don't understand.'

'Wah-wah-wah, here you go, same thing every goddam night. Get over it, kid. Seriously, when the fuck you going to start addressing the issue here?'

'I don't know what the issue is.'

'Jesus. It's like talking to, I don't know, a fucking plate of beans. It's like you evolved personally into this species that doesn't know the fuck how to use its brain.'

God, it really is freezing. And I need to pee. I try to raise my head to look around, but I can't. All I can see is straight up. If I just pee here in the forest, will anyone notice?

'You could do with losing a bit of weight, buddy,' says the voice to the side of my head.

The crow. It's a crow, although I can't see him. How do I know it's a crow? I must have heard that voice before.

'I just need to get some clothes.'

'Well get up and put them on, you dumbass.'

'And I need the toilet.'

'Jesus. You're like a fucking kid. Are you hungry? Does the forest smell weird?'

There's a flapping of wings, a rustling of the leaves. The crow passes through the edge of my vision.

'*That's* your cock?' he says.

'What?'

'That's it? Your cock? That itty bitty little thing?'

'Of course it's… What?'

I need clothes. I need to pee. I need to get up off this fucking, freezing, damp forest floor.

Start to pee. Can't hold it in any longer.

'There we go,' says the crow. 'Take control.'

34

Monday morning flits past, one thing quickly following another. A montage. A fucking montage of my life. Get up, hideously miserable, humour utterly wasted. Into the office, very early, sit and draft out a few words for the press. A snap conference in the morning, not much to say, not many of them there. Hopefully, however, that won't matter. We just need Clayton (or whoever the fuck else this is) paying attention, and if it is Clayton, we know he always pays attention.

A chat in Connor's office alongside Taylor, then the show for the press, then in with just Taylor, then back to my desk. Said the two lines I'd thought I'd say last night, not much else. The press guys who were there didn't seem terribly impressed. I wonder if one of them might work out the press conference was more about delivering a message than actually contributing anything to the narrative of the investigation, but hopefully they're more likely just to think we want to be seen to be doing our bit, while not actually doing anything at all.

And *phht*, suddenly it's eleven-thirty in the morning and it already feels like it should be the middle of the afternoon, and I'm sitting at my desk waiting for the e-mail to pop up, not really able to think straight, but it's nothing to do with anything much, just one of those fucking days when everything seems shit.

I want to go and talk to Philo this afternoon, but I really doubt she wants to talk to me, and yes, Jesus, I know she's dead and she's not talking anyway and she's not thinking anything about it, nothing at all, because, like we've already established, *she's dead!* so it's all a projection of myself, all of it. It's all about me, the self-obsessed, narcissistic wanker.

And you need to shut up!

Then here it comes, the long-awaited e-mail, the one we've been hoping for. Sit back in my seat, read the words over a few times. Morrow's not in, the desk opposite empty. Look into Taylor's office, where he sits at his desk, glance at Connor's door, which remains closed.

Forward the e-mail on, copying them both in.

Thank God! I can stop now! Such a shame you were too late for Rogers. Until next time, Sergeant...

As I send it, my eyes are on Taylor, his back turned to me where he sits. I can see the physical slump of the shoulders. The moment. Composing himself, shoulders straighten a little, and then we're back, and he's up, and walking through into the open plan. Stops at Morrow's desk, as ever.

'Suppose that's a good news/bad news situation,' he says.

'Not if you're Rogers.'

'The name doesn't mean anything?'

'Nope.'

'Right, I'll go in and talk to Connor, we'll sort out what we're taking to the Chief Constable. No matter how absurd, it looks like we were right. Bob Dylan album titles. Jesus... You get onto the system, see if there's anyone named Rogers been reported missing in Glasgow in the last few days.'

'I'll bring it in if I find anything.'

'Cool.'

And off he goes.

Take a second. Let my eyes drift over the words in the latest e-mail. Processing. Allowing this new information to sink into the misery of the day. Recalibrate. Try to stop internalising. Internalising is for sitting at home with a bottle of wine or a bottle of vodka. Internalising is for 2am, can't sleep, staring at the fucking wall. Internalising is for weekends with nothing to do.

Rogers!

Find the name straight away. Mr James Rogers of Rodden Drive, Kings Park.

Pick up the phone, call the local station. Answered by one of those fantastic, ball-crushing female police sergeants you get.

'Hi, Detective Sgt Hutton in Cambuslang.'

'Sergeant,' she says, the tone of her voice immediately signaling recognition. 'Nice TV slot this morning.'

'Thank you... You've got a missing guy called Rogers?'

Pause. 'Don't know the name, just let me check.'

Sit back, look around the office. Glance at the closed door of Connor's office. Wonder how Connor's enjoying the fact he's going to stand before the collected beaks of Police Scotland and say we've managed to bring an end to the Bob Dylan murders.

Jesus.

'Hey. Yes, we've got him. Reported missing yesterday afternoon when he didn't turn up for work. Was supposed to be in B&Q yesterday morning, didn't respond to calls to his house or to his mobile. No reports of him calling a doctor. His work place called it in, doesn't seem to have any family close by.'

'And someone's been round to his house?'

Slight pause.

'We knocked on the door, but the officers chose not to effect entry.'

I'm not going to ask why not. You don't go breaking into some guy's house just because he doesn't turn up at work. In fact, you don't really call the police in that situation, and if someone did and we reacted to it at all, it must have been because it was a quiet Sunday afternoon in Kings Park.

'Is there a problem?' she asks.

'Yep... we've got something... Those e-mails we've been getting? We got another one this morning pointing to Rogers. Too late for Rogers, that's what it said. No idea at this point who Rogers is, but we need to check this guy out, just in case.'

'OK, I'll send someone round.'

'Mind if I come over?'

'Of course not.'

'Cool. Be there in fifteen.'

Hang up, stare at the boss's door, contemplate just heading on out, but decide I'd better stick my nose in.

Knock, open the door but don't really go into the office. They look at me expectantly. Looks like I've got the room.

'There's a missing Rogers over in Kings Park. They haven't put his door in yet, so I'm going round there now.'

Taylor glances at Connor.

'We can leave it to the Sergeant,' says the boss, 'we need to draft something here. Call it in as soon as you're in the house,' he continues, looking at me. 'Including, obviously, a negative return.'

And I'm out the door, heading down to the car park.

* * *

It's a beautiful day. I don't think I noticed the weather when I came out this morning, I didn't see the glorious June sunshine. Too fucking miserable. That's what happens when you're forty-seven and you wake up having wet the bed because your head's a piece of worm-eaten, petrified fuck.

Four of us at the door. Detective Constable Hobbes, who seems like a reasonable bloke. Morrow, by another name, relocated fifteen minutes across town. And two female constables who I'm doing my damnedest not to objectify. I really am. Constables Clarence and Oates.

Oates unlocks the door on the fifth key attempt, and in we go. I prefer a well-placed shoulder myself, but it probably makes sense not to burst a door off its lock if you don't have to.

She steps into the hallway, this morning's mail on the carpet. Just a couple of white envelopes and a Lidl advert. Hobbes moves past her, into the front room. Walks straight in, and we follow.

A plain old room, nothing interesting about it, except the obvious gap on the wall, where the large TV screen – forty-two inch maybe – has been taken down, and another clear space on a dusty shelf beneath, where perhaps the DVD player used to sit.

Through into the room beyond, and now Hobbes stops in the doorway. The international sign of having found what we're looking for. He moves further inside, and we follow him in.

And there we stand, in a perfect line, staring.

The television has been attached to the wall in the small room. Too big really for the front room, it totally dominates this room. Pretty unpleasant porn is playing, presumably on some kind of continuous loop. A young woman, five or six guys. She doesn't look like she's enjoying herself.

Jim Rogers himself is on the floor, perched against the wall opposite the TV. The small dining table has been pushed out of the way to the back of the room. There are only two chairs, placed under the table.

Rogers is naked. The manner of his death is not immediately obvious. There's no blood. His penis is in his right hand, still erect it seems, although a quick glance suggests something has been inserted inside it to keep it that way. So, unnaturally stretched is probably a better description than erect.

His left hand is on a large bottle of Bowmore, which is nearly empty. If the rest of the contents of the bottle are inside him, that might point to one reason for him being dead. At first glance I thought there was shit smeared around his mouth, but then I notice the chocolate cake at his side. Most of it is gone too. And all around him, covering the floor, is money. Notes. Fives and tens and twenties. At a rough guess, several thousand pounds.

'Well, this is fucking weird,' says Constable Clarence after a minute or so.

Almost laugh out loud. You think? Hobbes gives her a quick glance.

'Fuck,' he mutters. 'This what you expected to find, Sergeant?'

Couldn't begin to know what I thought I'd find. It's got a seven deadly sins feel about it, doesn't it? *Se7en.* That's what I think. Gluttony and greed and lust, though maybe not all of them. And the sound of the girl getting fucked by several enormous, porn star-sized dudes suddenly seems even louder than it was when we walked in.

'I know we shouldn't touch anything, but could you put that off, Constable, please?'

I only ask because she's nearest. Oates. She glances at Hobbes for confirmation, he nods, and she takes the two steps to the DVD player, pulls the cuff of her shirt down over her finger and presses the off button.

Silence.

'I'll call it in,' says Hobbes. 'Can you look around, see if there's anything in the other rooms?'

Chocolate cake, money, booze and porn. Hmm... Bob did the *Seven Deadly Sins* song with the Wilburys, but that's not it. The seven deadly sins aren't represented here, not in their totality. It would be different from what he's been doing, and it would be copying the Brad Pitt movie. That's not Clayton.

Then out of nowhere the word pops into my head. *Desire.*

I'd thought it was almost too simple a title to have been used. Not sure, in fact, that it's not a bit of a stretch. How exactly is this guy going to have been killed by porn, money or cake? Alcohol, well that's fair enough. Kills thousands of us every year. It'll be my turn soon enough.

There I fucking go, making it about me again. Jesus.

35

This one has brought in the spectators, and I don't mean the gawkers who assemble at every crime scene. Those sad bastards are to be expected. The hordes who aren't quite fulfilled by *CSI: Garrowhill* on Channel 5 and need to see the real thing in action. Let them come.

This time, however, the suits have come to see. Connor is visiting a crime scene for possibly the first time in his entire life. Don't know much about the Chief Constable, but I imagine it's been a few years since he tossed on a SOCO suit and stuck his hand into the metaphorical viscera of an actual investigation.

Perhaps they came hoping the nasty porn would still be playing on the TV. They probably asked for it to be turned back on. Someone, somewhere, will of course have the job of watching it all, and more than once, to see if there are any clues to be had from the film. Won't be us, though, it'll go to one of the locals, in keeping with the general egalitarian nature of the investigation so far.

I'm currently standing on the sidelines, waiting to be called back into action. I should probably have already headed back to the station, but for now, I think I might actually need some direction.

Where are we going with is? Seven people murdered, plus the strange case of the missing psychiatrist. The latter is the only thing pointing to any peculiarity in Clayton's actions over the last week, and yet the potentially missing psychiatrist herself has no obvious connections to the random series of murders.

So we have nothing. At least, nothing on Clayton.

Coffee in my hand. Someone came round with them,

not sure who. One of our lot, though, not some random member of the public.

Taylor and Connor emerge from the house, squeeze pass a couple more SOCO's on their way in. Taylor eyes my coffee, looks around, doesn't spot the source of the tasty beverage.

Connor shakes his head, his cheeks puffed out. Lets out a long sigh. Hands in his pockets, looks around at the waiting crowd, all of them out of earshot.

'So what do we think, gentlemen?' he asks, his gaze over to the other side of the street, over the tops of the houses. Perhaps looking to see if he can see the floodlights of Hampden from here. Already looked. You can't. 'You've worked it out, and now he's going to stop? Was it really that simple all along? A simple, stupid, parlour game? The Bob Dylan murders?'

He grimaces at the artless stupidity of it. Unusually I find myself agreeing with him.

'If he's stopped,' says Taylor, 'then thank God. But it's not as though we can just let it rest because there aren't going to be any more.'

'No.'

'Anyone else getting anywhere?' I ask. 'I mean, any of the other stations?'

'No,' says Connor. 'I don't know who this is, but they're bloody good, I'll tell you that. Not a fingerprint, not a suspicious phone call, not a name online or in a diary or in a text message, not a piece of CCTV footage. Whoever this is, they've thought of everything. Bloody good. Bloody good...'

Yes, he is, just don't say that in front of a TV camera. I look around again, making sure everyone really is out of earshot. If some fucker's got a microphone... *Asshole Cop Licks Killer's Baws In New Establishment Shame.*

'Bollocks,' he mutters.

'What now?' I ask.

Taylor gives me a glance, then looks around the crowd of onlookers. Connor continues to do the same. Perhaps they're both clinging to the old maxim about the killer returning to the scene of the crime. Looking for the face in the crowd, the eyes that drop when they see the police looking, the person who turns and walks away under scrutiny. Or the killer with ball-breaking confidence, who stares down the police, somehow knowing he's untouchable.

And that's what our guy is, right now. Ball-breakingly confident and untouchable.

'We shouldn't be complacent,' says Taylor. 'He might just mean the bloody Bob Dylan murders are over. Maybe next he's going to do the Neil Young Murders, or the Winnie the Fucking Pooh murders for all we know. And we're going to need a more established, central point of the investigation. Rather than four or five teams working to the centre, we need one dedicated team, taking all the crimes together as a whole. It'll piss a few people off, but they have to do it. I don't care if we're on it, and in fact, since the killer is trying to drag you into this, Sergeant, you at least certainly shouldn't be.'

Pauses, looks at his watch.

'Sir,' he says, 'we're back to Riverside in an hour. We should get back to the station, finalise our pitch, aggregate everything we've got, and get in there. Come in strong and, more than anything else, practical.'

'Yes, of course,' says Connor.

Out of his depth, as he has been since he arrived, due to the proverbial series of unfortunate events.

Hmm, that's not a proverb, is it?

I don't feel out of my depth, but still, in terms of enthusiasm at least, I'm as far away from Taylor as Connor appears to be.

'Sergeant, you just keep on keeping on. Try and pin down Dr Brady, we need to find her. I want to be able to definitely rule Clayton out the game, or get something on him.'

'Right, boss.'

And so it goes.

36

Monday afternoon, warm day, standing on the doorstep of Brady's house. Back where I was yesterday evening, except the circumstances are completely different.

Yesterday I was looking in hope, and finding nothing. Today I'm back because I called her number and, out of the blue, she answered.

Look around as I wait for her to come to the door. Quiet street. Don't see anyone around. Not so much as a warm afternoon lawnmower in use. Maybe I can hear one in the distance somewhere, someone else's back garden, someone else's life.

Yesterday I spoke to three of the neighbours, all of whom had that inherent middle class suspicion of the police – totally different, of course, from the inherent working class suspicion of the police. Only the upper classes aren't suspicious of the police, because they know if there's any trouble, they can get the Queen or the head of the Civil Service or the Prime Minister to call off the dogs.

The door opens, I turn, and there's the vamp. Jesus. Same look as yesterday, this time built around a sheer white knee-length dress, holding a gin and tonic in her right hand.

How, you ask, do I know it's a gin and tonic and not a vodka tonic or a Bacardi and lemonade or even just a double lemonade?

Not sure, but I can tell. Call it a superpower.

'Sergeant, just in time. Come in.'

She stands back, not giving me a huge amount of room, and I brush past her, close enough to get the scent of the gin on her breath and the full waft of whatever body spray she draped herself in. And there's that old familiar feeling.

Momentarily close my eyes, my back still to her, as I examine the inner mental workings to establish if there's the slightest possibility I could try to carry out a proficient, coherent and professional line of questioning, and immediately acknowledge it's not going to happen.

I'm always about to leave the damn police anyway, right? What difference does it make if I do it in disgrace after getting drunk and fucking a witness?

Who said anything about getting drunk? And as for the latter, well I have my boss's instructions to which to adhere. Do whatever you have to do.

She walks past me and I follow her down a short corridor and into the large kitchen at the back of the house.

I already spent a few minutes in this place yesterday, when I broke in. It's the kind of kitchen you get in magazines, albeit not the kind of magazines I read. Floored with great slabs of stone, a wooden island in the middle with cooking implements hanging above, and all around sleek and expensive tools of the part-time chef's trade, tucked perfectly into beautiful units and sitting on marble worktops.

Even I like the damn kitchen, and I consider it cooking when I make a bowl of Cornflakes.

'Gin and tonic?' she asks, taking up position at the counter, beside an empty glass and half a lime.

'Vodka if you've got it,' I say.

'Just gin.'

'Gin it is.'

I stand and watch as she goes through the ritual of the gin and tonic, one-third to two-thirds measure, lots of ice, lots of lime. The dress is hugging her body, down to just below the knee. No bra, her nipples evident against the material.

She knows that while I'm watching her, I'm looking at her body, not at her make the drink. I'm undressing her, knowing that undressing her is something that would only take a few seconds to do.

She turns, hands over the drink, we clink glasses, take a sip.

'Shall we sit out in the garden?' she says. 'Beautiful day.'

For a moment I've lost the power of speech to lust. The filthiest, most enjoyable kind of lust. The kind you know you shouldn't have. Wanting something it's going to be dangerous to go anywhere near.

She opens the back door and leads me out. I stop for a second on the doorstep, eyes adjusting again to the bright sunlight, and look around the garden. As immaculate and big-ticket as the kitchen, like she had some TV makeover crew in for the week.

'Take your shoes and socks off, Sergeant, the grass feels beautiful on your feet.'

There's a table with a couple of chairs on a patio just by the back door, but she walks past them, barefoot across the lawn, to the end of the garden, where there is a small copse of elm trees. I do as I'm told, and follow. All around are beautiful plants, the names of which are lost to me, and which I barely notice.

In amongst the copse of elms there is a double swing seat. She sits down, looks my way, and I sit next to her. She sighs, moves the seat back, so that it starts swinging, and takes a drink.

I take a look around. A perfect spot, secluded from all the surrounding houses. The only place from which it is overlooked is her own first floor. The warmth of the sun is still on us, but we're protected from the brightness.

She removes her sunglasses, tosses them to the side onto the grass, rubs her eyes briefly, and then settles her head back, staring straight ahead. I glance at her, let my eyes run over her body, then turn away and follow her gaze.

'You've been asking about me,' she says. 'Is Mr Clayton really so bad?'

Take another drink. Sharp and strong. Swill the ice

cubes round in the glass. Business. We've got business to discuss. That's why I'm here. Police business, with a barefoot seductress, drinking gin and tonic, in a hidden copse in a fairytale garden.

'We think he is,' I say. 'We were worried about you. Your actions have been inconsistent.'

'Yes.'

'Why?'

She takes a drink. I join her. At this rate we're going to be heading back to the kitchen pretty quickly.

'You should have brought a pitcher,' I say, and she smiles.

'I didn't tell you everything.'

'We know.'

'But it's not necessarily what it seems.'

I leave that one out there. The explanation is coming. I really ought to be looking at her, gauging her mood, looking for the gut feeling she's lying, but it's not so easy when you're right next to someone on a swing chair.

I stand up, turn my back to the house, and look down at her. She holds my eyes, the drink goes to the lips, the ice cubes clink in the glass.

'Trying to exert some control, Sgt Hutton?'

'Tell me the story.'

Lowers the drink, holds it in both hands. Her fingers are going to be cold. Those cold fingers are going to feel fabulous on my skin.

Yes, yes, all right. *Concentrate!*

Despite having taken the positive step to stand up and look at her face on, I don't know it's helping my concentration. I may not be pressed against her now, but I'm looking at her, the legs crossed, the drink held in the slender fingers, the V of the neckline, her breasts beneath the thin cotton of the summer dress.

'I'm facing court action,' she says, and when finally it comes out, her voice is crisp, almost businesslike.

'What for?'

'If I tell you, you might get ideas.'

'I've already got ideas.'

'Of course you do.'

'Can you just tell me the story, please?'

'There have been a couple of complaints made against me, and finally the BMA put together a case, managed to add a few more to the pile, and now I've been suspended pending a full inquiry. That's why all my appointments were cancelled this week. I booked myself a small cottage, not far away, just the other side of Lennoxtown, and decided to hole myself up there.'

'What about Mr Clayton?'

'He wanted to continue seeing me, I told him it would prejudice my case if I did, and he said he would make it worth my while. So he has been paying me, and... well, as you can see, I've been making a lot of money doing what I do, and things are going to be rather uncomfortable without it.'

'But, like you said, won't it prejudice...'

'Yes, but then... all the complaints against me are absolutely true, so in fact, I really must make hay while I can, you see.'

We both take another drink.

'Sit back down, Sergeant,' she says. 'I'm really not hiding anything. You don't have to stand before me looking so accusatory.'

I think about it, decide where the stand is going to be made, and then come down on the side of the stand having already been made, then given up with barely a whimper.

I sit back down, and get the immediate feel of her leg against mine, neither of us pulling away. She leans forward, and now as I look at her the overlap of the V in her dress is parted and I can see her left breast, small and perfect, the nipple firm and dark.

Look away, but knowing she wants me looking. Wait, didn't even Taylor want me looking? Everybody wants me looking. So why am I staring blindly off into the trees, a gin and tonic at my lips?

I turn back. Her left elbow is on her knee, the drink

held in her left hand. I stare at her breast, imagine my fingers around it, my tongue on it, licking it, taking it into my mouth.

'I have sex with my clients,' she says.

Oh, Jesus, there we are…

'How many of them?'

'Most of them,' she says.

'And if I speak to the BMA they'll confirm it?'

'I'll even give you the name of the little bastard who's been after me for the last two years.'

'If you have sex with most of your clients, why has it taken so long?'

She turns and smiles, takes another drink, tipping the glass far back, not quite finishing it. She leans forward again, so that her breast is still evident.

'I'm good,' she says. 'None of them ever complain.'

'It's just the wives?'

'And the husbands.'

I get a glance with that, and then she looks away again.

'So obviously I slept with the first couple of BMA investigators who came sniffing around, and that kept it quiet for a while. But they wised up, and they put a vicious little middle-aged, sexless woman on my case. There was no chance of interrupting the investigation, and slowly…' she says, closing her right hand into a ball, 'she got me.'

'And Clayton?'

'Do I sleep with him?'

'Yes.'

'No, not Mr Clayton. I mean, he knows what I do with most of the others, but he's not interested. As a psychiatrist, he is a genuinely fascinating case, unlike most of the narcissistic simpletons one sees these days.'

'So why do you sleep with them?'

She finishes off her drink, tipping it back, before tossing the glass casually onto the grass beside her sunglasses.

'Two reasons,' she says. 'It's much more interesting than talking to them…'

I doubt anyone could argue that.

'And I'm insatiable. I'm your dream, Sergeant. I'm every man's dream. I can't get enough, and I really don't care. Seriously, they have help groups for this?'

Well, I'm not sure you need to be a qualified psychiatrist to know that little piece of insight into the dreams of every man, but she's bang fucking on.

'And now, I've been stuck alone in a small house on a hill all week, and the only man I'd talked to before seeing you and your boss yesterday was a client who only wanted me for my qualifications, and you know, Sergeant, I could have had you and your boss over the table right there and then. I went back to my place and I was fucking myself senseless with anything I could find.'

I may be getting toyed with, but right now I'll happily take it. She can toy with me all she damn well likes.

Lean forward, lips onto hers, and I can't stop myself reaching for the breast that has been sitting there so invitingly. Hand inside her dress, pushing the material aside, and my fingers close around the nipple. She moans at my touch, and straight away her hand is on my hard cock, grabbing it, squeezing it.

She breaks the kiss with a heavy moan.

'Jesus, Sergeant, just fuck me. Right now. There's plenty of time for everything else, but I just need your cock inside me. Come on!'

I stand up, lift my shirt off, and she's tearing at my trousers, belt and button and zip undone, then pulled off along with my NASA technology underwear. She's forward on her knees, briefly takes my hard, damp cock into her mouth, her tongue all over it, and then she's hauling me down, so I'm lying back, flat on the grass. She kneels over me, pulls the dress up to her waist, and now I see she came prepared, wearing no underwear at all, lowers herself onto my erection, and I thrust deep inside her.

'Jesus!' she says, not too loud, but a great sound, of desperation and relief and desire.

Her pussy is tight and soaking, and she starts working herself up and down. I reach up and pull the dress off her shoulders, and it sits on her midriff, perfectly framing her breasts.

I lie back and look up at her. Her eyes are closed, her movements becoming less frantic.

'God, I love that feeling,' she says.

I watch her breasts, and then lean up, taking her left breast into my mouth. I put my hands on her hips and start thrusting back at her as hard as she's thrusting onto me.

37

Sitting in the kitchen, I don't know how much later. An hour maybe. The sex slowed down, hardly became romantic or anything, but at least I stopped myself coming too quickly. Jesus, she looked fucking amazing sitting back on the swing seat, the dress at her waist, her legs open. Fucked her with my tongue for God knows how long. Every time she orgasmed, she'd squeeze my head tightly with her thighs. Could hardly breathe. Wonderful.

Drinking another gin and tonic, sitting at the island, leaning on the expensive wood while watching her make a sandwich.

'You're supposed to be telling me about Clayton.'

She hasn't put the sunglasses back on, which is good. She's changed her dress, but this one, simple, long, flowing, floral green and blue, is no less alluring.

The smile has gone, which I noticed as soon as she'd come back down the stairs. All through the interview yesterday, and through the early exchanges today, and throughout the sex, the smile had been there. Coming and going, delicious and attractive, mostly unreadable.

In the ten minutes she's been back in the kitchen there have been no smiles. A troubled look that – just like the smile – I'm unable to read. Perhaps this is her usual demeanour post-sex. She troubles herself with her insatiable appetite. Hates herself for needing sex to deal with any situation.

I mean, most people aren't insatiable, most people don't need to have sex with everyone they meet. I have my moments myself, of course, and I understand them. I know where they come from. Presumably she has her own reasons, but really, despite having a fucking ball the last hour, I don't care. Nevertheless I really ought to take something back to Taylor other than an air of gratification.

'He's dangerous,' she says.

Wow, there's a departure.

'What d'you mean?'

The small kitchen knife, slicing through cucumber, stops mid-cut. Eyes close for a second. Her hands are steady, though, and shortly she opens her eyes, continues with the movement.

'He tells me stories. I don't know whether or not any of them are true. About things he did at school. Killing people who made him jealous. Almost... they're almost too simple. Simple little stories, like they're out of a crime thriller, or they're taken from episodes of TV. I don't know if I should believe him. He's either telling the truth, in which case he's very, very dangerous, or else...'

She finally looks up. Her eyes are impossible. I don't understand this woman at all.

'Don't judge me, Sergeant,' she says.

'What d'you mean?'

'Don't judge me, because we had sex. Because I told you I have sex with everyone.'

'I'm not judging you,' I say. It's not the time for her to get introspective, or to worry about what I'm thinking.

'All men judge all women,' she says, the knife cutting a little harder onto the board. 'Especially after they've had sex.'

I'm not sure about that. The judging goes on *before* the sex. Afterwards... not so much judging.

'We need to talk about Clayton,' I say. 'If he's not telling the truth...'

Ham, cheese, cucumber, tomato and mayonnaise, your classic sandwich combo. You can't beat a sandwich after sex.

'He's delusional,' she says. 'The actions of anyone displaying that level of delusion are going to be highly unpredictable. It could be it never moves beyond his imagination, but it could be if he ever finds himself in a dangerous or stressful situation, and he believes in the past he has dealt with these situations in a certain way, that... If he believes he has already committed murder, or that murderous acts are trivial enough to be casually admitted to, there's nothing to say he wouldn't then carry out such an act.'

Slice of bread on top, perfectly cut from a thick loaf with one of those bread knives you see in supplements for several hundred pounds, then she slices each sandwich in half, places them on plates, and lifts them both.

'Shall we eat outside?'

She looks up, finally the smile is back, although this time a little forced.

'Bring the drinks,' she adds.

* * *

Taylor looks up as I walk into his office. Police work. It really is shit, sometimes. Here he is, nearly seven o'clock on a Monday evening. Hasn't had a day off in forever, will be in here again first thing tomorrow morning.

The papers won't give a shit. All they see are unsolved murders. If he took the day off, or the afternoon off, or stepped out the fucking office for two minutes to grab a cup of coffee, there would be a damned photographer there to record the moment for the *Lazy-Ass Polis Bastard Could Give A Fuck About Body Count* headline.

And right enough, he looks exhausted.

'You speak to her?' he asks. 'You have an air about you.'

'Yeah, she's fine.'

Close the door, take a seat.

'You look knackered,' I say. 'You should go home.'

He glances at his watch.

'Going to give it another half hour. Tell me about her.'

There's something else to tell him about, but I'm not sure yet. Need to think while I talk, even though thinking about it on the way over here hasn't really helped.

'Says her clients were cancelled as she's about to be struck off. She's been staying in a small cottage in the Campsies. Clayton pays her privately for daily visits.'

'Why she's getting struck off?'

'Sleeping with patients.'

'Hmm. Does she also sleep with investigating police officers?'

'Yes.'

'Did it help her talk?'

'Quite changed the mood. The woman we met yesterday, the one who was waiting for me today, I could easily imagine that woman being the one she described herself as. Wanton. Post-sex, it was like I was talking to someone else.'

'Maybe that's her way. Maybe she hates herself for it. You must be used to women hating themselves for sleeping with you.'

'Hilarious.'

'Don't mention it. What'd she say about him?'

A second, lower my eyes.

'This is what's troubling you,' he says.

'He talks a lot about crimes he's committed. Murders.'

'Plague of Crows?'

'No.'

'Lynch's case?'

'No.'

'What then?'

'It's fucking weird. I mean, we suspect the guy's been committing the Bob Dylan murders, aimed specifically at me, so why wouldn't he... why wouldn't he know this shit. It's just...'

'Sergeant...? What shit?'

'He told her about a variety of people he said he'd killed. Some guy in school he was jealous of, some girl at university who pissed him off, some guy he worked with who wanted to have a relationship...'

'And how's that all connected to you?'

'The school story. It happened when I was at Cathkin. It happened. Not in my year, but there was a guy killed in the fields down from the school, head staved in with a brick, just like Clayton described it. The–'

'Could it have been Clayton?'

'No! It was that little twat, John McGuire. It was McGuire. Everyone knew. Jesus, he was found with blood on his fucking hands.'

'Maybe Clayton did something similar.'

'I was at Glasgow Uni for four years. One person was murdered in all that time. A girl, been trying to remember her name, but it's not there. She'd been in the Conservative party. Killed, not raped, never found her killer. Clayton told Brady the story. And then – and this is the fucking weird clincher to absolutely say he never did any of this shit – he told her about killing some guy at work, dressed in a gimp suit, by thrusting a wine bottle into his mouth. Jesus, I worked that case! I worked the fucking case, second year on the job. And we got the guy. And no, no, there was no question about the killer. We nailed him. He confessed. There was DNA, there was CCTV, it was as clear-cut a case as you could imagine. The guy's still nicked. Clayton did not commit that murder. He's appropriating it, to make himself look... fuck, I don't know...'

'Why does he want the doc to think he's a killer?'

'I don't know. But they're all... they've all got some connection to me. It's like he's using her to taunt me. Just the same as he's been doing with the Dylan murders.'

I'm looking curiously at him, like I expect him to have an explanation. I sure as fuck don't.

'So why was she suddenly happy to break the doctor/patient confidentiality?' he asks. 'Those bastards usually dine out on that shit.'

'I don't know.'

'You think maybe you broke down the walls with your whole, damaged, Casanova thing you've got going on?'

'You're cracking me up,' I say.

He sighs heavily.

'Jesus, I fucking hate this guy. We could have video evidence of the bastard knifing someone in the face and we'd still be wary of him having faked it. He's got us, and the fucking suits, pishing in our pants every time we mention his damn name.'

'What d'you want me to do?'

'You're going to have to... first off, you're just going to have to look into all those old crimes, get the files out, maybe even speak to the fuckers who're in prison. Speak to people. Find out if there's the slightest possibility Clayton could have been behind any of it. After that... God, I don't know. We need to speak to Clayton again, but he can easily hide behind doctor/patient. Jesus... This bastard just runs rings round us.'

'Maybe we should just take him out,' I say.

He blinks, keeps his eyes on mine.

'What?'

'Kill him,' I say.

'Jesus. You're saying that in here, when not twenty-four hours ago we were wondering if he had the place bugged? Are you out of your fucking mind, Sergeant?'

There he has a point.

He leans forward, elbows on the desk, face into his hands, then quickly rubs them and looks up.

'Go home, Sergeant. Be in early tomorrow, write it up for me. Whatever you were thinking of doing now, don't. Just go home. You've done enough for the day.'

'I'd be pushed to say the last few hours were work.'

He waves me away, I look down at him for a few moments, but he's turned back to some paperwork and I've been dispatched.

Out the door, close it on him, annoyed at the dismissal and head back towards my desk. I stand and look at it, contemplate logging on and seeing if there are any more e-mails, mutter 'fuck it,' to myself, and then I'm out the door of the open plan and practically jogging down the stairs.

38

The thought's in my head now, once, twice, three times, keeps on coming back, as if Clayton planted it himself.

This torture would be over if I killed him. Me. Doesn't have to be some secret police unit that doesn't actually exist, (even though most of the population probably think the police have a secret assassination squad.) We don't have to call in a random US airstrike, following which we can have some official say, oops, sorry, we meant to hit Iran. We don't have to order some reluctant young constable, or pull a dodgy favour from some dodgy Glasgow gangster who still owes us one from some fucking dodgy deal we did at some point in the last twenty years.

I could just do it. Go and interview him, then kill him. Been a while since I fired a gun, but if I was close enough not to miss, well… I wouldn't miss.

There would be no point, and no peace of mind to be had, in trying to cover it up. I'd always be waiting; waiting for Clayton to come and bite me from the grave. I'd need to do it and then face the consequences, or do it and then turn the gun on myself.

Jesus, the thought of that brings blessed relief.

Taylor was right, though. I shouldn't have mentioned it in his office. That was just stupid. Unbelievably stupid. He really should have complete deniability. That's the trouble with me now taking the law, and Clayton's life, into my own hands. Taylor is liable to be caught up in it, and dragged down in the aftermath. I'd need to do it in such a way Taylor was totally detached. Mentioning it to him was a lousy start.

So, Sergeant, you're seriously thinking about it?

Sitting at home, at the small dining table I've occupied more and more since the one time I sat there with Philo. Just me, a bottle of wine, and Bob on the CD player. *Shadows In The Night*. It remains as ephemeral as it was last week, so as usual I'm playing it over and over. He's on his third run through the songs since I sat down, swallowing me up in his melancholy as we go along together.

Bottle of wine nearly empty, this on top of three hefty g&t's this afternoon. Drove home too. Fucking tube.

Turning the bottle around and around in my fingers. To be honest I didn't really get the notes of citrus and passion fruit. But yes, Mr Marketing Man getting paid at £500/a word, it is nice to drink on its own.

I had an all right few months after Philo, helped through by my lesbian buddy. But really, all that time I was just one crisis away from batshit crazy, and boom, here we are, the crisis has come calling on its miserable grey horse, gloom and depression quickly descending, sending me the way of the bottle and inappropriate sex. Sex with interviewees on desks, sex with witnesses, weird non-contact sex on a couch with a colleague. Perhaps, before any of this crap is over, I'll have come up with some other ill-chosen method of sexual congress, like sex with a victim's partner at the undertaker's.

Empty the glass, tip the rest of the bottle into it. Already wondering whether I'm going to open the next bottle, and knowing I will.

I want to talk to Harrison, she'd probably enjoy the story of the nymphomaniac psychiatrist, but I shouldn't call her. Not again. Not that I called her on Saturday, but it's too soon. This is a difficult time, but it'll pass soon enough, even if it just passes with me dead, either with my liver as the centrepiece of an exhibition or finally at the hands of Clayton. Whatever happens, it'll slip away, and the story of the psychiatrist and me will wait for another day. When it's all over, I still want to have Harrison around. I don't know how many times I could sit next to her naked and drunk and not fuck things up.

Tired, drunk, miserable, beginning to feel nauseous. Jesus fucking Christ. What if I do? Really, what if I get hold of a gun or a knife or a fucking vacuum pack of fucking coffee granules, go and see Clayton and shoot him or stab him or beat the living fuck out of him? What's there to lose?

Arms on the table, then rest my head on my forearms. As I make the movement, I catch the glass of wine and it tips, the glass tumbling on the table and breaking, and at the same time as my head touches my hands, glass shatters and the wine spills over the table.

'Aw, fuck!'

Straighten up, sit back, as the wine runs off, soaking into my trousers.

'Fucking hell.'

Can't be bothered moving. Jesus, what fucking difference does it make? Wine soaking into the old, fucking, stupid soak. Sit there, feeling the drip of the booze on my leg, the dampness spreading, and then put my hands and forearms back where they were and rest my head again.

Pressing my hands into the table I feel the sharp jab of broken glass.

39

Tuesday morning. Three plasters on my right hand. Tried taking them off this morning so I didn't look like a dick, and immediately started covering everything I touched in blood.

On the plus side, the crows took a night off. I think. Maybe I just don't remember. And if there weren't any crows, why weren't there? Maybe they've done their work. They wanted me to assume command over my own life. They wanted me to realise what it was I had to do. Put a bullet in Clayton, then do the same to myself. Everything over.

It's time to take control, and while I've yet to do it, I know now what it is I've got to do. And so, no more crows.

More likely, more mundanely, I dreamt about them and had just forgotten by the time I woke up.

Still no reports of any further murders around these parts. The bout of random slaughter on the streets and railway lines of Glasgow really might be over, and all because the boss and I worked out the killer was working around Bob Dylan album titles (with incidental help from the less-than-super superintendent). Fortunately that information hasn't yet reached the media – a miracle in itself – so we haven't had *The Bob Dylan Murders* graphic on the news.

Obviously it's good that the murders are done and dusted, but I'm kind of curious as to what he would have done next. Curious enough that I spent some time this morning going through the album titles and contemplating how it is one would murder someone after the fashion of

Street Legal or *Shot of Love*. *Christmas In The Heart*, where someone would be stabbed through the chest by a tree decoration or a giant Santa candle, is the one I think we missed out on.

Taylor's not known as the wisest man in Police Scotland for nothing. They've done what he was suggesting they would, by bringing all the cases together under one roof. We gave them Morrow, and he's off into Dalmarnock for the foreseeable.

The press are loving it of course. They'd particularly love it if there was another murder, but they don't necessarily need it just now. Seven murders in six days, all the work of one person? That is at least a month worth of headlines, and they've made up for a couple of days without a new death with sad tales from bereaved relatives, funerals and vigils, plaintive flowers beside the train tracks, and occasional angry mobs outside the Islamic Community Centre that used to be a church.

Tandy Kramer's dad is still around, somewhere. With the investigation being taken over by a new team – led by a DCI Collins – it was obvious they weren't going to let her body go yet. More questions to be asked, even if ultimately they never actually get her body re-examined. Mr Kramer, meanwhile, has taken the opportunity to speak to every newspaper going, the story of his relationship with his daughter and the heartache he feels – and the lawsuit that will be coming the way of the Police, Transport Scotland and the Scottish Executive – telling not quite the same story he told me.

Whatever. The guy lost his daughter. If he wants to make a play, if he wants to own the bereavement while spouting shit to the media, he might as well go ahead.

First word from Morrow is that things are a bit strained in Dalmarnock, but not as bad as they might be under the circumstances. He likes Collins at any rate, which is something. Trouble is, while the e-mails sent to me – and the fact the murders stopped as indicated – imply these seven deaths were all connected, they've found nothing else to join them, with the obvious exception of the two people dying together at the community centre.

Seven deaths, six acts of completely random violence. There are a few potentially useable pieces of evidence in there, every now and again, but they've all turned out to be on a par with our guy caught on CCTV. They mean nothing, they go nowhere. They are the killer perfectly covering his tracks, they are red herrings, they are ghosts placed in the machine to keep the police occupied. Like the ghosts Clayton placed in my machine, through the mouth of Dr Brady.

These deaths may look random, and perhaps some of them owed something to chance, but they had been planned well in advance. The killer knew what he was doing, knew when each murder was going to be committed, must have had an intricate plan mapped out. This wasn't him getting up in the morning, rifling through his Dylan albums and thinking, oh, OK, I'll do this one today.

So, yes, I wonder what would've been next. And who was the lucky bastard who escaped?

And the other thing. Should I be feeling guilty about not working it out earlier? If I had done, fewer people would have died.

Some time after eleven, Taylor stops at my desk, hands thrust deep into his pockets. Glances round the station.

'What are you doing?' he asks.

'Chasing up Clayton's backstory. Is it possible he was actually involved in any of those murders he described to Brady, or is he taunting? And if it's the latter, how in the name of fuck did he manage to find all that shit out?'

'Getting anywhere?'

'Believe it or not... no. I'm learning things I'd forgotten, but nothing about Clayton. This is just... what was that Woody Allen movie... *Zelig*, it's Woody Allen in *Zelig*. The guy has placed himself at the centre of the action, even though he wasn't there. Clever, clever bastard. And... well, I don't know. He knows so much about me, I can't begin to wonder where the Hell this is going to end up.'

'You think he got the doctor to seduce you, and then tell you this stuff, specifically yesterday afternoon?'

Puff out my cheeks, stare straight ahead.

'Where are we going to go with it, that's the question?' I say, looking back at him.

'Yep,' says Taylor. 'This is, indeed, the damned question. One of them, at least.'

He starts to turn, then says, 'Well, keep at it for now. Before we go anywhere with this I'd like to get right down to the bottom layer of it. Write me a report. Everything he said to the doc, how it ties in with your own experience, where he was and what he was doing at the time of each of the crimes.'

He starts walking away, then stops and turns back.

'And look... look, you know we're not supposed to be on this at all anymore. Do this thing, send the report over, and then we're going to leave it to the boys over in Dalmarnock. I'm going to need you to look at–'

'Sure,' I say, cutting him off. 'I'll give Ramsay a shout, see what's happening.'

'Thanks, Tom.'

And off he goes. I watch him for a second, and then turn back to the computer screen, which has powered down during my brief chat with Taylor.

A blank screen, nothing to be learned. That there, my friend, is an actual fucking metaphor if ever there was one.

* * *

Sitting in the canteen eating a ham and cheese panini, drinking a Coke Zero and eating a packet of sea salt and blood-of-my-enemies vinegar crisps. I'm not celebrating the fact we prevented further death after Sunday – because we probably should've worked it out more quickly – but I've yet to beat myself up about being so late to arrive at the party.

There's plenty of time for that. Maybe I need to read some misery stories from the families of the victims.

'Hey.'

Look up, and here comes my sergeant-at-arms, Eileen Harrison, sitting down opposite, a bowl of pasta and a bottle of water. Having not seen her previously today, I notice she's dyed her hair. The same blonde as before, but now the colour is richer, the roots lightened.

'Hair,' I say, approvingly.

She smiles and settles into the seat, pours water into a glass, and immediately starts twiddling spaghetti around her fork.

'What happened to your hand?' she asks.

'Broke a wine glass.'

'Drunk, or fit of rage?'

'Neither. Slumping in pathetic fashion, head down, onto the table while listening to Bob Dylan.'

'So Dylan is to blame for another injury?'

'It's fine. I won't be contacting his lawyers. Good day?'

'Hmm…,' she says, continuing to eat pasta. 'Got a woman who says her son has been slowly poisoning her by giving her thick cut marmalade.'

She sucks up a few strands of spaghetti which hang from her lips, briefly making her look like the Ood from Dr Who.

'She thinks thick cut marmalade is poisonous?'

'Yes. It's dangerous to eat too much of the skin, she says. Her son knows this, so is intentionally feeding it to her.'

'Why doesn't she just refuse to eat it?'

'He forces her.'

'And thin cut marmalade would be OK?'

'Yes.'

'OK. Good luck with that one.'

'Well, unsurprisingly it looks like she's on the Alzheimer's scale, and I've spoken to the doctor to confirm it. But on the other hand…'

'Oh, nice, there's another hand. Go on.'

More pasta, more sucking up of spaghetti strands. Try not to watch. She chews, dabs her chin with a napkin, although she didn't need to.

'On the other hand,' she continues, 'the doctor has admitted her health is on the decline and he can't explain it. And this is coupled with the fact the son is, well… he comes across as a bit of a cunt.'

'Lovely.'

'So, I'm wondering, you know… Maybe he's not poisoning her with thick cut marmalade at all.'

'Maybe he's poisoning her with something else?'

'Yes. And the marmalade's a distraction.'

That's the kind of thing that happens. Well, it's the kind of thing that happens in a certain kind of crime fiction narrative. I don't know if it ever happens in real life.

'I wondered if you wanted to speak to him?' she says, before sticking another huge forkful of pasta in her mouth.

'You in a hurry?'

'Absolutely stacked this afternoon,' she says, 'and I need to go down to Rutherglen for a thing. So what d'you think? I reckon it requires some detective work. Thought of you.'

Funny.

'Sure. Bring it to me when you've got the time. I'll speak to the son. Cunts are my specialty.'

40

Got nowhere further with Clayton, of course. Feel like I should be round there, pounding the fuck out of him, or shooting him, or doing something. Anything. Instead, Taylor told me to take a step back, and now I'm doing this. I'm here. I'm having to listen to this level of bullshit.

'Can I ask what the fuck this is?' says the Cunt.

'Ian! Show some respect.'

'Mum, shut the fuck up.'

'Don't you talk to me like–'

'If the fucking polis are coming into our house, then they can fucking expect what's coming to them.'

'I asked them here!'

'Aye, well, you should be in a fucking home. They can come and see you there.'

She turns to me.

'I'm really sorry, officer.'

I give her the don't-worry-about-it hand.

'Aye, you'll be sorry soon enough, mum. You, get the fuck out the house,' he says to me, then adds, 'unless you've got a warrant.'

A warrant. He says it because it's the kind of thing people say on the TV. As it happens, I do have a warrant in my pocket, the paperwork completed by my good friend Sgt Harrison, which was a bonus, as I hate paperwork, but she knew what she had to do to get me to take on the job. However, I don't need it yet.

'Who owns the house?' I say to him.

'Fuck off.'

'I do,' says the mum.

'I thought I told you to shut the fuck up?'

'The owner of the house, the principal named resident of the house, the bill payer, invited me in,' I say. 'And so I came in. If you want to call the police to get them to come and remove me, then you're welcome.'

'Fuck you, you pious cunt.'

I hold his gaze – just a regulation, *zip it, you useless, dumbass piece of shit* look – and then turn back to Mrs Thornwood.

'Why d'you think your son is poisoning you with marmalade?' I ask.

'Fuck, here we go,' comes from the cheap seats.

'It's the only thing I eat every day. Toast and marmalade, every morning for breakfast. And every day, every single day, I get twinges in my stomach within an hour or two of eating the marmalade...'

'Jesus suffering fuck...'

'... and every day I feel worse. I'm dying, Detective Sgt Hutton, I can feel it. As sure as you're sitting in front of me now.'

'We're all dying,' chips in the moron, 'you're just not doing it fast enough.'

'And you've been to the doctor to make sure it's nothing else, like an ulcer or...'

'I'm fine, I'm fine,' she says. 'Right as rain until this started.'

'When did it start?'

'When he got that new marmalade.'

The idiot snorts.

'You're aware my colleague took the marmalade away with her already?' I ask.

'Yes.'

'We've had it checked. It's fine,' I say. 'There's nothing in the marmalade.'

He laughs this time.

'What?' she says. 'What d'you mean there's nothing in it? There are huge chunks of skin, huge thick things.'

'Yes, there are, but they're not actually poisonous.'

'Aye, but I don't like them.'

'Jesus suffering fuck.'

'Maybe not, Mrs Thornwood, but that in itself isn't going to make you ill.'

'Well, what is then?'

'Fuck's sake...'

Beginning to doubt my decision to let this clown stay in here while we talked, but I wanted to see his reactions. Obviously I'm wondering if anything will happen when I leave, but I imagine they live in this perpetual state of ill-humour and abuse, regardless of whether the police have just been round.

We see this all the time, and of course there's nothing we can do. She probably needs him here for various things, and he's just waiting for her to die. No excuse to be the way he is, but some people are like this. We're here to make sure laws aren't broken, not to force them to be nice to their parents.

'You said marmalade is the only thing you have every day,' I say.

'Aye.'

'You said you have it on toast.'

'Aye.

'So you have toast every day as well.'

The arsehole barks out a laugh, the mum tuts.

'Aye, but the bread hasn't changed. It's still the same plain loaf.'

'And there must be butter on the toast.'

'Aye, but the butter's the same.'

'Jesus...'

'And you drink tea, there's milk in the tea, there's sugar in the tea.'

'Aye, aye.'

She stares off to the side with a quizzical look. Starting to think it through. I'm also beginning to think Sgt Harrison was just trying to get rid of some work. It's not like there's a great deal of detecting to do. Then again, if we're talking about attempted murder, then it's good the detective branch is in early.

'So,' I say, 'is there anything else you have every day, d'you think? So far there's toast, butter, tea, milk, sugar…'

'Coffee,' she says. 'I have my Nescafe.'

'D'you want to check her fucking bog roll 'n' all? I could have poisoned the fucking Andrex and the poison's being ingested through her arse.'

There's a thought. I wonder if anyone's ever done that before? Probably in a crime novel, although I'm not entirely sure what type. Some sort of rectal-death sub genre, popular with elderly ladies.

'What d'you put in the Nescafe?' I ask. 'Milk and sugar?'

'Sweeteners,' she says. 'And milk, of course. I heat the milk up.'

'Jesus, I've heard enough of this.'

I finally turn and look at the Cunt. He's been defensive from the off, but the more I ask, the worse he's getting. Still not sure I'm prepared to accept this clown is capable of slowly poisoning his mother, but then you can learn to do anything on the Internet.

'Tell you what I'm going to do, Mrs Thornwood. I'm going to take away all your basic foodstuffs…'

'No' you're fucking no'!'

'But what'll I do for a cup of tea?'

'Within the hour I'll get someone round here with replacements for everything I've taken away. They'll be newly bought from the shops, so you'll be sure they're fine. Is that all right?'

She's not looking like she thinks this is all right.

'You're not fucking taking anything, by the way.'

I turn and give the son a look, then turn back to his mother.

'There's really no need to worry, Mrs Thornwood. I'll get all your food checked, and very soon someone from the Police Service will be round with replacements. You'll be fine for tea and toast and coffee, and you'll know you don't need to worry about whether or not they're poisoning you…'

'You're taking nothing.'

I take the piece of paper out of my pocket, two pages of A4 folded in thirds. I mean, it could be a list of movie stars I want to shag for all he knows, but he straight away accepts the threat as it's intended, and doesn't even ask to see what's written. And then, surprise, surprise, he's on his feet and heading for the kitchen.

I look at Mrs Thornwood, giving the lad a moment to continue to be stupid.

'What's the matter?' she says.

'We're fine,' I say. 'I just need to leave you briefly.'

'Oh, all right. The toilet's upstairs on the left.'

I lean forward and pat her hand, then walk into the kitchen. And there he is, the next winner of British Master Criminal's Got Talent, tipping the contents of the bag of sugar into the sink, the tap already running. I walk up slowly behind him – he doesn't even seem to think I'd be coming – snatch the bag off him, turn off the tap, and step back.

He turns quickly, looking like he's about to go on the offensive.

'How far d'you want to take it?' I say.

He hesitates. You see the calculation running through their heads so often. Do they want to take the chance of adding police assault to the list? In this case, to be honest, he might as well. If he really is poisoning his mum, the daft bastard is facing attempted murder. Police assault won't really up the stakes that much more. He might as well go for it, but he's too stupid I reckon.

Maybe he thinks he can't take me. That would be odd.

I stuff the bag into my jacket pocket. Before he'd walked out of the sitting room I'd been about to give him the if-anything-happens-to-your-mum speech, but now there's no point.

Now, however, we get into the question of whether or not she's capable of looking after herself. Within a few minutes she'll be facing the fact that, despite their dysfunctional relationship and despite believing he was trying to kill her, she won't actually want him to go, because she'll be on her own and won't know what to do.

'Come on, Moriarty, back into the sitting room. I need to make some calls.'

'Fucker,' he mutters, and I let him walk past me, wary of him growing a pair and deciding to lash out. 'I'm calling my fucking lawyer.'

'You've got a lawyer?'

He pauses in the doorway, doesn't turn, then walks on through to the sitting room.

Trying to poison his mum using the sugar she put in her tea? Yep, Harrison was right. The guy's a cunt.

41

Walk back into the office just after six, having conducted further interviews with the lead suspect in The Case Of The Poisoned Sugar. Pause for a second by my desk, look around the office. Not much activity. Don't see Harrison. Taylor's door is closed, Morrow, who must have come back from Riverside, in with him.

Just about to insert myself in position when Taylor catches my eye and indicates for me to join them. I walk through and close the door behind me.

I look at them both expectantly, then Taylor indicates for Morrow to speak.

Taylor is behind his desk, while Morrow is standing by the window, like he's taking his turn to get a view of the carpark. Have a sudden notion this is Morrow in my place, Taylor's new sidekick. And why not? He'd make Taylor's life a damn sight easier.

Time for me to be leaving, I suddenly think, like the realisation is another nail in the coffin.

'Nothing to report,' he says.

'Ah,' I say, 'thought maybe you might have got somewhere.'

'Nah. There's a lot of industry, but for now they're just churning out pink elephants. Can't say it's a waste of time, because obviously it has to be done, but so far...,' and he lets the sentence go.

'White elephant,' says Taylor. 'Not pink.'

'Are you sure?'

Taylor gives him the look. See? That's the look he usually saves for me. It's as though he's already moving on, even though the moving on has so far only been taking place in my head.

'Anyway, a lot of people are coming up with ideas, it results in a lot of work, and so far…nothing…'

'Anyone talking about Clayton?' I ask.

Morrow holds my gaze for a second, looks at Taylor, I follow, Taylor nods at him, and so I look back expectantly. Sounds like someone's been talking.

'DCI Collins took me into his office this morning,' he begins, 'and we talked about Clayton for an hour. In fact, we talked about you for an hour mostly. He wanted my take on it all, on why you might have been getting sent the e-mails, on what I knew about Clayton, whether I thought it really was going to have been him who sent them…'

He stops talking, although his tone suggests there's more to be said. However, he really has just stopped, then when I raise my eyebrows at him, he shrugs.

'It's not unreasonable,' I say, 'so I don't mind you talking about me. I don't even care what you said. Is someone taking it on as a result?'

'Hard to say at this stage. The DCI didn't want *me* taking it on, that's for sure. As to whether he's given it to someone else… He certainly sounded sceptical about you're level of involvement, and seemed to want to think the e-mails were directed at the station, and therefore at the Police Service as a whole, rather than just you.'

'I hope you said that was bullshit?'

'I queried why anyone would randomly pick you out of everyone in the Police Service. However, it was like… his attitude was almost like someone seeing a ghost, or something inexplicable occurring. There's no rational explanation, or you don't like the only explanation there is, so you choose to park it to one side and pursue a completely different line of inquiry. One based on something more concrete, or at least, more palatable. That's the impression I got, but it's not to say he's definitely dropped the ball.'

Turns to Taylor – they've obviously already had this conversation – looks back to me.

'That's all I've got,' he says. 'Thought it might be of use, but otherwise, you know, everyone over there is just pissing in the wind.'

Taylor gestures to acknowledge Morrow is doing all he can. Long sigh.

Odd phrase, pissing in the wind. Usually it's used to refer to doing something that's not getting anywhere. But when you piss, all you're trying to do is void your bladder. Pissing into the wind achieves the objective just as well as pissing into a toilet. So it's not that it doesn't achieve anything; it achieves what you're looking for, but just causes unnecessary mess. So, for example, if you see someone scrambling eggs with their fingers, that might be a situation where you could say, you're pissing in the wind there, mate. Not so much this kind of getting-nowhere situation.

I notice Taylor watching me, and manage to snap out of it. He's going to say something, and then dismisses it, turns back to Morrow.

'Thanks,' he says, indicating with a head movement for him to leave. Morrow nods, turns, and walks past me out the door, closing it again behind him.

Taylor sits in silence again, elbow on the desk, rubbing his right eye. Other hand starts to drum.

'You were working a different case this afternoon?' he asks.

'Attempted murder. Investigation, proof, and confession ultimately all came within about three minutes of each other. It'll take the social services longer to sort out the leftovers.'

He taps his fingers. I know there's further conversation about Clayton to come, but will leave it to him to start it off.

'OK, back to the more pressing matter,' he says. 'If they're going to be ignoring Clayton... We'll do what we can until such times as told otherwise. I'm interested in this doctor of yours. Do some more digging. Find out if she's telling the truth about this BMA investigation.

Doesn't sound right, does it?'

'You mean, saying she had a sex addiction is almost like something she made up just for my benefit?'

'That, Sergeant, is exactly what I'm saying.'

Can't argue. I more or less thought the same thing as soon as she said it. At the time, however, I was happy to believe.

He glances at the clock. 'Make a start this evening, but don't work it too late. Try and have something together by tomorrow lunchtime…'

'Right,' I say, and I'm out the office.

* * *

An hour later I'm sitting in the bright shining offices of the practice run by EmMed International in the West End, waiting to be summoned for a chat with a Dr Cairns, the head of the medical practice which hosts our Dr Brady.

Dr Cairns is a woman in her late sixties, I'd say, judging from the photograph, with an air of ball-busting confidence about her. I'm standing with my hands in my pockets, slouching more than likely, looking down on the street below, when the door to the small, antiseptic waiting room opens, and I get the call.

The squirt from two days ago is still here, regarding me warily as he collects me, then leads me along the short corridor. He opens the door into Cairns's office, gives me the final disdainful look with which we police are so familiar – it's a bit like the Queen thinking everywhere smells of fresh paint – and I walk in to the small office of the doctor in charge. She looks up from a file, and offers me the seat across from her wooden, leather-topped desk.

The place has a nice sense of order, the smell of old books, shelves of them on either side. From the large windows you can see the university, although she sits with her back to the view. Her guests get the privilege. There are three family photographs on the desk, one single one of the husband, plus two different families of five.

'Sgt Hutton,' she says. 'You wanted to speak about Dr Brady?'

'Yes,' I say, settling into the seat. Haven't been offered a cup of tea or, indeed, any alcohol. Must be pushed for cash. 'I realise you won't be able to tell me much, but she's involved in a case we're working on at the moment and–'

'Not the Bob Dylan Murders?' she says.

There is what the ancients would have described as a pregnant pause.

'The what?' I finally say.

'I saw you on the news, Sergeant.'

'I never referred to them as the Bob Dylan Murders.'

'No,' and there's a nice smile on her face, 'I know you didn't. But that's what they are, even if no one's saying it.'

'How... I mean...'

She laughs lightly.

'I'm a Dylan fan, as are you, I daresay.' I nod, but it's only confirming something she was absolutely sure of in any case. 'Every time I hear about a suicide on the railway lines, I always think, ah, yes, blood on the tracks. Thought the same last week, of course. And then, over the week as these murders started piling up... I don't know, something just clicked.'

Fuck. She got there faster than we did. If I'd thought blood on the tracks right away, this thing could have been over by Wednesday. This here is a real Dylan fan. Taylor and I look like rank amateurs beside her.

'Then when you started your press conference with the words *before the flood*, well....,' and she makes a small hand gesture to complete the sentence.

'You haven't seen it mentioned elsewhere?'

'No,' she says. 'I thought someone would've picked up on it. That did make me wonder if it was just me, but it seems you've confirmed it.'

'We can't have....,' and I just let the sentence go.

'You don't want the media talking about the Bob Dylan murders?' she says. 'Don't worry, Sergeant, your secret's safe with me. But someone, I would think, will work it out eventually.'

'I expect so.'

'So, what did you have? Someone killing people after the manner of Mr Dylan's album titles, and you had to work this out? Your two or three mentions in your otherwise seemingly irrelevant press conference were your way of letting the killer know you'd made the connection?'

Jesus, she's seen right through us.

'You don't want to come and work for the police?' I say, and she laughs.

'I might be of some use if all the crimes you investigated had a Bob Dylan angle, but otherwise, I think my talents better serve me here.'

'You must have seen him in concert,' I say.

'Five or six times.'

I look surprised.

'I see. You'll have seen him over a hundred, I'm supposing,' she says.

'Well over.'

'Well, each to their own, Sergeant. I'm old enough to have seen Mr Dylan in his heyday. These days, these fifty or sixty concerts a year he plays that all you younger Dylan junkies overdose on so you can swap stories about how many you've attended, like guys in a bar comparing penis size...,' and she finishes the sentence with a dismissive wave. 'Mr Dylan just ain't what he used to be. I'll keep my memories where they are.'

'You weren't at the Albert Hall in '66? No wait, Manchester? Were you at Manchester?'

In actual, technical terms, this isn't really any different from jumping a witness on the desk, in that the job's equally not getting done, but chatting about Bob at least has a more wholesome feel to it.

'No, but I saw him in Glasgow in between.'

'Shit.'

'Actually he was rather good. I got his autograph too.'

'No way. You still got it?'

I automatically look around the walls of the office, expecting to see the small, framed piece of paper, the legend's scrawl preserved behind glass for future generations.

'Well, it wasn't really possible to keep it.'

She smiles again, and I'm so detached from my detective's brain – largely because I'm sitting here like some sort of brain-dead fanboy, who's lost all sense of reason – I have no idea what she means, so ask the question with a couple of raised eyebrows.

'He signed my thigh,' she says.

'No fucking way,' I say, quickly holding up an apologetic hand at the language.

'It was Mr Dylan, you could hardly be surprised.'

'Holy crap.'

She takes a moment, then looks to the side. I follow her gaze, and find she's looking at the clock sitting on the mantelshelf above the filled-in fireplace.

'Right,' I say. 'You're right. Dr Brady…'

Probably best. I mean, how far away was I there from asking if I could see the actual thigh that was signed by the legend himself? Not very far, to be honest, and if there wasn't such an air of grown up respectability about Cairns, I'd probably still have a go at it.

'Yes,' she says, 'I'm curious how she comes to be involved in these murders. We haven't seen her in over a week, so I do hope she's all right.'

'I saw her yesterday. She was fine. Well, physically she was fine, I'm not sure…' and there the words drift off.

I've come in here to talk about Brady, but it doesn't mean I actually know what I'm going to say, of course. Slightly thrown, not so much by Dylan fandom, but by the fact Cairns is on to us, that she knew what Clayton was thinking even before we did.

'I may not be able to answer all your questions, Sergeant, either ethically or because I just don't know, but please feel free to ask and discuss anything. You can be assured it won't go any further than these walls.'

'Right.'

Take a second, get my head in the right place – like that ever happens – and then, 'How long has Dr Brady worked here?'

'A little over two years. She'd been working in Germany for, I'm not sure how long, I think several years, and she applied for this post while she was still there. She's been with us since she arrived back in Scotland. I do remember her getting in from Frankfurt on a Sunday evening, and starting work on the Monday morning.'

'And she's well remunerated for her work?'

A pause, while she thinks this one over.

'I think her wages here are not really on the table of the discussion, but I do know she was in a very lucrative practice in Frankfurt.'

'Why did she come back?'

'That's a personal matter for Veronica. She left her family behind in Frankfurt. A husband and daughter. I imagine there was some sadness there.'

'Does she see them? You know if she travels to Germany much?'

'I believe so. In fact, I rather presumed that was where she went last week, and that her sudden request for time off work was perhaps as a result of some family crisis, or that some unexpected opportunity had arisen to spend time with her daughter.'

Eyes lowered, thinking this through. Not the time for it, though. Just need to be gathering information, try to put it all together.

'We saw her yesterday, and also on Sunday, so no, she's not in Germany.'

'And she was all right?'

'Like I said, physically, yes.'

'If you could tell me the way in which she might be linked to your murder investigation, I might know better if there is any way in which I could be of help.'

'We have a suspect. The name isn't in the public

domain, at least, not in terms of this investigation, although he is someone who's been involved in police matters before. Michael Clayton.'

Leave a gap to see if the name rings a bell, but there's nothing on her face.

'Dr Brady's story for the past week seems a little thin, and we're not sure about it. But she says she's been seeing Mr Clayton as a client for some time, and she's also been seeing him as a private patient every day for the past week.'

The brow furrows, Cairns leans forward on her elbows.

'I don't know the name, Clayton, but I don't know the names of all the clients we have here at the practice. But that does sound suspicious. Just give me a second.'

She lifts the lid on the laptop that's been sitting, closed, beside her, and I look past her head, out at the spire of the university, while she checks up on the names of Brady's clients.

If this isn't straightforward, if this isn't a simple matter of Clayton having a psychiatrist, then why did Clayton put us on to her? Why would he help us?

Help us? He wasn't helping. He was just using her as a messenger, to further taunt me.

There he goes, tying me up in knots again, and he's not even in the room.

She closes the laptop, head shaking.

'No, there's no Michael Clayton. Is it possible he was using a different name?'

'Yes,' I reply, 'but then, we asked Dr Brady about him, and she didn't react. If he's registered with you under a different name, she at least knows what his real name is, and she didn't mention any other.'

'Well, that makes no sense. Perhaps you were right to come and see me.'

'She also says she's under investigation from the BMA.'

The brow furrows again.

'What for?'

Don't immediately answer, partly because of my own part in this issue, then finally I internally roll an eye or two and get on with it.

'Having sex with her clients.'

Cairns looks surprised, then says, 'Good grief. Which ones?'

'All of them.'

'We are talking about Veronica here?'

'Yes.'

A second while she processes this, then finally the shoulders lift.

'There is definitely something fishy about all of this, Sergeant, I'm afraid. I obviously don't know the level of involvement of your Mr Clayton in these crimes you're investigating, but if he's got Veronica involved, then I urge you to get to the bottom of it with all speed. She has been an asset to this practice, and there has never been the slightest hint of trouble or of an investigation from the BMA.'

We hold the gaze, then her eyes drift to the clock again.

'I think perhaps you have some investigating to do,' she says.

'Yes, you're right. One more thing. You know if Dr Brady has any family in the city, close friends, anybody like that I could speak to?'

'Sorry, Sergeant, she's a good doctor, but we are in fact quite a disparate practice, even though we're all confined in this small, old building. I'm not sure she even has any close relationships with any of the other staff here. I'll ask around in the morning and let you know.'

I push the chair back.

'Thank you, Doctor, you've been very helpful. I must... maybe some day we could meet socially to talk about Bob. I'd love to hear about the concert in '66.'

'Give me a call, Sergeant, you know where to find me.'

42

Back into the office, almost eight by the time I get there. Need to find out about Brady's husband and child back in Germany, but that they exist, and that they're in Frankfurt, is all I've got. Taylor's not in his office, Morrow back at Riverside or has gone home for the evening, the superintendent's door is open, his chair empty.

Check of the watch, wonder how long I'll give it, wonder if it's too late to call Germany. Whatever, it's never too late to speak to someone, but it might just be too late to actually get hold of anyone useful.

I Google the doctor, and it seems odd it's taken any of us two days to do it. And there we are, 763 results (0.447 seconds), and the next hour or so will take care of itself.

* * *

Don't get home until well after eleven. Stopped for a Chinese on the way, lemon and ginger chicken with fried rice, pop it on the table as I walk past, heading for the fridge. Also dived into the off-licence for a vodka and wine top-up.

Found what I was looking for a couple of hours into my late evening stint back in the office, nothing but the duty constables for company. A report in German on a missing child. Dr Brady's missing child. No way that's a coincidence.

I called Germany, everyone I spoke to spoke English, which was a bonus – and naturally, spoke it better than me in a couple of cases – but I was calling late enough our time, and it was obviously an hour later with them, and I didn't get hold of anyone familiar with the case. Alarm clock will be set, and I'll be in early to crack on with it.

Already I've got Clayton kidnapping Brady's daughter, and then making her do stuff under threat to the kid. Why not? It's a theory, and hardly the most outlandish.

Not that it's given me too much enthusiasm for the task ahead. The days of suddenly getting the hint of a clue and thinking, this is it, this is going to drive us forward, are long dead.

Now I've got nothing. I need to get some sleep, and then I can get into it with Taylor in the morning. Maybe he can provide the enthusiasm, but it's hardly any more likely.

And I could just go straight to sleep, but why skip the opportunity for food and alcohol when it's there, regardless of how little it's required, and so here I am, at the table, wine and a glass and a fork. Contemplate putting on the TV, then decide as usual to go for some dear old Bob, trying not to think of Dr Cairns's thigh. *Oh Mercy* tonight. Slow, moody and sorrowful, just in a completely different way to *Shadows In The Night*, recorded back in the day when Bob still had a voice. Ha! Like Bob ever had that much of a voice.

Bite me, ye Bob Dylan fans.

Alcohol and a carry out, the national diet. Seems too late for me to make any other effort. My life is fucked, as good as over, and me, only forty-seven. I tried, I really did, but my one chance at redemption rested in the hands of someone who was killed within a couple of days of me realising what I could have.

And there will be no police redundancy. No pay off, no golden handshake. Stuck here, in this fucking awful job dealing with murderers and halfwits. All I can do is walk off into the sunset, bottle of wine in one hand, vodka tonic in the other.

Still thinking about Dr Brady, even though there's nothing to be done until morning. I didn't understand her, that was the thing. Didn't get her at all. I was blinded by my own lust to start with, I guess, but afterwards, when we were eating lunch, I had nothing. I don't even think she was putting up a wall to try and block my male superpower X-ray vision. She just sat there, talking or not, her mind working in a way I didn't remotely understand.

It'll be the kid. Introduce the kid into it, and it all makes sense.

Pour more wine, shovel more food.

We shovel Chinese carry outs, don't we? All of us. The only way to eat it differently is to use chopsticks, but there's something about eating a Chinese takeaway with chopsticks that just makes you feel like a bit of a dick, even in your own house, even with nobody watching.

The wine works its way quickly to my head. I relax, the tension of another crappy day in the stupid crappy office begins to fade. Another day over, another day in the bag, another day negotiated, another day nearer the grave.

I wonder about Dr Brady, and if she has indeed ever had sex with any of her clients. Has she been lying about everything, or does she keep that kind of thing from the boss upstairs, who once had Bob Dylan sign her thigh? I mean, you would, wouldn't you?

I'm disposed to believe Brady has been lying, but nevertheless, as I sit eating dinner, I imagine her having sex with a variety of clients in her office, male and female, and gradually those clients are replaced in my imagination by me, and I shovel Chinese carry out and fantasise about fucking the woman I had yesterday, on her garden furniture and on her office furniture.

* * *

As it happens, Dr Brady has never fucked anyone in her office. Not in a chair, not on the floor, not on her desk, not at the door... as Dr Seuss might have written, had he ever written a book about a psychiatrist not having sex with her clients.

She sits in her cage, her hands on her knees, her head

239

bowed. She's not looking at Clayton. She's not looking at the television, which has been set up just outside the cage.

Clayton is watching TV, his seat just beyond arm's length of the bars. Perfectly positioned. If she reached out and took a swipe, she would miss him by less than an inch. Not that she thinks about it.

'You should watch,' he says. 'You make a lovely couple.'

He turns the sound up, still not too loud, but loud enough.

The sounds of summer. A back garden. Birds in the trees. Cars in the distance. Two people having sex on a swinging seat and on the grass, in a small, secluded copse.

The couple are filmed from a bedroom window, and from a hidden camera in the trees. The microphone is in the structure of the garden chair. Great sound quality. The film has been edited, so it switches between angles.

The room is filled with the sound of her moaning, and of Thomas Hutton breathing heavily. She is lying back on the grass. He is kneeling between her legs, has hoisted her hips up off the ground, and is fucking her forcefully, the doctor nearing orgasm.

'This is a great position,' says Clayton, his voice slow and analytical, like a scientist dissecting a scene from a nature documentary. 'Your breasts are small, but this displays them beautifully.'

Despite herself she looks up.

'Fuck you,' she mutters bitterly, before quickly looking away.

'I don't know why you're upset,' says Clayton. 'Seriously, you look like you're having the most tremendous fun. As does Sgt Hutton, bless him.'

He smiles, his fingers entwined in his lap. The Dr Brady on the television cries out, trying not to make too much noise, her body juddering, as Hutton presses against her tightly, thrusting into her as far as he can go. The caged Dr Brady hangs her head, determined she won't cry. Determined she won't break in front of this man.

'Now,' he says, turning the sound off, but leaving the video playing, 'I don't wish to upset you, but I think it might be time to bring Sgt Hutton to heel, so I'm going to tell you what we'll do. I rather fancy one of those headlines where they imply that despite having lots of work to do, and a deranged killer to catch, the police are too busy having fun. So we're going to put this video online...'

She gasps, then quickly closes her mouth. There's nothing to be said, nothing to be done. He has dominion, and has already let her know just how pitiless he is. She cannot appeal to his compassion, for he has none.

'Obviously it'd be tremendous if we could put this on YouTube, it's the most wonderful platform, but we have to accept that YouTube just doesn't want this kind of content. Not even something as magnificent as this. So, what we'll do is use a proxy server and set up our own page, we'll get... What am I doing? You don't want to hear the mechanics, do you? You just want to know about the exposure. I mean, don't worry, darling, you look magnificent. Look, look at yourself!'

She doesn't look up. She knows what's happening, despite the sound being off. She knows Hutton has not yet ejaculated, she knows he barely let her finish coming before withdrawing, then thrusting his head between her legs and sucking and licking her, while she was still tender and not ready for it, so that she was spasming and gasping, delirious, the fury of discomfort and pleasure.

'Men are going to love you, women too, if they're not jealous. You look fabulous, darling. Hutton just looks like a brute, but you... you'll be the darling of the talk show circuit...'

'I just want to see Chrissie!'

She says it through gritted teeth, closes her eyes after the exclamation.

Shouldn't have said it. Shouldn't have let him see beneath the mask, let him see how much he was getting to her. And it had sounded so weak. But then, it was hardly a surprise, given the situation.

He stares at her, looking amused, his eyebrow raised, waiting for her to look back.

'Gosh, you really ought to have said. Would you like me to bring her up?'

Now Brady raises her head, the anger and hurt quickly lost to her surprise.

'She's here?' she says. 'Chrissie's in this house?'

Clayton looks surprised by the question.

'Of course! Where did you think she was? How many houses do you think I own?'

'Let me see her.'

Clayton stares, curiously, head tilted to the side.

'Let me see her? What *was* that? Was that an order? I hardly think you're in–'

'I've done everything you asked of me. Everything. Now please, can I see her?'

Eyebrow raised again, this time accompanied by an appreciative look.

'That's better. Much better. I think she might be sleeping though, I doubt she'll like getting woken up at this time.'

'Please…'

'You can see her in the morning. Now, I think it might be time for me to do some work. Things don't post themselves on the Internet, you know.'

'No!'

'There is no 'no', my dear. I've got work to do. If you want to complain, well you can, but then I can be back up here with your daughter's head in a salad bowl in less than a minute, and don't think I wouldn't. Do I need to tell you again what happened to the girl on the railway line?'

He talks through her gasps, the harsh breaths and restrained tears.

'Is everybody cool?' he says.

She leans forward, her hands in her hair, staring at the ground.

'Is everybody cool?' he asks again, his voice harder.

'Yes.' Voice strained.

'Good, good. Right…'

He settles back in the seat, glances at the television. Hutton is still where he was before, the doctor's thighs clenched around his head. Clayton smiles, lifts the television remote and turns it off.

43

'You know this is coming to an end, right?'

Have a strange sensation, just behind my ear. My right ear, I think. It feels sore. There's a pain there to suggest something or someone or some, I don't know, some entity, is stabbing into it. But I can't feel anything. It's a pain I'm familiar with, and the pain is usually accompanied by a sensation of stabbing. But there's no stabbing.

'What?'

There's a crow on my chest. The crow is talking to me. That also seems familiar, yet strange, at the same time.

'This whole thing,' says the crow. 'We're nearly done here.'

'How d'you mean?'

'I don't know, pal, I'm just getting this shit from you. If you don't know what I mean, then how the fuck'm I supposed to know?'

'But things don't just end.'

'Games of sport end,' says the crow.

'What?'

'Apart from baseball. Jesus…'

It feels cold. Why does it feel cold? The ground is damp, and I'm naked. That doesn't make sense either.

'Look, kid, you know things are coming to an end when you choose to end them. That's it. Your choice. And you know what choice you have to make, right?'

I don't answer. Looking straight up, the crow now at the edge of my vision. The branches of the trees are bare, and I can see the low, grey clouds. Looks like rain.

'We understand each other?' asks the crow.

I don't reply. The branches high over my head move

slowly in the chill breeze. There's a small movement in the leaves behind my head, as though something else is approaching from behind. I can't see what it is, but it doesn't bother me. I've got the crow to keep me safe.

And yes, finally, we do understand each other.

* * *

Standing naked in the bathroom, not long out the shower. Dried, teeth cleaned. Looking at myself in the mirror. Don't know how I do it. I mean, get women to sleep with me. Look at it. At that. At that, there, staring back at me. Saggy and ageing, only going to get worse from here on in. Love handles, bit of a paunch, chest going south, not a sign of a muscle anywhere.

Wonder what they think when they get to see me naked. *Is this it? Jesus, didn't realise you were this old? Oh well, too late now, you might as well add me to your list.*

Introspection interrupted by the phone. Stare at myself for another few moments, then walk through to the bedroom, lift the phone. Ramsay or Taylor. No one else calls this early in the morning.

'Sergeant, good morning,' says Ramsay.

'Stuart,' I say. 'Somebody dead?'

'You need to look on the Internet,' he says. 'Thought I should give you a heads up.'

'What's happening on the Internet?'

'Someone posted video of you having sex.'

Weirdly it doesn't immediately fill me with horror. Resignation more. I mean, it was bound to happen some time. And I hardly need to be too embarrassed walking into the office. Plenty of the women in there have seen me having sex in the flesh, never mind on video.

'Where?'

'Where did they post it, or where are you having sex?'

'The latter.'

'In a garden, on the grass and on a double swing seat.'

245

Fuck. Well, that figures.

On the plus side, Dr Brady is not a known witness, nor known to be involved in the case at all. Even the suits in Glasgow didn't know I was speaking to her. My Dylan-thigh-signature doctor aside, the only person really likely to be perturbed will be Taylor, and since he more or less ordered me to sleep with her, he's not really in a position to say anything.

That's just my natural positivity coming out there.

'OK, I'll take a look before I come in. Where do I find it?'

'Oh, you'll find it,' he says, very unhelpfully, and then hangs up.

Mutter 'bollocks' at the room, then into the bathroom. Deodorant, last glance in the mirror. Notice the stirring of my penis at the mention that the wee fella is now some sort of celebrity, roll my eyes at my own cock – as though it does genuinely have a life of its own – then back into the bedroom to get dressed.

Over breakfast of coffee and toast and orange juice and water, I find Ramsay was not lying. The video is very, very easy to find. Plenty of people are talking about it, and sure enough, plenty of the press are already taking the moral high ground, for all the world like none of them ever had sex in their entire lives.

There is, fortunately, no mention of the doctor, no mention of any involvement she might have with Clayton or our investigation. The perspective is entirely about, and entirely aimed at, me. Some expert somewhere has decided what the time is from the position of the shadows in the garden, and that it must have been filmed on Monday, (which it was), therefore what was I doing having sex at that time on a working day when there were so many murders to solve?

I start watching the video. Twenty-three minutes of nicely edited porn. It's not like I think I look great, but we make a good couple. It'll play well on Pornhub if it ever gets that far.

At some point while watching it, and getting turned on again, it suddenly occurs to me my family will be waking up to this too. Peggy, well, that's all right. She'll roll her eyes and wonder quite how we managed to last as long as we did together. But it's the kids. Last week of school. Both of them will be walking into the crucible of the playground.

Fuck.

The thought of it has the acute scythe of depression swinging down upon me, and I sit back. Almost put the video off, but I need to watch it all. I need to know what's up there, I need to see if there was any message left for me.

The video runs its course, beautifully executed, right to its conclusion. Finishes with a bang. And there's no obvious message, except the video itself.

Michael Clayton is in complete control. He even controls when I have sex, and he has cameras on hand to prove it.

The sexual excitement is long gone. Get up from the table and stand at the window, looking down on the drab street below. A dull morning, the heat of the start of the week having disappeared.

Wondering if I should call Peggy, and realise eventually my hesitation is because I don't want to make the call, not because there's a reason not to make it. Lift the phone.

'Hey,' I say.

'You sound terrible,' she says.

'Yeah. Look, I...'

'We know already.'

I don't say anything. There you are. Even they know. Everybody will know.

'Andy showed it to me... You've put weight on.'

'Are they all right going to school?'

'They're tough enough to take it,' she says, then adds, 'You didn't want to check for cameras?'

Not a lot to say to that. Almost throw in that it could

have happened to anybody, because it really could have happened to anybody. The thing I did wrong, which was sleep with someone we were interviewing in the course of the investigation, she doesn't know. Nobody will know. But *it could have happened to anybody* isn't worth saying. Because it didn't happen to anybody. It happened to me.

'Tell them I'm sorry,' I say.

She doesn't immediately say anything and I hang up.

Feel... wretched. That's the word. Stupid and wretched.

Phone in my pocket, jacket and shoes on and out the door.

44

Start thinking about it again on the way in. Killing him. Killing Clayton. Taking myself out as I go. Make sure the life insurance policy is all right before I do it – and I took it out a couple of years ago, so putting a bullet in my own head shouldn't nullify it – and then finish the two of us off in one go.

Decide to drive in. Not sure if there will be media hanging around the station, and I hate the thought of walking through them, but in the end there's no one there. They're much slower these days. Or, I guess I'm not interesting enough. If they had footage of Gwyneth Paltrow fucking Jennifer Lawrence they'd be quick enough off the mark.

Walk into the open-plan, go straight to Taylor's office, getting a wolf whistle or two on my way. Catch Morrow's eye, and he gives me a rueful, sympathetic look. Close the door, stand and await judgement.

Taylor hasn't even looked at me yet. Lays down his pen, settles back in his seat.

'You're a walking suspension-waiting-to-happen, aren't you?'

He sounds tired. Exasperated. The voice of a man who's seen enough, or of a parent who's seen enough.

I'd been sort of constructing my defence on the way over here. How exactly was it Taylor thought he could suspend me for this? Hadn't I more or less been following his orders?

The thoughts vanish, now that I'm standing in front of him. If I'd been going to do something unorthodox, or something veering dramatically from the standard police officer's investigative playbook, then he didn't want to know about it, and he certainly didn't want anyone else to know about it. It was up to me to make sure something like this didn't happen.

'It's not like I'm sitting here blowing sunshine up my own arse about my part in it, but–'

'Don't,' I say. 'I know you gave me some sort of green light to do anything to get her to talk, but I shouldn't have just walked in to this. I mean, with the Dylan thing... seriously, this person, Clayton, it must be Clayton, is out to get me. Me. It's about me. And he's owning me. I should be being careful, yet, as ever, I couldn't help thinking with my dick.'

He holds my gaze but doesn't dissent. Doesn't stop me. Does me the favour, at least, of not actually agreeing with me, but I'm not wrong.

'You need to go,' he says. 'I'm not, just yet, suspending you from duty, but you need to get out before Connor arrives.'

Glances at the clock, turns back.

'I don't care what you do today, but probably best if it's not related to the investigation. And whatever it is, don't go anywhere near Clayton or Brady. Go and play golf, go for a walk in the hills, go to fucking Millport and eat a snowball in the Ritz for all I care, just don't touch this.'

Hands in pockets, walk to the window, my back turned to him. Stand there in silence for a certain amount of time, something I quite lose track of. Cars arrive, one by one. Ablett and Jones. Milburn. I think her name is Milburn.

It suddenly strikes me that perhaps I've said my goodbyes. Not many to make, but I've done the round. I called Peggy to apologise. The kids won't care I never actually spoke to them. In fact, they wouldn't have wanted to. I visited the old church for the last time at the weekend. I paid my respects to Philo last week, and I know she won't want me going back. Now Taylor is telling me to go. One of these times he sends me packing from his office has to be the last. Perhaps this is it.

Maybe, when he told me to go to Millport for the day, what he really meant was go and finish this. Maybe when he expressly told me not to go after Clayton, he meant go after Clayton. It doesn't matter anyway, doesn't matter what he meant. I'm going. Clayton is out to get me, and he's going to be out there until I do something about him.

And he's beaten me, I'll give him that. I should be able to get him through regular police investigative channels, but I can't. I need to do something else. Go after him in a different way. And if, as a result, I get taken down too, well that's just how it's going to have to be.

'I'm sorry,' I say.

Last thing on the list. Apologise to Taylor. And he may not pick up on it, but I'm not just apologising for this. There are so many things over the past few years. Beyond counting.

He doesn't immediately respond, and I don't turn. Not sure how long I've been standing here. Maybe he got up and walked out at some point. Then finally there's the sound of his chair getting pushed back and then he's standing beside me, and here we are again, two middle-aged fuckers looking down on a dull carpark together.

At that moment, Gostkowski walks out and stands still, looking around. Taking in the day. Then she lights up her smoke, and folds her arms.

There's such an air of finality I wonder if he's going to come out with some sort of male bonding shit, but when he finally speaks, while his voice is infected with the same weight of despondency, he plays it as straight as I might have expected.

'Hand everything you've got over to Morrow before you go. He'll be heading over to Dalmarnock in about half an hour.'

I don't speak.

'Where are you anyway?' he asks.

'I am… closing in,' I find myself saying, and then can't stop the laugh.

The laughter goes, we don't look at each other. Both watching Gostkowski, although I daresay I see her through quite different eyes than the boss.

'The doctor has an ex-husband and a daughter who live in Germany. Frankfurt. Eleven days ago the daughter disappeared.'

I don't turn, but feel Taylor's eyes on me.

'Didn't manage to get hold of anyone in Frankfurt last night, but I don't doubt for a second Clayton took the girl.'

'Fuck,' mutters Taylor.

'Yeah. Fuck. The press would love to get hold of that angle. Missing kid, they love that shit.'

'Anything else?'

'She was lying about the suspension and being under investigation from the BMA. She's a good doctor, there've been no problems. I don't have all the proof, but I believe what we have here is Clayton using Brady's daughter against her. All part of the game. The trap.'

'Crap,' he mutters.

He steps away from the window. Stands in the middle of the small room, right hand worrying his chin, then, having gone through the available options, sits back at his desk.

'You need to leave,' he says, 'but give *me* everything you've got. I'll pass on to Morrow what I think he needs. If you have to write it up, go and do it now. Get on with it before Con–'

The door opens.

'Jesus fucking Christ!' shouts Connor, letting rip before even slamming the door behind him.

Well, that changes the mood in the room.

'Sir,' says Taylor, his voice steady. 'The Sergeant is just going to write up what–'

'I want you out the building,' says Connor, looking at me, ignoring Taylor.

While I've got nothing to say to the pompous prick, I don't immediately scurry to the door either. And though I say pompous prick – because it's not like he isn't one – I have to say that in this he has a point. I should be out the damn door, for all sorts of reasons.

'I need the Sergeant to write up where he's got to in the investigation,' says Taylor. Still no urgency in his voice, no attempt to rise and meet Connor at whatever pitch he's talking.

'What are you writing up?' asks Connor, still looking at me, still largely ignoring the boss.

'I met with the head of Clayton's psychiatrist's practice yesterday evening,' I say.

'Clayton! What the fuck? Seriously, Sergeant, you are going to very quickly get the fuck out of this station. I don't want to hear about Clayton, I don't want anyone talking to him, I never want to hear about that fucking man again. Get out! Get out!'

His voice is near a scream by the time he's finished. Being spoken to in a way maybe only one of my wives has ever spoken to me before. I'd deserved it then too. And while I took it from her, I don't feel like I want to take it from this dickhead. Especially when he's basically telling us to never speak of the perpetrator of the crimes we're investigating.

I don't move. His face is a mass of agitation, veins strained in his neck, fists clenching.

'Sergeant,' says Taylor, playing his own role in this little office drama, 'you need to do what the Superintendent says. I know who you spoke to, I can chase it up. You need to get out.'

'Get out!' spits Connor, like some weird, hissing, expectorating echo.

Jesus, I could just headbutt that cunt right now.

I stand my ground. I haven't moved an inch, or clenched so much as a fist or a jaw muscle. Just standing here, waiting my time.

I've been wrapping it all up, haven't I? Bringing everything to a conclusion. That's how it seems. Why not go out in a blaze of glory? Headbutt the superfucktard, spend a short period in a cell, leave with my head held low, then go and see Clayton, kill us both.

Who'd miss me?

I know I'm not physically bristling, but I can feel it rising inside me. The urge. I can feel the urge. I want to take this fucker out on my way past.

'Fuck,' mutters Taylor, and I guess the boss, having my back as ever, can read my thoughts. He's up and out his chair, he gets to the door, and he stands there, door held open, and now in the confined space of his office, Connor is pushed back a little, and Taylor is between us.

'Go, Sergeant, I'll give you a call later.'

Another few seconds, but there's nothing for it now. Now, in order to get to Connor, I'd need to fight my way past Taylor, and an ugly and unfortunate brawl would ensue, when what's required is a clean-cut headbutt, leading to an instant felling of the tree of authority.

And so, finally, when I move, it is quick and decisive and I just get it over with. ID card out the pocket, toss it onto Taylor's desk, then out the door without looking at either of them.

The open-plan has been quiet, waiting to see how it would play out, but I ignore them, the uncomfortable silence of the room, and soon enough I'm down the stairs and on my way.

45

So I'm ready to combust. Consumed by rage. Bursting, fizzing, hissing, anger spitting from me, feeling like my brain could explode out of my head in a bloody, fucked up, bitter, putrid eruption. I could lay into that cunt. Headbutt him and kick him, rip his fucking face apart, tear his flesh, crush his throat. I could take on fifty Connors, I could run headlong into the fucking orc horde at Helm's Deep, I could charge into a fucking terrorist training seminar on blowing yourself to fuck and take on every one of those fucked up, stupid fucking arsehole motherfucking murdering bastards.

And here I am. Sitting in a car in a carpark. And all I can do is put the car in first and wait for the gate to open.

Tightly gripping the steering wheel, knuckles white, I drive round the corner, managing not to wheelspin and not to angrily throw the rear of the car out, then park in a side street, out of view of the office.

And then, in the quiet surroundings of a small street in Cambuslang, with no one watching, and without even taking off my seatbelt, I let the rage spew forth.

* * *

Hard to break the inside of a car. Throat sore, fists sore. Maybe I broke a bone in the knuckle of my right hand punching the windscreen. Maybe, if I wasn't such a pussy, I would've broken the windscreen. Can you break a windscreen by punching it? I expect Dwayne Johnson could. Or, at least, he could in a movie. I'd have taken him on then, 'n' all, though things might not have ended well.

As it is, how did it end? The anger evaporated into the car and on out, into space. And I was left, sitting there, spent and hoarse and sore about the hands and fingers. The car survived the onslaught.

And now I drive home. Drained. Empty. Fingers tentatively gripping the steering wheel. The anger, the spirit, the fight, all of it, has been spent. Spat out, twisted and ugly and unpleasant, vomited into the ether, and now there's nothing left.

There are a hundred places to go, but I can't think. For now I just need to get back to the safe haven of my old sitting room, the place where fifty per cent of the sitcom takes place. Where I can sit in silence, a drink in my right hand, and stare at an indistinct spot on the wall. Not even Bob, not even the melancholic *Shadows In The Night*. Because I don't feel melancholic. I just feel nothing.

My phone pings as I'm driving, the sound of it fills the void for those brief few moments, but I don't pick it up.

Go through the motions. Changing gear, accelerating, braking, stopping at lights, foot down, clutch, automatic movements. Park, in the front door, up the stairs, open the door, into the house.

Stand in the silence of the sitting room. Aware the room smells stale. Late nights and cigarettes and alcohol. Open the window, look down at the street below.

Where is there to go from here?

There's one person standing in front of me, and it's not Connor. I may have burst my balls in rage at him, but he's not the problem. Connor is an insignificance.

Clayton. It's all about Clayton. So, when I leave here, when I can finally pluck up the whatever-it-takes to go and do something other than stand staring at the street below, there will only be one place to go. There will only be one thing to do.

Clayton has to die. That's all.

No one counts the seconds. No idea how long I stand here. Cars pass beneath me, a few pedestrians. There are people I recognise scuttling by, on the way to work, or on the way home from the graveyard shift.

The phone pings again, the noise muffled in my pocket. Turn finally, look into the kitchen at the digital clock on the cooker. 09:27.

It's never too early for vodka and tonic. Into the kitchen, large glass, lots of ice, lots of vodka, no lemon to hand, fill the rest of the glass with tonic, first taste of the day, a long swallow, and it's sharp and cold and bitter, and I stand there, glass in hand, feeling nothing, just me and the emptiness and the alcohol. The alcohol? The booze. It's booze. When you're drinking for the relief of it at 09:30 in the morning, you're boozing.

Finally take the phone from my pocket. Both messages from Taylor. First one:

Write your report, have it in by 09:45. Leave town. I'll be in touch.

The second:

Sergeant?

A moment, and then I write the reply.

I'm on it.

Grab the laptop, sit down at the table, another long drink, open up Word and start typing, my hand moving to the glass, the glass to my mouth, slowly, metronomically, almost once every sentence.

* * *

Late morning. Sitting on the sofa, looking at the TV. The TV is turned off, I'm on my seventh drink of the morning. The vodka is having the desired effect.

I submitted my brief report – if it could be given so grand a name – saying everything that had to be said, by 09:39, and have since been sitting in silence, only leaving the sofa to top up the drink. At some time after eleven I started eating peanuts. Not good to drink so much vodka at that time in the morning on an empty stomach. (Like it's good to do it on a full Scottish.)

Approaching midday, no obvious sign of intoxication.

Options.

1. Sit here until I'm completely wasted, fall asleep, wake up in the middle of the night feeling like shit, crawl into bed, perhaps having made a stop in the bathroom to throw up. Wake up tomorrow morning. Live. Die. Repeat.

2. Pack a bag, get in the car, head north. Check into a hotel. Do what I'm doing here, but with a view. Probably best to not do it straight away, on the back of seven vodkas.

3. Stop drinking. Sleep it off. Engage the case. Try to find a way to sort this out so that it ends well for me, badly for Clayton. Do the kind of thing a TV detective would do. Pull it out the bag when everyone assumes I'm screwed.

4. Accept I'm screwed. Life, career, everything else, down the drain. Drink heavily. Find Clayton. Kill Clayton. Kill self.

Number 1 promises long term misery. Number 2 seems too much effort. It would involve sobering up, making a decision. Number 3 seems so unlikely as to barely warrant its place on the list. Which leaves Number 4.

Number 4 benefits everyone.

Too late now to check a gun out of the armoury, which had been my initial plan for dealing with Clayton. Bullet in the eye. Now I couldn't get someone at the station to sign me over a stapler, never mind a weapon.

What are the other options? A knife. Strangling. Suffocation. Broken neck.

I'm no trained assassin. There's absolutely no reason to suppose that if I get into hand-to-hand combat with a man like Clayton I would come out on top. However, if I'm going to die, I really need to take him down with me. Otherwise it'd just be a waste, and there'd be nothing to stop him moving on to the next sorry bastard.

I could do with a gun, but a surprise attack with a knife ought to do it as well. If I turn up at his door then he would likely assume I'm there for further questioning of the suspect. He's been happy to welcome us in up until now, and there's no reason why it should be any different. He sees every engagement with the police as a potential lawsuit.

Maybe he already knows I've been kicked out, of course. That wouldn't be the world's greatest shock. We've never really understood the full extent of his capabilities, and for all we know, never witnessed him operating at full capacity.

Drain another glass, back to the fridge. No more tonic. I knew that after the last time, but I'd forgotten. Stare into the fridge, hoping it will make another bottle of tonic materialise, or help me find some tonic-substitute, whatever it might be. Finally close the door and turn to look at the almost empty bottle of vodka.

Yep, time for vodka on the rocks. Mixers are for pussies anyway. Another three ice cubes, then tip the remainder of the bottle into the glass. Hey, there's another bottle of vodka at least, so everybody relax.

Back through to my place in front of the TV, bumping into the door frame on the way. God, that's a stiff drink now, the second mouthful just as bad.

Tired. Decision time. Get in the car, round to Clayton's house, or sit here, festering in pathetic, drunken impotence. The other option, the hitting the road and getting as far away from Glasgow option, just isn't happening. This needs to be over, and that only happens if I stay. Sitting in this seat, or heading out into the city, I need to be near to Clayton. That's the only chance this thing ends, one way or another, and I need it to end. We all do.

Lay my head back. Make the decision to go, with my eyes shut and the alcohol kicking in. Not the best combination. I'm not going anywhere.

46

Wake up to the sound of the door closing. Eyes flicker, finally manage to focus on the room. Lift my head off the cushion, and immediately hit by the wave of nausea and the spitting, shooting stab of a headache. Head back down on the cushion. Jesus.

Still daylight, but then it's June. It's daylight until ten. It feels much later than when I passed out, but I've no idea how long ago that was. Deep breaths. The instant wave of nausea beginning to pass. At least I'm not going to throw up on the carpet. Just yet. Not just yet.

Did the door close? It doesn't feel like there's anyone else here. Did I just dream the door closing?

I can't move. That intention I had, that I have, somewhere deep inside, to get to Clayton and take him out, myself at the same time, the thing I was thinking about and planning as I sat here drinking neat vodka, is an intention for a different time. A different day. A different me. This me, lying here in abject poverty of spirit, well-being and competency, isn't doing anything to anyone.

What was I dreaming about? Did a door close in the dream? Maybe someone came in and went to another room. They're waiting for me in the kitchen or the bedroom.

Lift my head again. Jesus. The nausea races back, a blinding, spurting, gargling tsunami of puke waiting to burst forth. I don't want to be sick. I hate being sick. But it's going to happen, and all I can do is lie here, pointlessly drawing out, into as many futile seconds as possible, the period before I throw up.

If only Clayton was here now. If only the sound of the

door closing had been Clayton coming in, and he was standing over me, gun in his hand, ready to kill me, saving me from the fucking vomit.

And I'm off the sofa and running for the bathroom, hand clasped across my mouth.

* * *

Emerge from the bathroom forty-five minutes later.

I vomited. Sat on the toilet. Cleaned my teeth. Vomited again. Drank a lot of water. Showered. A long shower. Vomited the water. Drank more water. Cleaned my teeth.

Finally, into the bedroom and change my clothes, head starting to get back to normal.

Stomach is empty, I'm hungry, but I don't feel like eating. Some more water, maybe a cup of tea. That'll do for now.

Stand at the bedroom window, no thought for whether anyone actually came into the house when I was awoken by the door. Look out on the same view I looked out on earlier. The same street, going about its business in the evening. Slept all day. Almost nine pm.

So what does the rest of the evening and the night hold now? Likely won't get to sleep, which means I'll be up forever, staring at the ceiling, staring at the wall, staring into space. Maybe I can just sit on the couch and think about nothing. Let the evening and the night happen, let morning come, let one day end and another begin. Let Clayton do whatever it is he's doing.

Is he holding Dr Brady's daughter? Let others find out. Let others go after him. Let others establish the evidence. For now I've got nothing. The day, the bollocking, the anger, the drink, the sleep, the puke, it's all left me completely empty.

Back through to the sitting room, heading for the kitchen. A cup of tea. Do the next thing in front of you, that's all you can do. And the next thing is to make a cup of tea. The thing after that will be to drink it.

And there I stop. Standing in the sitting room. Total silence.

The door didn't close by itself. The door didn't close in a dream. The door that woke me up, was closed by whoever left the small item on the small dining table. It must have been there when I finally flew off the couch to run to the bathroom.

It's almost a nice touch. Under other circumstances, I might even have appreciated it, tying everything up so perfectly as it does.

It's a box for L'Oréal Excellence Crème hair dye, number 01, lightest natural blonde. The box is empty.

Hold it in my hands, and then set it back down on the table. Don't bother looking inside.

Walk to the window, look back down at the street. It's a calling card, as much as the big fucking bat in the sky. It doesn't make me angry, however. It doesn't do anything to me. Much too empty for that.

But fuck you, Clayton, and I'm sorry Eileen, and I'm sorry Dr Brady, but before I do anything, I'm going to have that cup of tea. Might as well try to enjoy it. It'll be my last.

47

11:27

Darkness has come. Darkness over everything. I stand at Clayton's door. He knows I'm coming, so what does it matter if I put the door in or ring the bell? But since he's expecting me, I presume the door will be open and it is for me to just walk in.

Try the door handle, and sure enough, it's open. Close it behind me. Stand in the silent darkness.

Take a moment. Try to sense the place. Sense where they are. I don't know what I'm thinking, as I haven't really thought anything at all since I woke up. Just going through the motions, one thing to the next. Do I expect to *feel* them? Sense their presence? To be able to go directly to the room they're in, using some sort of Jedi shtick?

Take another step or two, look for the light switch, turn it on. Nothing.

Jesus, Clayton. Having me walking around the house in the dark. How mundane, how utterly ordinary of you.

My phone pings, the sound shattering in the silence. Despite myself, despite my indifference, despite my determination that this is nothing out of the ordinary, just a matter of my life and death, of Clayton's life and death, still my heart jumps at the sound.

The message could be from anyone, but I know already. Hardly need to look.

No Sender, that's who. No Sender.

Open the message. It's a picture. A woman's face. A face burned into my head. A face I'll never be able to forget, one I would never want to forget. That I never deserve to forget.

How could Clayton possibly know about her? Jesus. How could he possibly have got hold of the photograph?

There was me thinking I was dead inside, that the bastard couldn't get to me. There was me thinking I was going through the motions. And here's Clayton to let me know I'm wrong, completely wrong. He has total dominion. He knows things about me I would've thought he couldn't possibly know. He knows where I am now. He knows what I'm going to do next. He knows how the next half hour, the next hour, the rest of our lives will play out.

All I had was my calm indifference, and he's removed that with one impossible picture.

'Clayton!'

Snapping into life, Sergeant? Pathetic life...

'Clayton! Where the fuck are you?'

Shouting, but my voice sounds small. Small and empty and pointless. *Come on you fuck, show your face. Get on with it, get it over with.*

The phone pings again, my shoulders slump further. I can't keep this up.

I hadn't been fooling myself in coming over here; I genuinely thought I could do it, that I could take care of it, whatever had to be done, no different from making a cup of tea. My foolishness came in thinking he wouldn't be waiting for me.

Open the next message.

Dear God, Sergeant, you are so slow! #unbelievable The basement, my good man, the basement!

#unbelievable. Fucking pompous arsehole.

Mental knots, leading me inextricably towards physical knots. I can still see that face, the picture from a minute ago, the face from twenty years ago. But I have to kick the picture into the long grass, throw it out the ballpark, do some sporting analogy or other to it, and just get on with this.

Having been all over the house during the previous investigation – when we felt so sure we were going to uncover an arsenal of smoking guns – I've been to the basement before. At the time it seemed disappointingly unremarkable. The basement is where you expect to find the room with the missing Lithuanian nanny, bound and gagged, or the equipment used to lead a life of crime.

Clayton's basement had been nothing out of the ordinary, home to cobwebs, a folded up table tennis table, and the usual litany of stored, but not discarded, items.

He knows I'm here, he's leading me on, something's about to happen, so the quicker I get it over with, the better.

To the far end of the hall, where there's a door beside the entrance to the dining room on the right, with stairs into the basement. Phone out of my pocket again. Look down at it. Stop to think. A virtual sigh.

Quick text to Taylor. It'll take him long enough to get here, and it'll all be over by the time he arrives. It's all going to be over five minutes from now.

Torch turned on, hold the phone forward to light the way, find the door, hesitate at the top of the stairs, then start heading down.

Clayton is completely in control. There's no sneaking up on him, there's no surprise, there's no getting the upper hand. Not yet, at any rate. He holds every damn card in the pack, and this thing goes the way he wants it to go. So, there's no point in walking slowly around corners, there's no point in hesitation, there's no point in trying to work out angles and look for signs. Whatever's going to happen, will happen at a time of Clayton's choosing.

I'm not here to solve anything, am I? I'm just here to get on with it, get this bloody awful business wrapped up and over with, so that others can get on with their lives and their jobs, and hope the women are all right.

Sgt Harrison and Dr Brady. That's why I'm here, tonight, right now. For them. Nothing else would likely have got me out the house.

Into the basement, phone held up around me. The table tennis table, the skis, the old set of golf clubs, the workbench. And, against the far wall with the old cabinet pushed to the side, an opening.

I don't even stop to think about why we didn't find this previously. Taylor can worry about that later, if it even matters.

Into the darkness of the passageway. Maybe it would help if I thought of this whole stupid business as an episode of Scooby Doo. In the end, however, I don't think I'll be pulling Clayton's mask off and revealing old Mr Watts, the janitor, beneath. *I would've gotten away with it, if it hadn't been for you pesky cunt.*

The tunnel is clean, walls of stone. It feels safe. Plenty of head room. I wonder who built it? Who is out there who knows Clayton has a tunnel leading from beneath his house?

Did he get a couple of builders in and then get rid of them afterwards? Likely, too messy. Too much chance for something to go wrong, for people to turn up at the last place they'd been known to be working. Unless he picked them off the street.

This is what Clayton does. He makes you think he's capable of anything. All he might be is some opportunistic fucker, yet in my head he's the Machiavellian master. He's every Moriarty that's ever been portrayed, rolled into one.

I'm not sure how long I walk, because I'm not sure I'm thinking properly anymore, about anything. At some point, thirty seconds later, or ten minutes later, or some time later, a flight of stairs appears out of the darkness.

Stop for a moment, take whatever the opposite of a deep breath is – that thing where you hang you head and just think, *oh for fuck's sake, here we go, this is it* – then up the stairs, turn the handle of the door at the top, and walk into the hallway of another house.

48

An ordinary hallway in an ordinary home. Not too dissimilar to the one I just left. I can tell it's ordinary, because there's a light on, a large lamp on a table halfway along the hall. The light on here, but no lights in the previous house. Further evidence he's just having a laugh.

This house smells old and comfortable. I lost track of the direction in which I'd walked, so can't think which of the surrounding houses I'm in.

A painting of Edinburgh on one wall, one of Dundee and the Tay on the other. An old portrait hangs near the front door.

I close the door behind me, but don't move. There's music playing in a room upstairs. Choral, religious possibly. The kind of thing you'd hear at evensong.

Jesus. Well isn't that mundane from the innovative murdering genius? The final act is to be carried out to a slow, dramatic soundtrack, like every hack movie you ever saw. Surprised it's not *Nessun fucking Dorma*.

Stand still. Is this house going to be as clean as the other, or is it possible this is where we'll find the proof of all Clayton's misdeeds? If that was to be the case, why don't I just run? Get out, establish where I am, get the police round, mob-handed?

Clayton the Machiavellian smiles smugly at my thoughts. That's exactly what he's wanting me to do.

The phone pings again. Quick look at the message. It's video, this time, and I don't hesitate. Might as well take a look. And there I am, having sex. But it's not with Dr Brady. This one is with her. Jane Kettering. The Plague of Crows. Me lying back, and her on top of me, those small breasts moving frantically in time with her body, and then me reaching up to grab one, taking the other in my mouth.

I watch it for a few seconds, then click off. If I remember correctly it wasn't too far away from the moment she zapped me with a taser. Been a while since I relived that particular pain.

I turn and look up the stairs. That's where the music is coming from, that's where I'm being drawn. Inexorably onwards and upwards. The sense of overwhelming defeat is getting stronger, so that it now feels inevitable. There's nothing I can do, nowhere else for me to go, no way out.

This guy knows my past just as much as he knows my future. The messages he's sending are so broad in scope, so humiliating, it seems he knows everything about me. He's there, whenever I do anything at all, to prick whatever balloon I happen to be flying at any given moment.

He owns me. He owns everything I do, and everything I say.

'Fuck it.'

Up the stairs, quickly now, two at a time. A bend in the stairs, then up onto the first floor landing. There are five doors off, one of them ajar, and it's from there the music is coming. Two strides, door open, and then into the room.

There is a small lamp in the corner, and the television is turned on, although the screen is currently blank. The DVD player screen, before play has been pressed.

Three people look at me. Clayton to the side, sitting in an old-fashioned, upright comfy chair. The kind of comfy chair that isn't very comfortable. Back straight, staring at me, as though his eyes have been looking at the door for some time now, waiting for my entrance.

Then there's a two-seat sofa, with wooden armrests, directly in front of the television. Sitting together on the sofa are Dr Brady and Sgt Harrison, side by side, bound and gagged. Blonde beside blonde.

They're looking at me, Brady with fear, Harrison with nothing. Dead eyes. Will be annoyed for allowing herself to be taken. Will apologise when all this is over, if we're both still around when all this is over. Just as I'll apologise for having dragged her into this fucking awful mess.

The music plays on. Beautiful and low, foreshadowing Death. Out of place here. Would be perfect in my old church at the top of the town. The church that belongs in my thoughts to me and Mary Buttler, the church to which neither of us will ever go again.

'Come in, Mr Bond,' says Clayton. 'Sit down.' Then he giggles.

I really look at him for the first time. He's holding a gun in his right hand, the gun resting in his lap.

'Look, Sergeant,' he says, 'let us not dally. You took quite enough time getting over here. We were all getting rather impatient, weren't we, ladies? The time for procrastination is over, if ever there was such a time. We're here to watch a video presentation. This is your life, Detective Sergeant. It's been so much fun investigating your past, it really has. Sit down, take a load off, and let's begin, shall we?'

He's smiling. I hold his gaze, but can barely stand to look at him. Glance at Harrison, who still gives me nothing.

'Well,' says Clayton, 'if you're just going to stand there.'

My life. A film of my life. I've already seen one of the photographs, I've heard the stories he told Dr Brady, I know how much digging he's done, down into the dark, awful pits of my past.

And then the screen flashes into life, and there she is again. The same photo, the same face, the same woman looking back at me. The Bosniak. The one who died. The one who got a bullet in the head while I watched. The woman I was ordered, at gun point, to rape. On whom I lay. Who was desperate for me to fuck her, so she'd be allowed to live. Who lay there helpless. Who got a bullet in the head for my weakness, while I, terrified and impotent, couldn't get an erection, my pathetic, helpless, useless cock, small and limp and as terrified as the rest of me.

The film freezes on the picture of the woman.

'Come now, Sergeant, please sit down,' says the voice of the snake from the corner. 'Make yourself comfortable. It's only twenty minutes. Plenty more interesting tidbits!'

I can barely take my eyes off her, and I almost stumble past the sofa, and slump down into the chair supplied for me.

'Excellent!' he beams, and then, with a single clap of celebration, he restarts the film.

And there I am, up on the screen, sitting much like I am now, watching TV, but with my dick in my hands. He had a camera in my television. He was filming me, in my own sitting room, from the TV. And so now I sit here, watching myself masturbate, and immediately I run through all the other things he's going to have filmed, the other people, and I wonder how long he's had it there, and if there's going to be sight of Philo, sitting at the small table, and I know there will definitely be footage of Harrison and me.

And then before I've even begun to fathom the depths to which he'll have trawled into my life, the scene changes to a camera running through a forest, and it could be a forest anywhere, but I know which forest it is, I know what happened in that forest, all those years ago.

Images flick past, one bleeding horrendously into another. Given that he started with the very worst, the forthcoming horror is not that this film will come to a head – it's not linear, images and scenes and photographs zipping back and forth – but more its overall, cumulative effect.

Me naked, drunk, talking to myself; me talking to Philo's grave; Philo kissing me goodbye; faces from the past, from Bosnia, from old cases; ex-wives; me and Harrison, naked and coming together; photographs of women I've slept with, women I've hurt; my children; the recording of me suggesting to Taylor that I kill Clayton; a recording of a phone call between me and Andy, my disinterested son, Andy hanging up the phone.

Clayton has been watching me for over a year, ever since the Plague of Crows business ended. Cameras everywhere. Phones bugged. And he's coupled the surveillance with raking through the past, digging up so much. And I sit here, forced to watch, wanting to look away, wanting to grab him and take the bullet or put the bullet in him, to finish this all off, but I'm fascinated and horrified, and I can't take my eyes from it.

Me having sex, me drunk, me feeling guilty, me fucking up a case, me fucking up a relationship, me fucking up my life, on and on, one scene or clip or photograph quickly jumping on to the next, the divine, choral music rising in crescendo, tears streaming down my face – on the screen and here, sitting in front of it – every life I've ruined, and none more so than this one right here, in this position, having allowed himself to come to this, this utter, fucking, wretched waste of a single fucking strand of sperm…

Finally I'm up off my feet, kicking the television, a boot right to the middle, but I'm closer to losing my balance than knocking it over, so I take a better kick, soul of the boot, and the set tips backwards, and then I lift it, pick up the set, pulling the plug out as I do it, and toss it away to the side.

'Fuck! Fuck! Fuuuuuuuck!'

The set smashes against the wall, with the final chord of the oratorio, or whatever the fuck that was we've just been listening to, then it settles with a crash, and suddenly the room is silent.

Dead silent.

Hands on my hips, head down. Eyes open, but I can barely see the floor through the tears. Jesus. Wipe my eyes, sniff, hand dragged across my nose, straighten up, finally. Turn round.

Clayton is up out of the seat. His face is dead. The face of a man delivering the final, crushing blow. The face of a man getting a job done. Perhaps the face of a man doing a job that, in the end, was so easy there's barely any satisfaction to be had.

He taps the barrel of the gun against his fingertips.

'How does it feel?' he says.

I give him nothing, except slumped shoulders. The women are no more than a couple of yards away, but they might as well not be there. At least, I think they might as well not be there. But he's in control. Everything is happening for a reason. Everyone is here for a reason.

'How does it feel?' he repeats. 'To be on...' He laughs, humourlessly. 'I shan't, I shan't. Too easy, too easy...'

And now, like a fucking wasted piece of washed-up useless sphincter skin, in the shittiest generic movie you ever watched, I fall to my knees. Head down, shoulders down, hands uselessly at my side.

'I'm leaving,' he says. 'This is an awful country. Going to the dogs. I mean, there are a lot of awful countries out there in the world, but it's time for me to move on. I rather fancy being the outsider. Living on the fringes, detached from society. Somewhere I don't understand the language. Bosnia looks nice... No, I'm teasing. It's fucking awful. No wonder you found it so easy to fuck up people's lives there.'

I'm staring at his feet, though I can feel his head, tipped to the side, staring at me like some kindly old uncle, standing over the lame dog before he puts a bullet in its head.

'Just a couple of small details to sort out before we're done. The presence of the two ladies won't have passed you by, I take it? You obviously got my clue.'

I don't lift my head, don't stare at him. I should be doing everything I can to save them, but I feel so empty, so bereft. I just want it all to end. Clayton can win. He can have what he wants, he can kill who he likes, just so long as I'm one of them.

'Obviously, it won't take much. One on top of the other, *blonde on blonde*, faces pressed together, then bound so there's little breath to take. A last few gasps, and then… well, another fine addition to the intriguing case of the Bob Dylan Murders. After that, time for just one more. You get it, don't you? I mean, you know what we're talking about? You understand your own death…?'

Time slows. Every sentence, every word, is another reach of his hand down inside me, ripping out my heart and my lungs and my stomach and my everything else.

'*Self Portrait*,' I say, the words forced out, and the fucker almost squeals with pleasure.

'Bravo, Sergeant, bravo. *Self Portrait*. Excellent. Still, let's not get ahead of ourselves. Look at me. Look at me, Sergeant. Come on.'

Slowly I lift my head. He's three yards away. Why don't I just go for him? He's got the gun, and the chances are he'd get the shot off and I'd be downed before I got to him. But I don't care anyway, do I? Right?

You don't care, you wasted piece of fuck, so why not just have a go?

'Before you die, I'm going to do you a favour. That's the kind of man I am. Decent. No, really, I'm perfectly decent, I really am. So, what is this favour, you're asking? Well, I'm going to give you the chance at redemption. How does that sound? Surely, everyone wants redemption?'

I've got nothing to say. I'm just the puppet, limp and useless before the master, waiting to do as I'm told. Is there anything I wouldn't do now, just to get this over with?

'Oh, I found them, Sergeant, don't you worry. I heard you tell poor, dear Philo your story, and I went to Bosnia and I found them. I found the ones you left behind, the ones who hadn't died. They hadn't forgotten. Of course they hadn't. And they certainly remembered the photographer, the Scottish photographer, who couldn't get an erection. One of them said it might have been funny if it hadn't been so tragic.'

He pauses, enjoying the moment. He's been planning it long enough, and now is his time. He has the floor, the

273

arch villain has his stage on which to monologue.

'Haven't you always wished you could have that night back, Sergeant? A do-over? I mean, really, haven't you relived it a thousand times? Ten thousand. When you relive it, when you think about her lying there, does it give you an erection?'

I see the gun move in his hands. He's baiting me, possibly wary of me snapping, and getting ready to deal with a charge.

'Well, now's your chance.'

A smile, and I really don't know what he's talking about. And then slowly, his head and the gun turn towards the two bound women.

'Now we already know you're happy to sleep with the good doctor. But Sgt Harrison... I don't know, I felt you left so much on the table when you sat together on the couch. So much potential lost. So, Sergeant, this is your chance for salvation. It has been my intention all evening to kill them both. To trap them together, blonde, indeed, on blonde. But I will spare them, or rather, you can spare them, if you do what you failed to do to that poor woman – who would otherwise still be alive today – in the Bosnian forest.'

I hold his gaze, from my position of abject poverty, and then look round at Harrison. We stare at each other across the short distance of the room.

'Fuck her, Sergeant,' he says from my right, his voice suddenly cold, zigzagging back and forth as it does, as he plays me. 'Fuck her, or she dies.'

49

Gun in one hand, he takes out his phone with the other, looking at me expectantly.

'Well, Sergeant, we have film of so much else! When this footage is used in the documentary of your life, you want the final moment of triumph to have been captured, don't you? The scene of deliverance. Every good film has one.'

Brady has her eyes closed. She's crying. I wonder where her daughter is. At least we have that, at least Clayton hasn't dragged us all so low, that there would be a twelve year-old girl sitting here, subjected to the X-rated garbage of my life.

Harrison is steady. Good on her. Not taking any of this arsehole's crap. She's worth a hundred of me.

'Take her gag off,' I say. Looking at her, not him. The words could be an order, but I'm so bereft of spirit, so damned empty, they sound like a sad and hollow last request.

'Hmm,' he says. 'Intriguing. Well, yes, why not, eh? That rather sounds like a plan. It'll make lovely television. I hope you've got a decent script though, there's the potential it could be maudlin. No one enjoys maudlin.'

He goes behind her, finds the end of the piece of tape strapped around her head and across her mouth, and then quickly unravels it, ripping it out her hair at the end. She cries out at the shock of it, then quickly bites her teeth, pressing her lips together, annoyed she made the sound.

I don't doubt Clayton. He's a calculating, weird, sick fucker, but strangely there's some code about him. I trust him in that. If I do as he's telling me, he'll let them live. If

I don't, we all die.

And so, as I look at her, I'm not thinking about the awful night in Bosnia. I'm thinking about a few evenings ago, sitting on a sofa with Eileen, desperate to sleep with her, as turned on as I've ever been. Maybe even more turned on than usual, given I was having to deny myself.

Here, in the demon's pit, with two bound kidnap victims and a mad fucktard with a gun in his hand, and me on my knees, utterly crushed, I'm forcing myself to think about watching lesbian porn with my best friend, trying to force some life into what is currently the deadest organ in my body. Or, at least, tied for dead last with my brain.

'Don't trust him,' she says, her voice hard and cold. 'You can't fucking trust him, Tom.'

Jesus. She's not going to make it any easier. She doesn't want me to do it.

Of course she doesn't want me to do it!

I already had words in her mouth. I imagined her telling me she'd really wanted me to do it on Saturday anyway, I imagined her encouragement. Something to make it easier. Something to cause a spark.

'I can't let you die,' I say. Head down, staring at the carpet.

'We're all going to die anyway.'

'I believe him,' I say, looking up.

Behind her he squeals quietly, and the sound stabs into the side of my head. Squealing with delight.

I just want it all over. All of it. For me to be dead, and for the sergeant not to be dead with me.

'Don't you dare, Tom,' she says. 'Don't you dare do what he wants.'

'Tut tut tut...,' comes the voice from behind. 'Now, now, Sgt Harrison, you have to remember your place in this little drama. Maybe you don't know the story, perhaps that's the trouble. The Sergeant here was forced to rape someone, or else the victim would be shot. She, in her desperation, pleaded with him to rape her. Questionable, then, of course whether you could call it rape in my book,

276

but let's not get into legal technobabble…'

Just shut up. Please. Stop talking.

'So, if we are to truly offer the sergeant redemption, you have to go along with it, Sgt Harrison. This isn't about you, you know! Nor, I should add, is it about me. Let Sgt Hutton do what he has to do. You know–'

'Shut up! Just shut the fuck up! I'm doing it!'

'Oh, my goodness!' he says, faux shocked. 'Extraordinary!'

And I approach her on my hands and knees. Jesus fucking Christ. There's your next fucking metaphor. There's your life in one all-consuming instance of desperate awfulness.

I glance up at her as I come to the couch. A last look and she closes her eyes. Clamps them shut. I rest my arms on her legs – she's wearing jeans – hesitate, and then part her legs.

Pushing forward into the abyss, even though I know I'm not going to be able to do it. I know I'm not, and it'll be for exactly the same reason as before. It's not a matter of whether I should. It's not a matter of playing along to the gunman's whims. My penis is no more willing now than it was back then. And Jesus, why would it be? If it couldn't get an involuntary erection in my mid-twenties, it sure as fuck isn't going to now.

I reach out, hand on the zip of her jeans. This, for some reason, feels like the Rubicon. We're here, we're fucked up and messed around and used, and we're fully clothed. As soon as I start undressing her, this is it. Cross this line, and nothing stops until I'm lying on top of her and my useless fucking cock has made its final decision.

I need to recapture the feeling. This is where I wanted to be the other night. She was right there, next to me, the most unbelievably erotic situation I could imagine, and I was desperate to put my hand on her thighs. They were there, naked, pressed against mine, and I couldn't touch.

I squeeze them, press my head against her left leg. She is steady. Tense, but not a hint of a tremble. She's not telling me to stop anymore. He's controlled her, just as much as he's controlled me these last few days.

As if to remind me of his presence, he squeals again. I look up, and there he is, out of reach, gun in one hand, phone in the other. He lifts his eyebrows at me in encouragement. We're all friends in this together. I look back up at Harrison, eyes still closed, face set hard.

The past floats away. It's gone. Dead and gone. I'm not reliving the past, any more than I'm giving myself redemption. All I'm doing is giving in to the whims of a fucking freak.

Why did I even start thinking about it?

There are tears on my face, and I press my head more firmly against Harrison's thigh. Just for a second. Then finally, finally, I make a decision and grow some fucking balls for the first time since walking into the room.

It's not about making a grab for the gun, attempting some dramatic act that turns the scene on its head, leaving the women released, and me standing over Clayton. Just the balls to finally not do what this lunatic is telling me to.

I get to my feet, lean forward, press my face against Harrison's cheek for a second, whisper, 'Sorry,' in her ear, then kiss her briefly on the lips and stand up.

She looks up at me, her expression suddenly changing. I glance at Brady – the last woman with whom I'll ever have sex – almost forgotten, bound and gagged on the sidelines, no more than six inches from Harrison, and then finally I stand upright and look at Clayton.

'What's this?' he says, the phone lowering.

'I'm done.'

'You're done?'

'Yes.'

'Hmm… well I think that means I put a bullet in your head, and then strap the two women together, shortly afterwards leaving this place with all three of you dead. Are you sure that's what you want? Are you sure you want it on your conscience, the very last thing on your resume?'

'How many bullets are in the gun?'

———

'Curious,' he says. 'Just the one. Why?'

'Give me it.'

He smiles. Has a look about him like he's on fucking *Crackerjack*.

'Ooh, interesting. Explain.'

'My death, this whole thing, this was to be the last act in the Bob Dylan Murders. *Self Portrait*. Well, the video isn't a self-portrait, really, is it? You made it. If a self portrait is what you want, I have to die by my own hand. So give me the gun.'

The eyebrows are lifted again.

'And how–'

'We're renegotiating. I'm not going to do what you want with the Sergeant, but I'll do this. Give me the gun, I shoot myself, you free the women, and then you can be on your way. Live whatever life you're going to lead. I'll be dead, I won't care.'

'I'm not sure I entirely understand the concept. So *I* give *you* the gun? And you kill yourself? And not me?'

'Yes.'

'And why would I trust you? Why wouldn't you just shoot me?'

My shoulders are slumped. I've had enough. Can barely even bring myself to talk.

'I'm already suspended. This would be just what I needed. A murder trial for putting a bullet in your face. I'm done, Mr Clayton. You win. It's all yours. All of it. Every fucking thing you want out of this. If you want to put a bullet in my head, then on you go. Here I am. But I thought you might take a little more pleasure out of me doing it to myself.'

His lips are pursed. Thinking about it. And I'm not lying. I don't care, I really have had enough. I want out of here, and this is the best route.

'I just don't want to take Sgt Harrison, or Dr Brady, with me. Give me the gun, you'll get your *Self Portrait*, and we're done.'

'Hmm...,' he says, and now the phone is back in his

pocket, the gun lowered, and I can see he's thinking about it. I've nothing else to add though. Not trying to persuade him, not trying to do anything further.

'Very well,' he says finally. 'Yes, yes… Let's try this. Sounds exciting. Two foes taking each other at their word. Rather splendid.'

He pauses, there's a genuine look of curiosity about him – he's finally, after all this time, considering something that wasn't part of his plan – and then he holds the gun forward.

'Gosh,' he continues, 'I do believe I'm rather nervous. That hasn't happened in quite some time.'

And then the gun is in my hand.

I don't know guns, been such a long time. This seems old, the kind with a barrel. Like the old Westerns, or Clint in the *Dirty Harry* movies. But smaller. I push the barrel out and check, and sure enough, one bullet. All he thought he'd need.

Not a shooter, Clayton. He kills with malice aforethought and absurdity and grotesquery. A bullet in the head isn't for him. Except when he has manipulated someone else into putting the bullet in their own head.

'You have the gun, Sergeant,' he says.

'Tom!'

I don't look at her. Eyes on the gun. No fight in me. I've given up. Just want it all to be over. And it could be over if I killed him. At least, this little drama would be over. But I trust him, as much as he seems to have trusted me.

If I kill myself, then the sergeant, the doctor and the doctor's daughter, wherever she is, this invisible, kidnapped girl, will all be safe. I kill him, well yes, the women will still be safe, but it leaves me standing here with a gun and more blood on my hands. It doesn't matter what Clayton has done – and the chances of us finding proof of all of it will be damned slim – I'll still be the police officer who put a bullet in the head of an unarmed man. The investigation, the media, the trial, the bullshit.

And I'd still be here, in this fucking awful world of injustice and terror and famine and illness and war, I'd be on my way to prison, and all those fuckers out there who mistrust us and everything we do would have one more giant excuse for hating the police.

'Sergeant,' he says. 'It's time.'

The seconds pass. The music comes back, as though someone has just turned it on, but it can't have gone away. I just hadn't been thinking about it. I haven't heard it in several minutes. Sounds like a choir of angels, the perfect thing to hear before I pull the trigger, and send myself down where I belong, into the pits of Hell.

'Tom! What the fuck are you doing?'

I look at her. Sgt Harrison. Saying the right thing, just as Sgt Harrison usually does.

'Put a bullet in his knee, cut our bonds and call for back-up! Tom! Come on...'

Her voice starts to trail away at the end.

'You fascinated me, Sgt Hutton,' says Clayton. 'After your outburst at my able assistant during that frightful crows business, I couldn't help but examine your life. What had led you to such an attitude? Fascinating. You really, truly are fascinating. A smorgasbord of psychological disaster.'

He laughs lightly. He's laughing at me? And I'm the one with the gun in my hand.

'Right, right, enough, Sergeant, time to get going, we can't be dilly-dallying around any further. The text you sent to DCI Taylor will be coming to bear fruit soon enough. Chop chop!'

Jesus, he really does know everything.

He holds my gaze, then takes the phone back out his pocket. This is it, then. I can feel the relief. At last he's shut up, and this can all be over.

Place the gun in my mouth, momentarily catch my lip between the steel and my teeth, turn the barrel upside down so that it's pointed upwards into my head. Towards that fucked-up, booze-binged, sex-addled brain, the one that deserves no more. No more than this.

'Tom!'

Eyes closed. It comes to this. And do I believe him, as I give him what he wants? That he'll release the women, before disappearing off into the night? And how much longer before he resurfaces, to carry out further monstrous crimes? How many more lives will he destroy?

Do I turn my back on justice so easily, so that he once again, for the third, or the fifth, or the tenth time in his life, walks away, untouched by the law?

Hand surprisingly steady. One small movement of my finger on the trigger and it's over. One bullet, one death; one life that few, if any, will mourn.

Fuck it.

Open my eyes to look for the last time at my tormentor, the man who has hounded me and killed me as sure as it's him who has the gun in his hand.

He stares back, cold and hard, no hint of smugness, no hint of triumph. Just a face in a crowd of one.

Ah fuck it, fuck it, fuck it! Fuck it! How can I give this cunt the satisfaction?

When I pull the trigger I have to be alone, I have to be doing it on my own terms. It can be tomorrow or next fucking week, but not now, not with this bastard looking at me.

Gun out the mouth, and I toss it on to the floor. It bounces briefly, shallowly, and then comes to rest between us.

We look down at the gun together, then our eyes lift so we're staring at each other.

I win. That's the thought that comes into my head. He led me here, through twists and turns and connivances, all with the intention of us arriving at this moment. Me with a gun in my hand, yet me at his mercy.

This is all I can do. This is the only way I can come out of this situation on top. By not pulling the trigger.

There is a second, while this latest development feeds into the situation, while he processes it.

He had planned for me to shoot myself.

Perhaps he planned, as he handed over the gun, for me to shoot him.

Now, has he also planned for me to toss the gun onto the carpet?

'What'd I miss?'

We turn to look at the door, and there he is, a late arrival to the party.

'Ha!' barks Clayton, in his buffoonish way. 'I fucking knew it!'

50

Taylor quickly looks around the room, taking in the situation. Me, deranged and weeping, the television tossed and busted, Harrison and Brady bound to the sofa, Clayton, owning the room, completely in control, despite being armed with nothing but total self-confidence, and the gun on the carpet between us. If anything, marginally closer to Clayton.

A few seconds ago the gun didn't matter. Clayton gave it to me, I tossed it on the floor. Neither of us seemed to care who had it. Now, however, Taylor has walked in on the party.

Am I in a position to get the gun before Clayton? Does he hold another concealed weapon?

Fuck. This has brought me back to life. Didn't take much, did it? When I'm consumed by self, I don't care. Very easy to let go, because there's so little to let go of. But now Taylor's walked into the middle of the scene and the previous dynamic is out the window. No honour amongst thieves now.

And so we stand, eyes moving between each other and the gun, absurdly like Eastwood, Wallach and van Cleef in that damn, fucking movie, and the heavenly choir still sings beautifully in the background. Jesus.

'Isn't this weird?' says Clayton, and he's smiling now. Fucking smiling, the bastard. 'I mean, isn't it? Weird and wonderful. The three of us standing here in some fucked up abortion of a Mexican stand-off, and there are two hostages just sitting here, wrapped in fucking duct tape like, I don't know, sausages in clingfilm. Well, it's remarkable.'

He doesn't get anything from either of us. We're both making the same calculation. Who gets to the gun first? In this respect, at least, Taylor is out of the equation, being that extra few yards away. His part, such as it is, has possibly already been played. Has he called for back-up? That's what will be running through Clayton's mind.

'Blah blah blah,' he says, waving his fucking hand again, and I could break those bloody fingers, 'this is all very well and good. And I wish we could stand here chatting. Time to go, however, time to go. I must say I'm disappointed you betrayed me, Sergeant, I really am. I thought we had a bond.'

Oh, for fuck's sake!

I dive for the gun. Don't even think there's any positive thought in that direction. Just happens.

Clayton is quicker. I'm a lumbering, unfit fool, he has the moves. The bastard has everything.

Foot to the gun barrel, presses down, pushes the grip off the floor, and it's in his hand. I'm upon him in the same movement, the gun is fired, the explosion of it booms in my ear, but the bullet doesn't hit me.

Tumbling back onto the floor, me on top. He brings his head down, but misses the sweet spot. Instead a clash of foreheads. Press my nails into his wrists, and then, another unthinking moment. Bite his hand, like a fucking kid fighting.

And then Taylor is there, swinging, and Clayton and I are torn apart. I fall away, head hits against something, and Taylor is on top of Clayton, driving him backwards, driving strong and hard, and then Clayton's head thumps into the wall.

Can see it in his eyes, straight away, a knockout blow, and his head falls forward. The eyes are still open, but the fight has gone out of him, along with his awareness of what's happening. For good measure, Taylor brings his fist up, a swift uppercut, under Clayton's chin, smacking his head back against the wall again, and now Taylor steps back, lets him go, and Clayton falls to the floor.

He steps over him, making sure he's down and is staying down, speaks without turning round.

'Get me some tape, Sergeant. Come on!'

Off my feet, stop instantly.

The doctor, looking shocked, her face still wrapped in silver tape. Harrison next to her, eyes open, looking up at me, a large soaking patch of blood on her side.

'Jesus, Eileen.'

'I'm good,' she says. 'I'm good.'

She doesn't sound good.

* * *

And so the next few minutes pass in a blur, a flurry of desperation. The roll of tape flung at Taylor; Taylor binding Clayton; me removing the bonds from Harrison, as careful as I can, careful but desperate, and then ripping them with little care from the doctor, so she can attend to the Sergeant; the call to the nearest station; Harrison lying on the floor, her buttocks raised so that the side wound is elevated above her heart, the doctor holding a compress against the wound; me running out of the room, running around the house, looking for the invisible girl, the girl without whom Dr Brady would never have been involved, and finding her, two rooms along, neither bound nor gagged, but asleep behind a locked door; taking her back to Brady, then taking over from her, kneeling beside Harrison, keeping her talking, making sure the flow of blood has been stemmed.

And all the while, weirdly, bizarrely, the music plays on, while Taylor watches over Clayton, and Clayton lies still, now bound by his own tape.

And then suddenly there are footsteps outside, growing in volume and number, and then the room is full, and people are shouting, and someone in green is pushing me away from Harrison, and I squeeze her hand, a last touch of the fingers, and then I'm pushed back and I will have no further part to play in the sergeant's own small tale of survival.

I step away, the scene playing out before me, still alive against all expectation. Clayton in handcuffs, on the floor, the paramedics beside Harrison, Brady and her daughter, still hugging, the swarm of officers, and Taylor barking at them not to touch anything.

'Crime scene, crime scene!' he shouts at one point.

Epilogue

Three days later. Small dinner table, Chinese carry out, a bottle (or two) of Sauvignon Blanc, my turn to go to Eileen's house.

She looks fine, not even pale. Just fine. Her movement's a bit stiff, but just sitting here at a table eating dinner, you'd never know anything was wrong.

The crows are gone. We're done, for now. Three night's sleep, restless, uneasy nights, but no crows. Gone for good, though? I doubt it.

Maybe this little episode is over. But what happened in Bosnia, that'll never be over. And if Clayton could go out his way to investigate my past, someone else could too. And everything he found out will be on his computer, and the computer is now in the hands of the police.

And even if it's never mentioned again, it doesn't matter. What happened back then still happened.

Clayton, for his part, will not go easily to prison, and once he's there, there's nothing to suggest he will rest on his past triumphs. Clayton's story ain't finished, not by a long shot. The crows, however, have decided to give me some respite.

I've just sat down, having been in the kitchen getting plates and glasses and cutlery and distributing the food. Arrived five minutes ago, kissed her, shared one of those looks women give each other in American romantic dramas, then we hugged briefly, until she winced, then she sat down, and now I've joined her.

'Getting shot looks good on you,' I say.

'My mum didn't think so. She thought I was near death and should be in hospital for another month.'

'How is she, by the way?'

'In her element.'

'She always knew you'd get shot if you joined the police?'

'Yep.'

'You should have been an accountant?'

She laughs, nodding.

'What about you?' she asks. 'You on actual suspension yet, or is Taylor managing to keep you as his pet sergeant for a while longer?'

'Fuck off,' I reply, taking the joke. 'And yes, I'm suspended pending a full investigation into my habit of sleeping with people involved in an investigation. It's been noted, apparently, that this isn't the first time. And while the doctor might've been only acting to protect her daughter, she still aided a murderer, and the procurator's looking at her for now. She'll be fine. Me...? Whatever. Anyway, Taylor has my back, as ever, just as he'd have yours if you needed him to.'

'I know!'

'Totally bummed, though, I'm not now going to get to complete the work on my taskforce. Or start it, for that matter.'

'There goes your MBE.'

'Exactly. Total bastard. Meanwhile, the boss says they're turning up a decent amount of shit on Clayton's files. Enough to really nail him. Apparently there's been the odd muttering from above asking why we weren't listened to sooner.'

'Jesus,' says Harrison.

'Yeah, I know. Still, good to hear someone realises we haven't been crying wolf for the last year and a half.'

'Well, about time. You think you'll still have a job?'

'I don't know. Just have to wait and see. Given the level of budgetary savings they've all been asked to make, kicking me out and replacing me with a sixteen year-old constable'll save a pound or two.'

She nods in agreement. Food is eaten, thoughts

thought, or not. A lifted glass of wine, conversation lapses. Talking about the case feels like going through the motions. Has to be done, but that'll do, Donkey, that'll do, the case is over – until the inevitable, convoluted, God-awful trial – and it's time to move on.

'How about you?' I ask 'How long you signed off for?'

'A month.'

'Seriously? They know the bullet passed straight through, right?'

'Fuck off!' she says. 'And don't make me laugh, it hurts.'

'At least a couple of those weeks must be sympathy weeks, though?'

'Exactly what it said on the doc's sick note. What about you?'

'I have to appear before some dick in a suit to answer preliminary questions, three weeks on Monday. And not before.'

'You're getting paid all this time?' she asks.

'Including overtime.'

'I bet. What you going to do with yourself?'

Jesus, it's just like, there you go buddy, there's the fucking question. Three days ago you'd got yourself into a place where you'd been about to put a bullet in your head. So, what are you planning to do instead? Go to the pub? Binge-watch a couple of boxsets?

'What about you?' I say, to avoid the question.

'Not sure. Mum wants me to go there for a few days. Or, well, forever actually. I think if I do go, she might break my legs and pull a *Misery* on me, then get a series of attractive male doctors to attend to me in the hope of curing my accursed condition.'

'So you're not going to your mum's then.'

'Nowhere bloody near.'

Another silence, more food, more wine. There's a solace in talking to Eileen Harrison I didn't think was to be found. Nevertheless, the gun that rested so comfortably in my mouth will not easily be forgotten. That I did not pull the trigger was as a result of not wishing to give Clayton the satisfaction, not because it wasn't the right thing to do.

'So, we're still talking to each other,' she says after a while.

I hold her gaze. I wondered coming over here how awkward it was likely to be, and it seems strange that so far it's not been awkward at all.

'Even though you turned down the chance to have sex with me,' she continues. 'I mean, I was strapped down, and you still didn't want to do it. You, who's had sex with more or less every woman you've ever met.'

'Bugger off.'

'I thought the venue and the circumstances were pretty romantic,' she adds.

'Certainly how I envisioned it when I've fantasised about you in the past.'

A beat, one of those rom-dram looks across the table.

'Thank you,' she says. 'Again. You keep not having sex with me. I appreciate it.'

Jesus, don't say that, Eileen. Don't appreciate me. I don't deserve it. Let's just be normal. Two normal people, talking about normal stuff over a normal carry out.

'There was a lot to take in on the video he showed us,' she says, and the jokiness has completely gone from her voice, as she doesn't yet share my desire for normality. Maybe she's right. 'You going to tell me about it?'

Don't reply.

'Might do you some good to talk. I suspect, being a man 'n' all, talking about it isn't really your thing.'

She's right, of course. Can't say I haven't been thinking the same thing. Because I have to do something. Talk or die. Maybe both.

'The video's already doing the rounds of the station, I expect,' she says. 'I can imagine they're all loving that. You and me–'

'Taylor's doing what he can. He wants the investigation into this side of it undertaken by a complete outsider, trying to make sure it doesn't get passed around, because, of course, it's not just what we saw, it's all the potential files and Jesus knows what else on Clayton's computer. We'll see, see if it works. He got me a copy of the disk, which was big of him. He thought I should talk to someone about it, though he didn't offer up himself.'

'Has he watched it?'

'Nope.'

'You *want* to talk about it?' she asks.

'Seems to be the way forward.'

'You want to talk to *me* about it?'

Hold her gaze across the table. Mind a total fucking rollercoaster. Well, a dumbass, fucking rollercoaster that only ever manages to be on some sort of level pegging before plummeting miserably deeper into the abyss. There don't appear to be any available highs.

'You're the only name on the list of candidates,' I say. 'But not today.'

'Sure.'

'Today's for unbridled meaningless chit-chat.'

'And drinking.'

'Yes, of course.'

'Shall we watch it again?' she says. 'In better circumstances? You can talk me through it.'

'Yes. Yes, we can. Jesus… And I'll stop it on every frame, every photo, every fucking clip of a damned forest, and I'll tell you why it's there… and… and I don't know what state I'm going to be in by the time we get to the end of that, and I can't begin to imagine how long it'll last…'

She reaches out and squeezes my arm. Fuck, I think I might be about to start crying again. Fucking Hell, Hutton, get a grip.

'But not tonight,' I manage to say.

'No, I thought we'd watch *High Society* tonight,' she says, and there's the change of tone, Eileen rescuing me from the next descent.

'What?' I ask, smiling as I do so.

'Bing Crosby and Frank Sinatra. And Grace Kelly, of course.'

'I know. But why?'

'It's an antidote to modern life. It's old-fashioned and romantic, and Grace is utterly gorgeous in it. But, you know, gorgeous in a way that makes you want to fall in love with her, not gorgeous in a way that makes you… you know, the other thing. It'll do us good. Some wholesome, 1950s romance.'

'Wholesome?'

'Yes!'

'Apart from the fact one of the reasons Grace Kelly's character is considered aloof is because she disapproves of her father having a mistress.'

'Shhh.'

'And if we ignore Bing Crosby not kicking the tail off being thirty years older than her, which is kind of creepy.'

'Shhh. It's romantic. I love that movie, and you're not spoiling it. It'll do us good.'

I let out a long sigh, take a drink of wine. Hold her gaze across the table. Some 1950s romantic decency. Maybe she's right. I certainly don't want to think about Clayton, and I don't want to think about the catalogue of depressing psychological horror contained on the disk.

'That sounds nice,' I say.

'Good. Grace Kelly it is. And we might as well plan a getaway while we're at it. We both need cheering up.'

'Really?'

'Some r&r. I've got a month off and you've near as dammit a month. We should go and recuperate by the seaside.'

'Like 19th century poets?'

She laughs. 'Yes, exactly. Like 19th century poets.'

'Millport?' I say.

'God, no,' she says. 'I was thinking the south of France. Or Brittany, at the very least.'

'How about a Swiss lake?' I venture. 'That's what the poets would've done.'

She laughs, takes a drink, lifts the bottle and tops up both our glasses.

'Settled,' she says. 'We shall take to the Internet after dinner and map out a plan. We'll be drinking champagne and eating olives in the shadow of the Alps by this time on Friday.'

We clink glasses, we laugh, we drink. Normal, jokey, surface conversation, covering up the hurt and the turmoil and all the shit that lies beneath.

Maybe this is all that the upward swing of the rollercoaster is. Idle chatter, passable food, decent wine, chat with a friend. There are no fireworks, there's just doing what you can to get by, and letting someone else help you every now and again.

'Mountain air,' I say.

'Exactly,' says Sgt Eileen Harrison. 'Mountain air.'

By Douglas Lindsay

The Barber, Barney Thomson

The Long Midnight of Barney Thomson
The Cutting Edge of Barney Thomson
A Prayer For Barney Thomson
The King Was In His Counting House
The Last Fish Supper
The Haunting of Barney Thomson
The Final Cut
Aye, Barney

The Barbershop 7 (Novels 1-7)

Other Barney Thomson

The Face of Death
The End of Days
Barney Thomson: Zombie Slayer
The Curse of Barney Thomson & Other Stories

DS Hutton

The Unburied Dead
A Plague Of Crows
The Blood That Stains Your Hands
See That My Grave Is Kept Clean

DCI Jericho

We Are The Hanged Man
We Are Death

DI Westphall

Song of the Dead
Boy In the Well
The Art of Dying

Pereira & Bain

Cold Cuts
The Judas Flower

Stand Alone Novels

Lost in Juarez
Being For The Benefit Of Mr Kite!
A Room With No Natural Light
Ballad In Blue

Other

For The Most Part Uncontaminated
There Are Always Side Effects
Kids, And Why You Shouldn't Eat More Than One For Breakfast
Santa's Christmas Eve Blues

Printed in Great Britain
by Amazon